ADVENTURE AWAITS

VOL 3

EDITED BY

DEREK POWER

First Edition
Published by
Breaking Rules Publishing Europe, 2021.
This is a work of fiction.
Similarities to real people,places,or
events are entirely coincidental.
Adventure Awaits volume 2
978-91-986841-7-9
Copyright © 2021 BRPE

"Adventurer" -- he that goes out to meet whatever may come. Well, that is what we all do in the world one way or another.

~ Allan Quatermain by H. Rider Haggard

DRUID BOOKS

ASHLEIGH CATTERMOLE-CRUMP

Garden City Books sat unassuming on a busy London corner. Most eyes flicked from the coffee shop on the left to the overly-priced department store on the right. The owners, Frank and Robert kept their own hours and entertained a litany of magical creatures, leaving Holly Parks to deal with their run-of -the-mill human customers; offering recommendations on the latest romance novels, ordering school textbooks and arranging book covers in increasingly elaborate displays. Some locals refused to shop here—they much preferred a *'regular, human shop thank you very much!'* to the druid-run Garden City. Holly had always been unsure why—Druids held the key to thousands of years of knowledge and logically, they staffed most libraries and bookstores. Deciding to close early, Holly flicked over the sign on the window. As soon as she touched it, the window collapsed in on itself, tiny shards of glass seeming to hover in mid-air for a moment before tinkling to the floor. Holly flung her arms over her head and ducked, waiting for whatever or whoever had smashed the glass to make themself known. There was complete silence, the street outside continuing on as if the store did not exist.

Before Holly could move, the ground began to shudder, and a cavernous crevasse appeared under her feet stretching the length of the dusty wooden floorboards. The sides, red with fire were radiating heat, and as Holly leant over in surprise, flames rushed at her face. She was used to strange happenings, working for a druid and all, but this was something else entirely.

"What in the bloody hell-"

Frank crashed through the broken door, followed by a shellshocked Robert.

"I-I couldn't see who it was!"

Holly's hands flapped the way they did whenever she was about to be engulfed in panic. Holly was still panting from the fright of it all, looking between the men and the floor for some sort of confirmation that this was really happening.

When, as a stammering, newly fired 27 year old, Holly had entered the bookstore to ask for a job, she was drawn into the wisdom and the excitement of the shop. Holly's heart wanted more than anything to be drawn into the ranks of druidism, to be the bearer of true wisdom, to know the power Frank had shown as he whipped book after book off the shelf, reciting their contents in an attempt to test her nerve.

Sharing a knowing glance, Frank and Robert shimmied over to Holly, their shoes beginning to steam from the heat. Holly stood hovering near the exit, the strange disquiet in the empty shop magnifying the sounds of her shuffling feet. She daren't move for fear of being swallowed by the fiery cavern that Frank and Robert didn't seem particularly worried by. She opened her mouth to speak several times, but nothing came out. Seeing her questioning glance and impending panic, Frank sighed heavily and reached into his desk drawer, handing Holly a large flat book. The cover was glossy black, a thin silver edge to save the corners from damage. The covers, void of any word or mark, were cardboard and there appeared to be nothing between them, simply a fancy manilla folder.

"What's this?" Holly asked blankly.

"Open it," directed Robert, his usually friendly demeanor disappearing.

Swallowing the rising thickness in her throat, Holly sucked in a deep breath. *Wait, was she being fired?!*

Frank and Robert were both staring at her, a strange expression on their faces. She wondered what she had done this time. Had that stroppy fae from the pharmacy cast a spell when she wasn't allowed to touch the 'proper' books? Oh god, had she left the kettle on the stove again?

Before any of them could speak, from deep within the wide abyss, fiery letters burst into the sky:

Retirement imminent, Frank Reese. Apprentice Druid required to report 9am.

Suddenly the rings on Holly's fingers felt oddly

tight, her asthma causing a crushing sensation in her chest. Frank nodded down at the book in Holly's hands. Clearing her throat, she gingerly placed the book on the counter and opened the cover. It contained nothing but a single blank page. It was completely unremarkable, but for the fact that as she scanned the paper, words appeared, ghostly at first then growing stronger and stronger, floating beneath the page as if on water. The words became fuzzy as she tried to concentrate on them, the more she tried to catch them, the more unreadable they became until Frank reached out a long, hobbled finger, the words forming into sentences under his touch:

The Druid's Pledge

The holder of wisdom, the one who will promise to stand at the gates of knowledge even when ignorance beats against. Their fortitude proven against evil, the heart measured against temptation, the mind tested against any and all threats. Your test will begin when you sign below. It will end with a new druid or a dead human,

Sign at your own risk.

All the nights they had spent together in preparation for Frank's retirement, there was no mention of an exam, especially one that could kill her. Frank cleared his throat; his eyes were focused on something fascinating out the window. Holly's mind was still computing. Frank had promised her she would run the shop one day…but really? She had to pass a test before she could become a full-fledged druid?

Before either Frank or Robert could answer Holly's questioning gaze, a figure appeared, rising from the cavernous hole, his smoky body spilling into the shop before solidifying into the form of a pimply teenage boy. His fingers were encircling an elegant silver cigarette holder, clinking against several golden rings as he casually strolled over to them as if it were perfectly normal to appear in a bookshop from a hell portal.

"Ah gentleman, nice to see you both looking so... young," the apparent teenager spoke with a Welsh accent and an air of importance. The ground closed again, leaving only a smoking crack in the wooden floorboards.

"Bryce. Is there something we can help you with?" Frank's voice was even colder than usual.

"Just checking you got my message. Not long left for your post, time's a--ticking!"

His eyes caught sight of Holly, his lips blowing a circle of smoke through her greying hair. His towering figure loomed over her, his breath smelling of smoke and fire.

"Is this her?"

His face gave nothing away but he stepped even closer, tipping his head towards her.

"Bryce. Demon," he announced, holding out a dainty hand. "You're taking her test?" Frank asked, before Holly could shake it.

"Indeed I am! Talk about lucky."

He continued looking Holly up and down before spinning around to grin at Frank. A sudden swoop sounded in the distance and through the open door several ravens cascaded inside, landing on the demon's shoulders.

"Boo!" he snapped his head around at Holly who

began to shake, the only thing keeping her standing was the edge of the counter under her sweaty hands.

"Well...I'm sure you all have a lot to talk about. You and I are going to have a real good time," his gritty voice scraped against Holly's ears as he ran a finger down her cheek.

"I'll see you in the morning, beautiful," he announced. "Make sure you say your goodbyes. You won't be back."

He swept his overly tall frame back through the door and disappeared into a swirl of cloud. The oxygen seemed to follow him out of the room.

Frank was pacing sternly, his eyes seemed sunken and tired. He and Robert were packed for Costa Rica, his apprentice was preparing to take over his post and he had prepared for every eventuality. Yet he stood, shoulders slumped, muscles braced as though he expected something to physically attack him. His face was downcast, reading the pledge over and over, although Holly knew he had memorized it long ago. He had purposely kept it a secret from her. Did he really have that little faith in her that he would spring this surprise on her rather than offer her a chance to prepare?

"What kind of test are we talking about?" Holly grimaced, her face reddening into a thick mask of sweat.

"The tests are always different. They're run by demons, and Bryce is a real prick of a demon. It could be anything from a game of tiddly-winks to a cage match with a dragon...but there's always an answer somewhere. They're not allowed to make them unwinnable. I... I know you'll succeed."

"What if I refuse to go?" Holly felt the palms of her hands slick with sweat. "You can't, I'm afraid. The contract you signed when you started working here...it says you're required to pass a test before you're given the ability to govern the shop and its knowledge. Otherwise the demons can keep you in hell."

"Then, I guess I don't have a choice," Holly's voice wavered, betraying her worry. She internally cursed herself for not reading the fine print. Frank grabbed her hand and held her gaze.

"My contract is due to expire, I only have a day left before I must retire. If--WHEN-- you succeed, the shop will be yours, and you're the only one I would trust with this place. I've become rather attached to it after two centuries."

The morning sun rose quietly as Holly negotiated her way through the noisy, smog-filled London morning, lingering outside Garden City Books to appreciate the smear of deep pink across the horizon. She entered and sat in the familiar chair collecting the black book and running her hands over its smoothness. Just like the night before, it sucked the air from her lungs but this time when she opened it, a separate sheet of paper fell out. The words began to sway back and forth before arranging themselves into neat rows. Typewriter-ink fingerprints were smudged on the corner and Frank's scrawling signature, in deep set blue ink, was at the bottom of what appeared to be runes. No wonder she hadn't read the fine print. The emptiness boomed around her. Frank and Robert had left at the stroke of midnight, after a solemn goodbye. Now, as Holly picked up a pen, the symbols began to move once again, slowly slipping below the surface until the page was blank. A dribble of ink fell onto the book, collecting in a pool before rearranging itself into the shape of a single holly leaf.

It occurred to Holly as a sandstorm suddenly appeared around her, that she was not properly dressed for a demon battle to the death. Her crocheted cardigan felt heavy and her leggings stuck to her legs. As the sand fell to the ground, grains blowing through the shelves, Bryce the Demon appeared. Holly vaguely wondered why he hadn't taken the fiery portal this time.

"Ready?" he asked, seeming almost bored. He must've had a long night of terrorising people. Holly nodded, swallowing.

"When I click my fingers, our battle will begin. Kill me before I kill you."

Holly swallowed and nodded. He glowered at her, clicking his fingers menacingly, fire and brimstone in his eyes. Nothing happened.

"Baha just kidding, this ain't a movie!"

Bryce swaggered over and lingered uncomfortably close to Holly's short frame before reaching into his pocket. He took out a lighter and held it in his hand for a few moments before clicking it. The two of them began to descend through the floor as if taking a ghostly elevator through the darkness. Noting the look on Holly's face, Bryce spoke up.

"Humans find the portal a little scary," he said.

"They get annoyed when the skin is flayed from their face. Plus, the elevator's less claustrophobic."

After what seemed like an eternity, Holly's feet bumped into the ground and she saw they were in a cavern lit dimly by flaming torches, edged by an ink-black lake, tiny ripples flowing outward towards nothingness.

In a dark corner of the cavern flames flickered to life in a series of torch brackets. Three wooden doors without frames, apparently leading to nowhere, sat in the sand. There was a barely readable tarnished plaque nailed into each. Bryce nestled himself into the sand and took out a scroll. He began to read.

"Hear ye, human! You are here today to face your toughest battle yet--what the? Who wrote this garbage?" He threw the paper aside.

"Pick a door," he announced, unceremoniously.

"What's inside?" Holly asked, the thickness of her words mirroring her foggy thoughts.

"Well I can't just tell you that. What would be the point of the test?" he sounded exasperated. Was she really the stupidest human he'd ever tortured?

"There are three doors. Each one leads to a different place. All you need to do is find your way back through the door at the other end-kind of like a maze, but ya know-I like to give you a choice of deaths."

Bryce was now leaning against the dank walls, bored. Was this his day job? How many people had he defeated in this cavern? Holly narrowed her eyes, waiting for the catch. Bryce held out his hand.

"You've got an hour, if you don't get back through the door, I'll leave you in there to die. Won't take long mind you, I imagine when I leave and the room collapses, you'll go with it, not sure to be honest. Never tried it myself."

Holly couldn't think. She wasn't sure what she was expecting but it certainly wasn't this. What was on the other side of the doors? Was a tidal wave about to crash down from the blackness? Would the walls start to close in and crush her? Was he lying? Would she be crushed to smithereens even if she escaped?

"That's it?" Holly asked, suspicious.

"Indeed. We demons may be horrible but we're nothing if not honest. Your hair is freaking hideous by the way. Well? Go on."

"Righto, get to it. You just need to find your way back through the door, understand?"

Holly nodded.

"Ah, I actually need you to say it, you know *out loud*. Otherwise it doesn't count. Legalities and such, you get it."

He was chewing on a perfectly manicured pinky nail. *How old was he*? Holly wondered. *Did he choose to stay this age forever?*

"I understand."

Closing her eyes, she took a deep breath and tried to shove the overwhelming panic from her mind. Pulling out an inhaler, she sucked in a deep breath in an attempt to loosen her chest. "Tick tock love, haven't got all day."

The contrast of Bryce's youthful accent and his overly dramatic velvet cape would have seemed comical if not for the seriousness of the situation. Holly wished Frank was here. She recalled his voice telling her about the 'rules' of druidism. No two druids can exist in the same space, an insurance of sorts against any possible attacks from the underworld. He was surely sunning himself on a beach somewhere by now, safely in the golden years of retirement. Holly stepped forward, and with all the confidence of a rat with a paw on some mousetrapped cheese yanked open a door.

Once, when Holly was nine, she had been on a hot air balloon. She had been so terrified her breath refused to come out and, in her panic,, she had almost toppled over the side of the basket. That was the closest she had come to the feeling of shock she felt as the door snapped closed behind her. It was as though the carpet was ripped from beneath her feet, a pneumatic tube of darkness sucked her into a rabbit hole, her scrambled body emerging into a sudden sandy heatwave. Holly felt the grit of the beach in her socks as she scrambled to her feet, quiet waves splashing up onto the rocks that appeared to lead to a jungle. Holly realised that at some point in her morning, her watch had disappeared, and she had no way of knowing how much time she had. Making her way across the sand and rocks to the edge of greenery, she looked around feeling beads of sweat gathering on her face. She ran her hands dry under her armpits before examining her surroundings. Trees and grasses grew wild for miles, was the door somewhere through them? Before she could think too much, the waves sounded closely behind her. The tide had risen several meters in only a few seconds. The water receded once again, before splashing in around her ankles. She felt the water seep through her pants. Slapping an icy feeling against her skin, the heavy pull almost dragging her under.

Holly remembered the time her parents had taken her to the beach in Brighton. The waves had washed up against the sandcastles her mother had pushed together with her toes. They had gently eroded from the bottom until the top collapsed. Now, she found herself wondering if that's what would happen to the island. Would the waves just lap up the beach until the whole island was underwater? She couldn't wait any longer, her feet began to force her up the sand into the jungle. Panting, she looked around, trying to distinguish some kind of path, clue, anything. Grasses cut along her shins, she didn't look down, but she could feel the sting of blood soaking through her leggings.

Ahead of her Holly could see the trees swaying violently. Realising there was no wind, her heart shuddered wondering what was ahead. As the water pulled back, she continued onward, brushing aside sharp grasses and overgrown weeds. The sun seemed to disappear behind thickening treetops as she ploughed on. Just as she managed to trip over a patch of thick toadstools, a creaking sounded from high in the trees and a log the size of a car swung through branches to land squarely in her chest. Propelled backwards, Holly landed in a soft wet mud puddle that squelches up her back and into her hair. Her head knocked against a rock, the dizzying, spiralling sky pin holing into black.

Blinking her eyes open again, Holly's first thought

was how much time had passed. She had no idea how long she had left to find the door and she was pretty sure at least two of her ribs were broken. Before she could rise to her feet, a shuffling and a loud chorus of voices chanting swelled up somewhere in the darkness. A fiery torchlight invaded her line of sight, the flickering fire lighting up the face of a figure dressed in tattered furs thrusting their way through the underbrush.

"Woman! You are trespassing."

The woman's voice was strong, her lips a deep purple against her skin that appeared to be shimmering against the flickering flames. From somewhere in the darkness, a voice echoed in Holly's ears.

"Lock this one away, I'm not much of a fan."

Bryce the Demon stepped into the moonlight. He jerked his head and the woman stepped back, two of her companions gripped Holly's upper arms and hauled her upright. Holly wondered if they would kill her or if they were simply there to stop her from reaching the door to freedom. Before her train of thought was fully formed, one of the women thrust her short bronze dagger against Holly's throat. There was a gag placed in her mouth and she was frogmarched away through the dark, the cackling of Bryce following closely behind.

"Well, that was short-lived!" he cackled as Holly was dragged up a steep, forested hill.

"Urgh! Let me out! This is not fair!"

There was no answer to her screams and Holly clattered the bars of her cage in frustration. The lock was large and seemed to be fused against the bones that Holly hoped were animal and not human. Peering around, she saw no one anywhere in sight. Banging her shoulder against the lock, her skin bruising, she eventually cracked through the bars, collapsing to the ground below. Softened slightly by layer upon layer of moss, her body creaked with the impact of the ground. Somewhere in the distance, a squall of birds rose into the air. Hearing the panicked screams of her captors, Holly took off, brushing aside thorned bushes and slippery tree branches. The treetops obscured any light, any clues to the whereabouts of her goal were buried in her breathy panic. Slowing enough to rub her eyes clear, she forced air through her lungs. The sounds of Bryce and his soldiers ducked in and out of the forest, whispering around Holly until she had no idea how much distance was between them. She didn't know how high up she had been taken but the sounds of the waves had diminished, was the tide still rising?

A rustling in the trees close by shocked Holly into action, but her feet were not fast enough. The fur-dressed woman barrelled into Holly, taking the two of them off the mossy drop, rolling over and over until the pair lay splattered across a dusty rocky outcrop. As Holly shielded her face with her arms, she caught sight of the woman in the dim light. Her skin shimmered with dragon scales, her elbows sharp claws that protruded from her cloak. Shocked, Holly was too slow to stand and she felt the woman's fist connect with the hardness of her cheekbone.

"No one leaves this island, no one! You must die."

She spoke menacingly but her voice was soft and even, as if stating an obvious fact. Before Holly could plead her case, a noise fell through the leaves in the distance. Somewhere up there, where they had fallen from, there was something moving. Something huge. Not wanting to wait to meet the noisemaker, Holly scrambled to her feet, searching around for any kind of weapon. The dragon-woman stood watching as Holly's shaky arms found a rock. The woman laughed.

"Oh, it's just not as satisfying when you don't even try!"

From high above, a pair of large swooping dragon wings parted the forest, uprooting skyscraper-trees and trampling any sign of birdlife. Holly, rock grasped in her hand began to run, not sure which direction she should head in. The dragon-woman, still laughing was close. Holly turned and instead of aiming her rock at the incoming dragon, she hit squarely out at the woman's face, sending her tumbling into the bushes. An angry squawk from above rained down upon Holly as she kept running. He turned only long enough to see the dragon had landed in search of its mistress and had lost interest in its prey completely.

The trees ahead were thinning. It was the only way Holly could tell the direction she was running in might have been leading somewhere. As she pushed past the last few saplings, she felt brightness in her eyes as her feet stumbled on the ground below her. Dirt splattered itself through her eyelashes and she felt the rocks under her scatter away. Pulling herself upwards she saw she was on the edge of a cliff. Her arms propelled herself backwards to grip onto the thin branches, her battered hands holding herself steady. Dirt puffed around her as she stood swaying between an angry demon and a sheer drop to certain death.

Frank had told her there was always a solution, she surely couldn't die here falling from a cliff dropping into nothingness. Staring around, examining every crevice, every hole. Could she climb down somehow? Was there a bridge?

As Holly saw the shadows of her pursuers advancing, her fingers found a mossy, fraying rope. She remembered the time Frank had sent her to self-defense lessons in an attempt to build up her physical confidence in the event she ever had to deal with an annoyed customer who harnessed more magical power than herself. Looking back, Holly hadn't realised how strange it was a bookstore clerk had required increased physical confidence. Frank had known, he had spent years preparing her for this moment.

"Jesus, really?" Holly muttered to herself as she tested the strength of the rope. "Righto."

She hissed a breath through her teeth so she wouldn't hyperventilate and turned just ss Bryce emerged from the forest, his face lit by a flaming torch flashing through the darkness. With no other option, Holly leapt. Unsure where she would land if she fell, her hands burned as the fibres grazed into her palms, the cliff disappearing behind her as she swung into the depths of the unknown.

As Holly landed, she half expected the ground to collapse, or the trees to burst into flame, maybe a pit of snakes. Instead she landed into complete silence. Patting herself down, she checked for cuts and broken bones, but she appeared to be whole. As she crept forward, checking the ground for booby traps, the moon crept out from behind a cloud, lighting the way ahead. Hearing nothing, Holly stood on a rock to look around, her hands bruised and shaking. Squinting at her surroundings, Holly saw something dark looming against the forest backdrop. It was the door!

"Finally," Holly muttered; her throbbing feet relieved at having a destination to head for. No sooner had she taken her first step than her body froze once again. A high-pitched, primal squalling sound was rising through the trees, higher and higher until it felt as though the noise itself would shatter her into tiny glass shards. Her hands over her ears, Holly searched for the source. With no other option, she began to run for the door, eyes focused, her feet slipping closer and closer. When it was finally within reach, Holly let out an audible sigh, her panting matching her pounding footsteps. She was so close. As her hand reached out for the doorknob, a figure the size of a house crashed down from somewhere in the darkness above. With another high-pitched squeal, a burst of flame shot from within the toothy jaws of the dragon that was now cutting off her route to the prize.

Clambering behind a rock, Holly watched as the dragon shattered and burned plants and shrubs and rocks under her great feet. Holly had never met a dragon before, but she knew that while they were vicious and dangerous, they were almost completely blind. She recalled the huge volumes of magical knowledge Frank had examined her on and quite often slipped into normal conversation. He had once casually mentioned that his mother was once taken by sirens after his father angered a mermaid, she had been saved by a dragon who had traded her sight for returning her to her family. Holly shook Frank's memory from her head. He had done his job; she knew what she had to do. There was no use worrying about disappointing him now. As another flash of fire ripped through the trees, Holly noticed the ground below her feet. It was a matted mess of twigs, manmade materials and something sparkling.

"Mother fu- really?" she sighed. They had put the door inside a dragon's nest. Crafty. Her palms moistened, her hair had long since matted in the sweaty heat. Try as she might, she could not slow her breathing. Instead she stood upright, feeling her heart straining against her ribcage. All she had to do was sneak past him and get through the door. If he couldn't see her-maybe she would manage it. Glancing out from her hiding place, Holly noticed the dragon was blindly stamping as anything and everything, a poor seagull charred to a crisp as he flew too close to the jaws of fire.

Rifling through the contents of her pockets, Holly pulled out her work keys. They jangled for a moment before she clapped them into her fist, cursing herself for making noise. With the deep black and silver scaly beast ahead of her, Holly daren't take her eyes off the dragon. The door could disappear at any time. Holly's breath quickened, her toes tingling as she forced herself to stay just a moment longer. Her feet wanted nothing more than to sprint towards the door, taking her chances against the dragon.

"Ok," she whispered to herself. "Ok, think. There's an obvious solution here, where is it?"

Her fingers ached from flexing. Forcing her eyes closed, she tried to imagine her way out. She felt the heavy keys in her hand, silenced by her tightened fist. Mind whirring, Holly glimpsed the wings of the dragon flapping in agitation, not able to find the human who had encroached upon her nest.

A sudden whistle from somewhere high above, Holly felt the wind from the dragon's wings almost knock her down.

"Come here my darling!"

A familiar voice pierced the darkness and Holly saw the figure of Bryce silhouetted against the moon, beckoning the dragon to his side. The jewelled scales flapped into the air, swooping upwards to collect an increasingly angry Bryce. The demon, whose sinewy young form frightened Holly even if he were not atop the back of the dragon.

Holly knew she had no choice. It was now or never. If she didn't take her chance now, she was done. Clutching her keys, she flung them as far into the forest as she could, the metal clanging against rocks and tree. Bryce and his dragon spun at the sound, pelting towards the source of the noise. Holly, feet planted into the soil, launched herself upwards and began to skid and slip across dirt, crushed gold and mossy wetness. The door loomed closer and closer, and only as she was almost within reach did, she turn around. Her foot slipped against one of the rocks, causing her to cry out and the dragon to spin around mid-air.

"There! Fly!" Bryce screeched through the air, steering the dragon downward. Stumbling through the pain Holly hauled herself closer and closer to the door, her hand finally gripping the bronze knob just as a flame jettisoned towards her. The last thing she saw before the swooping, nauseating nothingness was the anger and fire of the pursuing demon.

Tumbling back into the cavern, Holly landed ungracefully on her backside, the blackness of the lake lapping at her legs. Bryce made a strange, annoyed noise as he marched into the cavern behind her and pulled out the lighter again. Without a word, he scowled and threw the set of keys at Holly, which she caught in midair--the most athletic feat she had managed that day.

When the invisible elevator dropped her back into the sun-drenched bookstore, she was alone. Bryce apparently did not want to stick around for the celebration. She wandered over to the lonely desk and saw a glimmering magical postcard from Costa Rica, the likenesses of Frank and Robert were waving and smiling up at her from their beach chairs.

"So, you think you can handle it?" Holly slapped her hands down on the table, making the middle-aged man in front of her jump.

"Y-yep, t-totally" he stammered.

"Yep, totally?" Holly closed her eyes and grimaced at the direction the English language had taken. "I've worked in this stop for a hundred and fifteen years and I'm about to teach you more knowledge than you ever knew existed. Don't make me regret it."

He nodded eagerly, pulling out his electronic notebook. Holly sighed and tapped the bookshelf beside her. She pulled out a large, perfectly bound book titled 'How to Defeat a Dragon-Riding Demon'.

"We do things the old-fashioned way around here."

THE MEDUSA COIN

DEBORAH DUBAS GROOM

With slow sinuous movements, the two sisters slithered behind the beaded curtains. From their vantage point on the second floor, they watched the first-floor shop, staffed by a smiling and attentive clerk, who would greet the tourists and offer them tea as they entered. The locals never shopped at store like this one.

Visitors would sift through richly coloured silk scarves, marvelling at the quality, examine bowls decorated with red tulips and crescent moons, admire the romantic hanging lights and buy cheap souvenirs featuring the nazar to ward off the evil eye.

The sisters paid little attention to these tourists with their cruise ship stickers on their shirts, selfie sticks, rumpled clothes and sweaty upper lips. These people were of no use.

The sister's focus was on one small medallion sitting on a deep purple, velvet cloth in a glass case beside the cash register. Whoever was called by this piece would be of very great interest indeed. The sisters had waited eons and if the castings were right, their wait was about to end.

Sarah, basking in the sun, closed her eyes in appreciation of the breeze that came off the Bosphorus. Sitting in a cafe beside the colourful heaped spices of the Egyptian Spice Market, she faced the Galata bridge and watched the dozens of men and youth lined up with their bait buckets and fishing poles. To her left were the tiny booths with striped awnings that sold grain to feed the flocks of pigeons that strutted through the square. Woman in raincoats and headscarves would give their children the pans of seeds to throw for the birds. Sarah watched as one sweet little girl in a long red sweater, pink and white striped leggings and yellow sneakers, ran. She shrieked in delight, her dark tangle of curls flying wildly in every direction, as she was caught up in the flapping of wings.

Sarah's eyes crinkled. Istanbul had captured her from the first time she'd sailed into port and seen the minarets rising through the fog. In quick order she'd been ensorcelled by the palaces, mosques, colours, music, art and the people. She loved the taste of chocolate baklava, the flaky pastry of borek for breakfast, coffee strong enough to wake the dead and markets full of ruby red pomegranates, beautiful orange red lentils, and the shocking pink of watermelon opened with a machete.

The sky was a brilliant turquoise, and the cloud were bleached white. Her delicate scarf fluttered in the breeze. She was enjoying the excitement of being back and hearing the hum of the city. She lifted her tea in its tulip shaped glass, when, without warning, she felt a shock of alarm, and the burn of adrenalin splashing through her. She swung around in her seat and knocked her handbag onto the ground, scaring the cat that had been lurking under the table, hoping for scraps. Sarah scrambled to pick up the spilled contents of her bag, all the while trying to practice her square breathing. She couldn't be having a panic attack, not here. Faces that had turned to see what was happening, went back to their meals, and nargile pipes. As she grabbed the tube of lipstick that had rolled away, she saw her lunch date walking through the throngs of people racing through the markets, crossing the bridge and heading to the ferry terminals.

Sarah gave a frantic wave, and Christine, in a trademark khakis and tank top, smiled widely, and parted the crowds, her blonde curls contained with an orange headband and her arms covered with a matching shrug. Before Sarah could say a word, she was wrapped in a hug that ending in laughter. Christine had an easy grace and confidence that people responded to. The waiters smiled at the reunion. They'd been concerned that Sarah was eating alone. Now they could unfurrow their brows and go on with their business.

Christine's face turned thoughtful as she stepped back and got a good look at her friend. Being a topnotch medical administrator, who also had a gimlet eye for details, she saw the soft purple shadows under Sarah's eyes. Her auburn hair hung loose around her face, her skin paler than usual and her emerald green eyes seemed anxious. Her dress, though still showing her curves, hung looser than normal. She seemed diminished.

Sarah had always been the heart of the friendship, so insightful, endearingly funny, and happy and then, half a year ago, her husband Phil left. No one had realized how bad things were until he packed his belongings, and within the month was sending out housewarming invitations for himself and Moira, his secretary. Sarah had talked and Christine had listened, and though Sarah was subdued, she seemed OK. A few months later things took a sharp downturn.

Sarah became more and more introverted, until one night she called Christine at 2 am, sobbing and begging for help. It was a bad dream but the same one over and over again for weeks. She couldn't sleep. Every night she found herself painting the face and flowers from the dream over and over again.

The corners of Christine's ocean blue eyes pinched briefly. The two friends sat at the patio table and clasped hands. After twenty years of friendship they didn't need the small talk. Her eyes searched Sarah's.

"Have the dreams been doing this?"

Christine had been one of the few people Sarah would trust to hear her when she started being plagued.

"I tried warm milk, exercise, sleeping pills and counselling. The images scared me. It's like they could see me."

She'd finally had to take a sabbatical from work.

Sarah smiled ruefully.

"Well, I'm here now. If anything can banish it, I'd say a little time with you, and a painting holiday on the Turkish Riviera should do it."

When Sarah had confided about the dreams, Christine told her about her trip to Anatolia to be part of the dig site. She suggested they meet up. She reminded Sarah of the painting trip she'd been mooning over, fresh air, fresh food, a couple of cooking classes with the famous Ozlem Warren, the most gorgeous scenery and plenty of swim breaks. Sarah jumped at the idea and had reserved her spot that night. Now here they were, the smell of grilled meat and peppers filling the air, and it was irresistible.

The women squeezed each other's hands and let go to pick up their menus.

While they ate their barbecued chicken wings, a craving Sarah had had since her last trip, Christine told her about her working vacation.

"You know I've always dreamed of being an archeologist."

Sarah nodded and laughed, remembering the old fedora Christine used to wear.

"So, this is a career change?"

Christine smiled.

"Ah, nope. I found out that the medical training I did when I was in the army qualified me to apply as on-site first aid personnel for one of the museum's teaching programs. I applied and found out I'd be working at, get this, Golbekli Tepe."

Sarah lifted an eyebrow.

"How did you manage that? Isn't it one of the oldest sites in the world?"

"Yes, and I don't know but I took it before they could change their minds. This afternoon I'm going to go meet professor Kara at the Archeological Museum in Gulhane. He'll be in charge of the research. Why don't you come? I know you are a sarcophagus groupie."

Sarah groaned. As a young girl she'd gone to a King Tut exhibition and tried to hide in the museum so that she could sneak out later and spend more time looking. That had earned her a grounding and having to send a hand-written note of apology to the museum.

"Do you think professor Kara would mind?" She loved the Archeological Museum.

I haven't met him, but I'll tell him you're a travel writer and maybe he'll even give you a tour." The conspiracy now in place, the women paid their bills, and began walking away from the market, picking up some pistachio Turkish delight and joking with the merchants who tried to lure them into their shops.

Within the half hour the ladies had walked through the impressive gates and entered the grounds of the museum and mounted the steps. Sarah couldn't help but gawk like a tourist every time she walked through these halls. There were remnants of civilizations that no longer had known languages, and it even had a baby Sphinx. Christine noticed the colour returning to Sarah's cheeks and the lightness in her laughter. She was determined to see this continue.

After obtaining the right visitors' badges, and a few twists and turns, they spotted a group of men standing at the entrance of a workroom.

"There he is."

Christine waved and a short, older, stocky gentleman, with pince-nez glasses sitting on his hooked nose, and wearing a light linen suit, looked up. His face was wide and jowly and had a slight Mediterranean skin tone. His salt and pepper hair had a light wave and parted in the middle. Sarah, in her nervousness stepped up, hand extended.

"Hello professor Kara. My name is Sarah Prophet. I hope you don't mind. Christine invited me along." Sarah could feel a flush creeping up her neck.

"She's been telling me about the dig, I mean, not anything that's confidential. Christine wouldn't do that, but it's just an honour to meet you." She hoped her smile was disarming.

The gentleman frowned, then motioned to the man beside him. Sarah stepped back, her eyes flitting over to a younger, taller and trimmer man in a crisp white dress shirt with rolled up sleeves, a gold watch and tan slacks, not that she noticed, and a smile directed at Sarah. He stepped forward and extended his hand.

"Thank you Sarah. It's nice to meet you. I am Michael Kara."

Sarah turned fully pink and stared into the eyes of the most handsome man she'd ever seen. They were a vivid blue, the type that could change colour. She did her best to snap her mouth shut. Vitality radiated from him. His face could have rivalled any of the statues in the hall. His jaw had firm clean lines, and his tanned skin accentuated the musculature in his forearm and made her want to trace it with her fingers. His eyebrows were strong, clean lines that peeked out from the dark curls that fell rakishly across his forehead. His lips quirked and his eyebrows lifted. Sarah realized she was still holding his hand and was even more chagrined when she realized that she didn't want to let go.

"I'm sorry!" He dimpled in response.

His smile widened, and the entire party looked back and forth between the two.

"Let me introduce my colleagues. The gentleman you greeted is Spiro from the Benaki museum in Athens." Spiro inclined his head and murmured her last name. His eyes, indistinct behind his glasses, gave away nothing.

"This serious young lad is Johansen, one of our interns, and Ari is assisting Spiro."

The young men gave the briefest of nods but didn't attempt small talk.

"And on my left is Herman."

Herman was about 6' 250 lbs., headphones around his neck, and wearing a Hawaiian shirt over a t-shirt with the words, "Should not be left unsupervised". Bright red and gold hair stuck out in every direction and his eyes formed crescents over apple cheeks. He grinned impishly as he put an arm around Christine.

"Hey Sarah, thanks for delivering the visual relief for the trip."

He let out a quick grunt as Christine's elbow landed a neat jab to his side. Michael laughed as Herman faked a collapse.

"Welcome aboard Christine. You'll do just fine with

this crew."

He looked at Sarah, and her face began heating up again. Ancient monoliths were becoming increasingly enticing. She gave herself a shake. What had gotten into her?

"We're just going to the discovery room to look at the progress they've made processing some of the thousands of pieces uncovered while digging the tunnel between the European and Asian sides of Istanbul. Would you both like to join us?"

Herman piped up.

"Yeah, he won't tell you, but this has been Michael's baby for the last year, right prof?"

Michael narrowed his eyes at Herman, and then gave a quick nod and motioned for everyone to go in. Sarah and Christine couldn't say yes fast enough. This was not the time to play it cool. Michael put a hand behind Sarah's back and ushered her into the room. It took all of her will power not to lean into his bronzed arms and rub herself like a cat against his chest. She burst out giggling at the thought, so much for being an introvert, and then immediately lost herself in the wonder of the artifacts. A couple of hours later, which seemed like minutes, Christine had learned more from Spiro about her role on site, and with a few more diggers joining them, it was time to go. Christine wrapped her arm around Sarah's shoulder and whispered,

"Sooo, you and professor Kara were very cosy over there by the pottery shards. Are you thinking about changing your trip and doing a little sifting and cataloguing?" Sarah smiled.

"His wrappings are rather nice." They stifled their laughter as he wandered over.

"Ladies we have a rooftop table booked in Sultanahmet tonight, I'll give you the name if you'd care to join us for dinner, at about 8 pm?"

"We'd love to," blurted out Christine, refusing to make eye contact with Sarah, and with that she steered her friend across the foyer, and down the stairs, and into the garden of statuary on the grounds.

It was 4 pm now so that left them time to have a rest, wash up and join the team for dinner. They headed out the gate, past the tramline, and were continuing up the congested side streets, past miniature graveyards with turban topped gravestones, when they heard a voice. The ladies looked down to see a small frantic child clutching at Christine's sleeve. They knew to keep their purses tight to their bodies, as it was a common trick for one child to be a distraction while others picked your pockets.

"Please lady come quick. My baba is bleeding. Please help me."

Tears poured down his stained cheeks and there was something more in his eyes. He looked terrified. His multicoloured sweater had tattered cuffs, his pants hung loosely, and his navy sneakers were worn. He shot continuous looks down a little curving pathway. Christine looked at Sarah and she nodded at the boy. Christine had her medical backpack with her, so it was possible that they were chosen because there really was an emergency. As the boy led them to a small first floor flat, they could smell the illness. They decided it was best if Sarah stayed outside. After a couple of minutes Christine emerged wearing a face mask and her hair pulled back in an elastic.

"This might take a while. He's got bites all over, and some are infected. It's like he was attacked by rats. I'll have to disinfect everything and then stitches."

There was no question that she would help. Sarah understood. She admired her friend. Sarah would stay nearby to make sure Christine was safe, and didn't getting carted off, or as they used to joke, tossed into an old fishing boat, though Christine had enough training to take down most assailants. She'd defeated more than one surprised young buck in sparring practice.

Sarah looked at the broken blinds and floral net curtains in the windows, the weeds and bits of grass growing where the pavement met the building, and the sparkling stucco on the outer walls. She began to meander down the pathway. Next door were tiny shops that sold vacuum cleaner parts, beside that rivets and buttons, and then leather strips for belts. Everything was grey and taupe, and tarnished metal. She looked across the street and her knees buckled.

Her eyes filled with tears and her lips pulled back in a grimace of horror. She knew she must be having an attack, but it was there. It was the face that had haunted her night after sleepless night. On the opposite wall, carved into a dark wooden door was the woman with the blue face surrounded by flower. The eyes staring and dark, and the lips partially open as if about to speak. The door had no handle so it must just open out. Sarah backed herself against the tiny storefront windows. She would not touch the door. There was a price for that in the dream, but this wasn't a dream. It couldn't be here. She shivered violently. She was hallucinating.

"Come."

Sarah jumped, her pulse pounding erratically. It was the small boy, looking grim and there was an odd glimmer of anger. He reached for her hand, but instead of bringing her to his home, he led her to the front of the shop that ran along the main boulevard.

Sarah stopped at the entrance and looked up at the name plate but couldn't read the writing. When she looked down, the boy was gone. Instead, in the doorway appeared an eager smiling face, with shining round eyes, beckoning her forward. The lean young man continued to rapidly wave her in, stepping behind her to close the door. Sarah's stomach clenched. She'd never hear the end of it if she was the one carted off.

"Hello lady, yes please. Come in and enjoy. Chai? Apple tea?" Sarah wanted to say no, but to be polite she said that chai would be fine and thank you.

"I'm Ibrahim. Where are you from? How do you like Istanbul? Is there anything I can help you find?"

Sarah trembled and pressed her fingernails into the palm of her hand. She couldn't afford to fall apart now.

"Yes I, well, I wanted to ask something."

Ibrahim continued to nod, staring at her with a fixed smile.

"It is about the artwork on your side door."

As if someone had thrown a switch, Ibrahim froze. His eyes became large and glazed. He began panting, his lank hair falling in front of his face. His head making violent jerking movements. Sarah's eyes widened as she darted backwards. He spoke in an echoing voice.

"You saw the door?"

Sarah's eyebrows raised. She took another step back and hit against the front counter. She began to take side steps to get around him and to the entrance. Her voice became pinched as her desperation mounted. She reached into her purse, fumbling for her keys to use as protection if needed.

"I don't think you're well. My friend has a medical kit. I'll get her and she can take a look at you."

A loud rattling and hissing sounds issued from up the staircase, and the bead curtains made jarring, clacking noises. Ibrahim shot a look of terror upwards and then there was a second of silence. Sarah decided she needed to make a break for it and get back to Christine. She tried to sprint past Ibrahim when a turquoise light flashed a narrow beam out of one of the front display cabincts. Sarah flinched and swerved towards it, and impossibly, locking eyes on the face of the woman from her dreams. It was a coin, a coin set into a pendant. The face had turquoise eyes and a soft vulnerable mouth. The hair was not quite flowers, she could see that now, and the lips had a hint of fangs. She'd never seen a Medusa coin like it. Sarah pressed her palms against the glass case. She felt a feral desire to touch it. She'd never felt so compelled by anything in her life, even though every nerve in her body was screaming for her to escape.

Ibrahim, open mouthed, watch her with an expression of fear and disbelief. Was it for sale? Before she could ask, Ibrahim withdrew the chain and pendant, and held it out for her. She looked from his hand to his distorted face.

"Yes, its very nice, but how much is it?" He blinked at her.

"You asked about the door."

Now Sarah blinked. Slowly she responded, not wanting to repeat whatever had triggered Ibrahim.

"Yes. I guess thats why you thought I'd like it."

Without registering the speed at which he moved, Ibrahim was behind her and reaching around her to latch the pendant. Sarah struggled, knocking racks of chains and earring to the ground.

"Don't do that. I didn't say yes. I don't even know the cost. Get away."

Ibrahim pushed her up against the counter. She kicked out, a shelf of ceramic crashed to the ground, and a mannequin in sparkly belly dancer clothes toppled over. She tried reaching him with her keys.

"Stop that. You can't force me to buy it. Let go. I'm calling the police."

Ibrahim fumbled frantically, forcing the necklace in place, while gibbering and crying.

"You asked about the door. You saw the door."

Sarah used her body to push back. A stand of postcards toppled over.

Ibrahim was sweating and swearing, his voice at a fevered pitch. He sprang away from her, the pendant now around her neck.

"There is no door. Don't you understand? You can only see it if she calls you."

As soon as the words left his mouth he screamed in

terror, a light shot out from the coin, and hit Ibrahim's mouth. His lips began to turn grey and he collapsed into a leaden heap. Sarah screeched, tried to pull off the necklace, and was lanced with pain. Her fingers reached around to the back of her neck and felt the chain adhered into her skin. She heard movement from the second floor and bolted for the door, securing the pendant under her dress top. She didn't care if the police stopped her for non-payment. She ripped open the door and ran towards the flat of the wounded man to get Christine. As she turned the corner, her friend was walking up to greet her.

"Well that was unexpected. I hope you weren't too bored. Thanks for waiting."

Sarah, panting, opened her mouth to speak and found she didn't know what to say. She'd seen a door that wasn't a door, was forced to accept a necklace she couldn't take off and the man who accosted her was hit by laser beams from the pendant. She looked over to the side of the store and, oh yes, the door was gone. Her nightmares had followed her to Turkey and were hanging around her neck. As she and Christine continued on their way, two sets of eyes followed their progress. They closed the shop. It was time to make ready.

***

The night view from the rooftop restaurant was breathtaking. The Blue Mosque was lit from below and the gulls called out to each other as they circled the minarets. Sarah had decided not to say anything yet. She could not get the image of poor Ibrahim out of her mind. She feared he was dead, and somehow, she was a part of it. She put her one hand to her chest and clutched the edges of her silver threaded pashmina to keep her warm. Christine smiled, misunderstanding her friend's distraction.

"I'm sure he'll be here soon, and you look stunning."

Sarah had picked a Greek inspired soft grey dress in a silky material, with an empire waistline, a very high side slit and cording wrapped around twice. She put her hair up in combs with long tendrils hanging down, enough to cover the necklace. Her lips shone with a light shell-pink lipstick and her emerald eyes were fringed with just a hint of mascara.

"This is such a different look for you. Usually you wear your happy floral maxi dresses, and this is almost mythical." She gave her a sly sideways glance.

"Clever girl."

What Christine didn't know is that Sarah didn't remember making this or buying it. She wasn't even quite clear about doing her own hair. Christine, on the other hand was practically glowing in an apricot wrap dress that showed off her runners' legs. She was the picture of good health and energy. She loved being in the middle of the action and being alive. Sarah started to return the compliment, when suddenly her vision blurred and was overlaid with a different scene. Christine wasn't on the roof anymore. Christine was falling down an embankment, rocks were cascading all around, and she landed in rushing water. She was flailing and reaching for one of the two branches that jutted out from the other edge of the stream. The weight of her clothes was pulling her down. She grabbed the first branch, it broke off in her hand, and she was swept into the cave and down the falls. Sarah screamed and ran to grab her, when arms wrapped around her waist and yanked her backwards.

Startled, she saw the entire restaurant, patrons, staff, the team staring at her, her worst fears realized, and then there was Michael, who had kept her from pitching headlong over the side of the building. His eyes were wide with concern and confusion. He was breathing heavily, and his hands were still on her waist. She began to shake, and he folded her into his arms, holding her to him.

"You're OK. What was that? What happened?" He stepped back, not letting go.

"You almost went over the side of the roof. I saw you standing there looking, well you look like a goddess, and then you screamed."

Sarah opened her mouth to speak, but then was surrounded by the rest of the team and Christine. Sarah shut her eyes.

"Please, I'm sorry but I wasn't here. I mean I saw Christine fall. The earth was trembling, and she fell into water, heading for a waterfall. She grabbed the first branch, but I was trying to tell her it was broken and to grab the second one, and." Sarah stopped. She'd never wanted to hide more than she did now. Michael looking impossibly sexy in his jeans and dove grey dress shirt and he still had a steadying hand on her arm. Spiro was looking at her with almost a hint of fear, Ari his assistant radiated affront, and Herman was the only person who seemed relaxed.

"So, Sarah, did you get into the raki early, or was it like a vision or something? Either way, if you're OK,

I'm having kabobs. Who's with me?"

Sarah could have kissed him. Herman broke the spell and they all gathered around the table. One of the local students, Bulent, began telling stories and the conversations turned to other digs, flying carpets and treasures.

"Golbekli Tepe actually means Potbelly Hill." Herman chimed in.

"Yeah. It's right beside Old Man's Crevasse." The team responded with chuckles and groans. These were old jokes. The mood settled and they sat under the vine covered trellises, eating and talking, and gazing across the rooftops to the sea of Marmara. Sarah knew that something had changed. Spiro continued to regard Sarah with an intense stare that became increasingly unnerving. Her nerves already frayed, she decided it was enough.

"May I help you sir? I'm sorry for the earlier disturbance but it wasn't normal for me either." Spiro leaned back and whispered something to his assistant who nodded, looked at Sarah and left down the stairs. Spiro looked back at Sarah, blew air through his lips and shrugged his shoulders.

"I'm not so sure this is the first time. You saw something did you not? You have some sort of prophetic gift you think?"

Slowly his eye looked at her with a shrewdness that was at odds with his manner. Sarah blanched. She did not want to have this conversation. Off to the side she heard Herman.

"This is so cool. Oh man." The team became silent, sensing the friction.

Christine laid a protective hand on Sarah's arm. She looked around at the others at the table.

"Sarah doesn't have to answer that. She's here for a rest. She hasn't been sleeping well and I'd appreciate if you'd all just let her be."

One of the students, Johansen, looked at Christine.

"Well as long as she's not coming to the site. We can't afford to have her going and hurting herself or someone else. Sorry if you aren't well but we don't need a druggie."

Sarah's cheeks burned with shame, and tears threatened to cascade over them. How could this night have gone so wrong?

"I've never done drugs in my life, but you don't have to worry. I'm not going to your site." Michael's arm tightened around her shoulder.

"Mr. Johansen, that was out of line. I want people on my team who can be objective and examine the evidence before making decisions and presenting them as fact. You have definitely brought your suitability into question."

Johansen's body became rigid and he leaned back to consider the implications of Michael's words.

In the corner of the terrace there was a carpeted lounging area, decorated with hand painted tiles, and red and gold cushions, It was a place for people who wanted tea or coffee and a nargile, or as the tourists called them, hookah pipes. It was lit with hanging Moroccan lanterns. Michael stood up and led Sarah, Christine, Spiro and Herman away from the few other diners who were openly listening, and to the couches. The students and other workers stayed at the tables.

Sarah took a moment to feel the cooling in the air, a respite from the heat of the day. She raised her chin, breathed deeply to centre herself and began.

"Most of my life I've had feelings, that tended to come true." Herman laughed.

"Me too. When I got here, I felt hungry and I was."

Christine gave him a slap on the arm. Sarah gave a tiny smile.

"Thanks. That makes this a little easier to know I'm not alone."

Herman gave a little nod of the head. His eye sent a private message of support.

"I'd get a feeling in my gut that something was going to happen or that someone was ill. I don't know. It never made much sense. It learned it was just easier not to say anything." She looked away. Spiro nodded but didn't comment.

Michael's eyes found Sarah's.

"So, what brought you here to Turkey?"

His tone was low and so compassionate that Sarah had to stop from brushing his lips with hers. "I've been having dreams, bad dreams. It has been months and I knew I had to do something to make them stop."

Christine moved her hand off Sarah's arm and rubbed her shoulder.

Spiro came to attention and faced them, hands together and legs a bit apart to accommodate his girth.

"Tell us about this dream if you please."

Sarah looked at the cityscape, the Hippodrome with its obelisk, Topkapi palace and the cruise ships in the distance.

"The dream is always the same. There's a door in a tree, etched with a painting I created, or I thought I created. It's a woman with a blue face surrounded by flowers. I step forward to run my fingertips along the recesses of the carved panel, like I need proof that it's real, even though I'm in a dream. There is a soft light emanating from the skin. The flowers are small delicate buds. They have a phosphorescent glow, but the green seems wrong, like radioactive glass. Then my knees start to get weak, and my head is forced to bend, like in worship, or prayer. I don't know if it's a shrine or a holy place, but I start to pass out and I know that I can't let that happen."

As Sarah continues, shadowy figures begin to filter onto the terrace.

"I'm scared. I start to panic, and I want to leave. It's really dark, too dark. I don't want to stay in the too dark. The roots of the tree start thrashing, and I try to push off the damp grass, but I can't feel the earth. I start to fall and then I wake up."

Michael puts both arms around her as she shivers.

"I just want it to stop. I thought if I got away for a while, spent time in nature, painted something besides the woman with the blue face, I'd keep from falling apart."

As the group sat silent, seven men appeared behind Spiro. Spiro stands.

"I am sorry Sarah, but you have seen the woman with the blue face, and I am afraid that we can't allow you to answer that call."

Michael face darkened, his jaw clenched, and white

lines formed around his mouth.

"Spiro, what is wrong with you? Earlier tonight you questioned Sarah about having visions, now you are threatening her for having dreams? I don't know what this is about, but it stops now."

As if on command, the strangers move into action. One of the men pushed aside the low table to reach for Sarah, Michael jumped swiftly to block him. The teacups go flying, shattering against the tiled wall. Sarah felt a sharp pain, like a bite, and a thin turquoise line shoots out and hit the advancing man in the neck. He screamed and a grey patch spread to his shoulder as he crashed to the ground. Spiro jumped up and moved faster than a man of his age and size could usually do. His eyes widened as he sees the pendant that has fallen forward on her neck. He looks at Sarah with a blistering glare, filled with unbridled fear and hate.

"Where did you get the coin? That is stolen property from the Greek government. You will give it to me now. You are a thief. Gentlemen, restrain her, but don't look at the coin."

Christine jumped up to block the next man coming to grab Sarah and flips him back over the couch. Sarah calls out.

"Wait. It's not real. It's a knock off. I got it at a shop in Gulhane."

Christine, bracing for the next attack, looks over at her.

"What shop? I don't remember it."

"It was when you were helping the man with snake bites. I went into a store on the corner." Christine stops and stares at her, open mouthed.

"How'd you know they were snake bites? I told you rats, but it was snakes."

Sarah shook.

"I don't know. I don't know what's going on. I didn't steal it. A man forced it on my neck and now I can't take it off." The room was spinning.

She stumbled back as a man jumped on the couch and was knocked off by Herman tackling him to the ground. The staff raced up to grab the remaining pipes to take them to safety. Management was screaming for everyone to get out and they could hear the wail of police sirens. Spiro was urging his men on and yelling into his cell phone.

"Yes, she has it. It's already bonded. Where were the watchers? She has to be taken now. I don't care. Use whatever force is necessary."

Spiro looked around wildly for Sarah, screaming at his men.

At the other end of the terrace Sarah, Christine and Michael were sprinting down the back-kitchen stairs, and out to the back alley. Once they hit the ground both Michael and Christine rounded on her. Christine went first.

"Would you like to tell me what the hell is going on? Someone forced something around your neck, and you didn't bother to mention it? Snake bites? You can't take it off?" Michael went next. Cradling the pendant in his hand, despite Sarah's scared protests,

"Where did you really get this? This is no knock off. This is older than almost anything in the museum.

The only place you could have found something like this might be at the museum,"

He stopped, looking like he's never seen her before.

"Maybe something undiscovered from the ocean floor, something from the tunnel?"

Sarah, already shivering went deathly cold.

"You think I stole something from the museum?"

Michael's eyes swirled with blues and greys, hurt and anger.

"Give me a better story Sarah. One I can believe."

Christine shoved Michael.

"Look I just met you, but I've known Sarah for decades and she's no thief."

Michael didn't take his eyes off of Sarah while addressing Christine.

"A minute ago you didn't know about the necklace, the supposed attack and yet somehow she knew about what injured your patient. I'd say you don't know everything about your friend. I think we need to take a trip down to the police station, check out this store, and the necklace will need to be examined by the experts. I'm sorry Christine but she may have just been using you to get access to the museum."

Sarah's mouth open and trembled. Christine quickly touched her arm.

"Well I think we've got bigger problems right now. There are still strange men probably running down from the restaurant, and they are willing to hurt us. Michael, I'll go around the left side of the building and you go around the right and we'll see which way is clear. When we know we'll get back here and grab Sarah. You good with that girlfriend?"

Sarah nodded miserably. Michael had stopped looking at her. His face closed.

Sarah crossed the alley and tucked herself into the shadows of a doorway. She watched two men scramble down the stairs, both holding weapons. She wanted to shout out to her friends, well at least one friend, but that would only get her killed. How could this be happening? This morning she was strolling through the weekly market in Kumkapi, on the north shore of the sea of Marmara. It brought back memories from when she and Christine met, sharing a cheap apartment when they were students on an international exchange program. Now she was facing the possibility of a Greek or Turkish jail, and Michael, the first decent guy she'd met since Phil, might help put her there. Wondering if she should make a break for it, she started to inch around the corner and was flanked by two cloaked women. Their height was staggering, and their faces were hidden.

"Sarah Prophet, your time is short. If you wish to live you will come with us."

Sarah didn't know whether to be terrified that they knew her name or laugh at the bad acting. It was when they blew the powder in her face, that she saw the fangs and passed out.

"Sister, she wakes."

Sarah's eyes flew open when she heard the voice. She knew it instinctively. It had been part of the background of her dreams. She awoke reclining on a set of floor pillows in reds and yellows. The room was rocking, and she could hear the lapping of water on the other side of the wall. Pendant lanterns lit the space and the floors were smooth like marble, but nothing compared to her hosts. Their hair cascaded in riots of black curls and their faces seemed elongated with the tips of fangs peeking over the top of their lower lips. Their eyes were rimmed with kohl and when they blinked a second set of clear lids flicked up and down. Sarah might have been able to look past these things, except that instead of legs, from the waist down they were snakes.

Sarah tried not to recoil as they slide towards her. She reminded herself that if they had wanted to kill her, they could have done it in the alleyway. Were those wings? She guessed that explained the no top thing.

"Your time is short, little one and there is much to do."

The one chided the other.

"Sister, where are your manners? I am Eurydale and this is Sthenos. We are Gorgons, as I am sure you know." Sarah didn't know, but her fear suddenly calmed.

"In your blood you know. We were the protectors of the oracle. Most only know of the one Gorgon, our sister Medusa, who was slain for her beauty."

Sarah startled. That was a new one. She'd heard that Medusa was so ugly that her looks turned men to stone. As if they'd read her thoughts from her face, Eurydale continued.

"No, she was beautiful, but because of it, she was attacked and the goddess Athena, whom she served, gave her a weapon to protect herself from men who would take what was not freely given. What you have around your neck is one of the last drops of her blood."

Sarah had been clutching the pendant and quickly let go.

"I'm so sorry. That's horrible. Please take it back. I didn't have a choice." She struggled to pull it off, but it was stuck.

"It is too late for that. You have the necklace because it called to you. You need to use that blood for a special task."

Sarah stopped and saw from the intensity in their eyes that this was not a request. She decided on trying another tactic.

"Look, I'm not saying I won't help you, but I have to find my friends. I'm in a bit of a mess and maybe you can explain to the police that I didn't steal the necklace, though I guess you don't go out much."

Sthenos narrowed her eyes and Sarah figured now might be when they bite her head off. Eurydale responded.

"You do not need to worry. Your friends are here. We thought you might need some help completing your task."

Sthenos stayed with Sarah while Eurydale carried in Michael and Christine and deposited them on the floor. Seeing her strength, Sarah realized that escape would not be an option, even if they weren't at sea, and they also had wings. She crawled over to her friends and undid their bindings.

After several moments, screams and orientation, all three faced their captors.

Sarah shook her head in bewilderment.

"So, all the dreams, Christine's job and the necklace were all to get me here?"

Michael, though not touching her, seemed to have thawed, but was still tense and alert. Christine was still looking shell-shocked, blonde curls in disarray.

"So, what do you need from me? If you have the blood, why can't you find her yourself?" Sthenos gave a fang-filled smile.

We are immortal. Our sister was not. We cannot use the blood because the protections do not allow us access. It needs to be a human who can bond with the blood and only someone with oracle lineage can do that. The blood will help you to find and wake our mother."

Michael's eyebrows shot up.

"Excuse me," he said, shifting into a defensive position.

"Echidna, the mother of all monsters? Present company excepted of course."

The Gorgons broke into what must have been their form of laughter. The sounds raked through their bodies. All three guests paled. Michael spoke again.

"With respect, this would be a very bad idea for the human population."

Sudden Sthenos was at Michael's side, a golden-green coil around his neck.

"And what you do not understand is that Typhon, the father of those monsters, is waking up and unless Echidna is returned to him, he will tear apart the world looking for her."

Reacting instinctively, Sarah reached out and placed

her hand on Sthenos' arm. The coil immediately retracted, the Gorgon looked stunned and darted over to her sister. They conferred, looking at Sarah with new eyes.

"So, it seems that your oracle blood is no longer dormant. Our sister's blood is also warming to you."

Christine finally spoke out.

"So, if she has oracle blood, which is a new one, then you have to protect her, right? You have to listen to her? So if she says you have to take us home and fix the Spiro problem you have to, right?" Sarah shook her head violently. She didn't know if she could influence them twice.

A blue sheen began to glow from Sthenos's face as she sidled up beside Christine.

"Little sister you do not quite understand the situation. The coin, once worn by an oracle, activates the blood. The wearer has 24 hours to use it or absorb it. There's no going back."

All three sat in stunned silence. The boat creaked and the lantern swayed, and the painting holiday seemed to drift away.

Tears dripped unbidden down Sarah's cheek. She was not strong enough for this. There was no right answer. She looked at Michael's face and she saw the apology in his eyes, and the hurt at being so powerless to take this from her. She looked at Christine who'd always been the strong one, the brave one, the one to come up with the most daring ideas and always make sure it was safe. How could she protect her friend?

"So, I have 24 hours to find your mother, wake her up, hope she doesn't eat me, reunite her with your father and hope he doesn't eat me. After that the world will have a plague of monsters, present company excepted. Or I can fail, Typhon awakes and destroys most of the world looking for Echidna and I become a Gorgon."

The sisters looked at her unblinkingly, their coils writhing slowly.

"That is not completely correct. The 24 hours started this afternoon as soon as you killed poor Ibrahim."

Michael and Christine whipped around towards Sarah and jumped back. In unison they yelled,

"You did what?"

"No, no I didn't! The pendant did it when he started talking about the blue faced woman. I didn't recognize the image because it wasn't Medusa, it was Echidna, and if I only have 18 hours left, and I don't know where she is, its pointless."

Overcome with misery, she dropped her face into her hands.

Meanwhile, the sisters leaned over a map they'd spread out on an old captain's desk. Sarah was glad their hair continued to cover their chests. They pointed with blood red nails.

Michael and Christine looked at each other. The Gorgons were pointing at Golbekli Tepe.

He shook his head.

"That doesn't make any sense. The gods are Greek. Why would they be in Turkey?"

Eurydale answered.

"Typhon was so big his head brushed the stars. He fought Zeus and defeated him. The gods, became afraid, transformed into animals and fled to Egypt. When they went, in revenge, they took Echidna and hid her so she couldn't cry out to Typhon. In his grief at losing her, Zeus was able to defeat Typhon and put him to sleep, some say under Mount Etna and some say the Euphrates. We won't tell you exactly where he is, but either location would not turn out well for the humans."

Sthenos slid forward.

"What you need to understand human, is that Typhon is stirring."

All three sat and thought about the tremors that had been going through the region for the last several months. It was nothing new, but the frequency was increasing. Christine put up her hand.

"So that still doesn't explain what Gobekli Tepe has to do with it?"

The sisters seemed to sigh.

"There are 200 monoliths in 20 circles. You humans dig and dig but there is nothing there. Most are portals. They connect us to the immortals who have gone to sleep, or must never be born, and things that would destroy your minds even to hear their names."

Christine lowered her hand.

"Sorry I asked and Sarah, if you have a prophecy about these unspeakable things, now is not the time to share it."

Sarah looked at the sisters.

"It takes over 18 hours by bus to get near the site. We are in a boat. How can we get there in time?"

Sthenos smiled.

"Being a monster has some benefits."

The sisters, in unison, leaned over and blew powder

in their faces, and the three passed out.

"Wake!"

The command crackled through their heads as all three sat bolt upright, greeting the rising sun on the rise in Golbekli Tepe, near the camp. Christine clutched her backpack, which had been in her hotel room, Michael also had a bag full of supplies and Sarah had a pale blue, finely woven cape embroidered with wings. Most of the site was still shrouded in shadows. As the three started to walk down to the site Sarah took the lead. Light came from the pendant, pointing the way. Her face began to shine as she lifted her palms. Michael and Christine exchanged looks.

"Nothing freaky here," muttered Christine and then they heard the clicks.

Flanking them on both sides, was Spiro and eight armed guards. Spiro, dressed in local garb, stepped forward, the sun reflecting off his glasses, his long tunic flapping, his hair bound.

"I am sorry it had to come to this but as soon as I heard mention of the lady with the blue face, I called my compatriots and had a plane ready to go. We had an idea where you might be headed."

He motioned to the men in mountain tribesman dress, all with rifles pointed. Michael's fists clenched.

"Spiro you don't know what you are doing. You don't know what is at stake."

Spiro's smile slid off his face.

"It is you Michael that don't understand. For thousands of years a coalition of families from Greece, Turkey and Egypt have watched over this site and performed the rituals to keep the gods slumbering. We cannot allow you to wake Echidna and bathe the world in fresh monsters and the horror they will bring. You must not wake the gods."

As Spiro spoke, he became more animated and his eyes burned with fanatical zeal.

"The gods have no mercy and they must not be allowed to rise. The portals must stay shut."

He waved his hand in the air.

"Shoot them! Shoot them all."

Suddenly the ground shook violently, and a part of the hillside fell away. Some of the riflemen fell into a breach, screaming on the way down, others were hit by rocks exploding from the ground, and another managed to get on his knee and point his gun only to be grabbed from above by something with talons and wings. Michael reached for Sarah as they struggled to follow the beam, when a second convulsion hit, and Christine was thrown down an embankment. Soon they heard the splash. Sarah raced to the edge.

"The second branch. Grab the second branch."

Christine was carried out of sight and bullets shot at the dirt beside them, dust flying and gravel scattering. There was nothing more they could do for her now.

"Sarah we've got to go."

They ran, following the light, into a newly open cave. They stumbled down a drop off, landing on thick, glowing moss.

Grim-faced, Sarah looked at Michael. He could

guess what she was going to say.

"This is exactly like the dream."

There was no more time to decide.

"Maybe it wouldn't be so bad to be a gorgon," she joked weakly.

He reached out for her.

Michael took her face in his hands. She closed her eyes and rested her forehead on his. She pressed her lips against his mouth, and savoured the warmth and passion in his response. They held on as if they were drowning and her heart shattered from needing regret. She looked at him trying to memorize his face. She smiled softly.

"Worst timing ever."

Pain sprung into his eyes. She turned from his embrace and faced the door. There was no handle, but she knew how to enter this door that was a portal. The pressure to merge was almost unbearable. She heard the flapping of wings and the last few blasts of gunfire. The eyes on the pendant glowed a violent green that matched the colour in the door. Sarah went to her knees and let herself be drawn in.

Once inside she saw the still form of Echidna, mother of monsters, the half viper and dragon, laying on a carved slab. Her face was beautiful, her body like that of her daughters. She lay in a thick, translucent gel, in a state of half-life.

Sarah made her choice.

Moments later the door fell open and the Gorgons rushed in, claws extended, but Sarah raised a hand and pointed to Echidna. She was no longer restrained and could move even though she slept.

"What game is this?" raged Sthenos.

Behind her were Michael, and Herman, with his arm around a very wet Christine, wearing his jacket. They stood deathly still waiting for her answer, her friends unable to get around the Gorgons.

"I was given an all or nothing choice and decided that there was another option."

She paused, giving Sthenos and Eurydale time to calm, their eyes filtering from red to black.

"I gave your mother 3/4 of a drop of Medusa's blood and let the other 1/4 be absorbed. She is free just not awake. You can take her to Typhon and go and watch over her."

The Gorgons looked at each other. Sthenos spoke.

"We may not forgive you for refusing to restore our mother, but she is free so we will stay our hands. Also, since you now carry a remnant of our sister's blood, she lives in you, so we claim you as family. From today our connection will stay, but the dreams of our mother are gone." Michael stepped up, his face haggard but his eyes hopeful.

"So, she's OK? What if she gets mad at me?" The sisters chortled. Eurydale smiled.

"She does not have Medusa's weapon, and if she gets mad at you, buy flowers."

Michael grinned ruefully.

 Sthenos added,

"And don't forget who her sisters are."

Michael gave a quick nod and took a brisk step away from them.

Sarah looked at the Gorgons and felt a surge of affection.

"So, what happens to me now?"

Eurydale picked up their mother, and Sthenos answered.

"Having a mix of oracle and Gorgon blood will make things…interesting."

Michael ran a hand through his hair, gave Sarah a searching look, and stepped up again.

"So, does that mean the we can be an us?"

From the front of the cave Herman snorted.

"You were mated from the first minute you two met. It doesn't take an oracle to figure that one out." Christine rolled her eyes.

"Can we please get out of here so I can find some dry clothes and get something to eat? I'm starving."

Herman grinned. "That's my girl." Christine shook her head.

Everyone walked out of the cave towards the tents. Spiro was nowhere in sight.

Christine looked at Herman.

"How did you get here so fast anyway?"

Sarah watched as they retreated and caught the faint glowing outline of wings on Herman's sneakers. Herman looked back at her and winked.

Sarah looked at Michael and her eyes flew open wide.

"Oh no!"

The tip of her tongue found two tiny points at the ends of her top canine teeth.

Michael looked at them and gave a wicked grin.

"You know, they are kind of sexy."

VOLUME 3

Sarah decided to put his claim to the test. As he proved his point, she wondered if she could convince Michael to take a little R &R at the antique pools of Cleopatra and help create some new dreams. What could possibly go wrong?

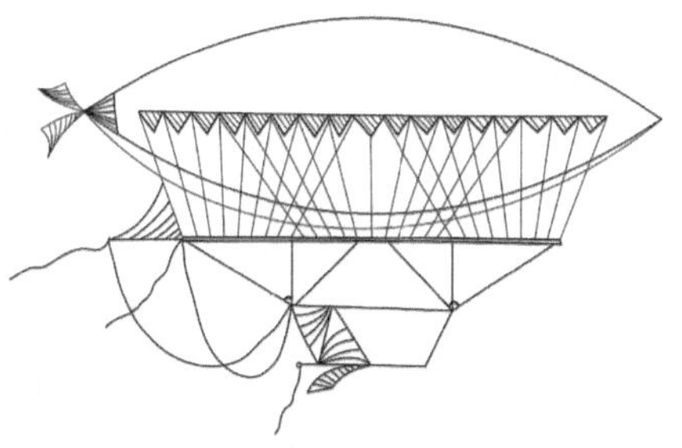

AROUND THE WORLD IN 80 DIRIGIBLES: LEG ONE

SCARLETT LAKE

Hyde Park

Violet couldn't believe her eyes as she looked around the wide-open green space that was Hyde Park. In her life, she had never seen such a spectacle as this, and she never thought she would again, even with the adventure they were about to undertake. This was one of those 'take a mental picture' moments, an image she hoped she could still remember when she was a little old lady.

"Violet!" she hears called over the throng. Looking around, she sees the Doc waving her over in that frantic way he does when he gets excited—like a kid who has just discovered the candy store.

"Come on, Edison," Violet says to the four-legged beast stood loyally at her side, who reaches up past her waist in height. She runs off towards the Doc, otherwise known as Doctor Everett Wellington, scientist and inventor extraordinaire. Edison runs alongside, his long legs flying around comically as his tale swings erratically from side to side. Together, a girl and her dog run through a maze of airships, great and small. Some as large as houses with stretched fabric balloons reaching up into the sky, pulling strings taught ready to take flight. Others are as small as horse carriages designed to only transport two people, with smaller balloons being batted around by the large ones as they fight for airspace. She weaves her way through the gaps in the ships, eyes wide with excitement as she takes in the competition.

"No more larking about, young lady," the Doc says as she skids to a halt at the base of one of the largest ships in the entire park. Their ship. She blows her long brown hair out of her eyes and stands up straight before the Doc throwing a mock salute his way. Edison, stands to attention by her side, lifting his paw just like his girl.

"I wasn't larking, Sir," she replies, the side of her hand still against her forehead and her shoulders as far back as they will go.

"Then what were you doing?" he asks with a slight, almost unnoticeable smirk and a twinkle in his eye as he stands at the base of the ramp leading up to the Queen Victoria. A couple of days ago she asked him why he named their ship after the current lady of the throne, and he responded with…

"I'll tell you, young Violet. When you ask a lady to

borrow one of her dragons so you can compete in an around the world race to win the title of The Greatest Dirigible Inventor, a cash prize and a bottle of the best Scotch this side of the Thames… she has a few conditions."

Violet thought that Victoria had leant one of her dragons as a thank you for the Doc catching Jack the Ripper. Not that anyone knew he had, besides Violet herself, Victoria, a constabulary or two and the Ripper himself, it was all very hush-hush. Oh, and Edison knew, of course, he's in on all the gossip. She had heard Mr Holmes kicking off one night when she was supposed to be asleep but wasn't. Instead, she was up reading, prepping for their upcoming adventure, when she heard Sherlock's voice filter through the vent grate in the corner of her room. She only caught a few words, but it sounded like he was upset that the Doc beat him to the catch and made him look like a fool. Not that he needs much help in that matter, anyone who's anyone knows what a drunken lout the famous Detective has become. Sad really.

With Doc Everett, Violet has leant to take what he says with a pinch of salt. He's a little on the eccentric side… who's she kidding? He's a LOT on the eccentric side. But with a bit of kookiness comes the brain of a genius, one who longs to escape the laboratory and head out on adventure-filled travels around the globe. That's the real reason for entering the competition. Not to win some lame title or the cash prize, but because he wants the adventure. An excuse to travel the world in his airship that's powered by a dragon. To see the sights, he's only read about in books. And to do it in less than eighty days so he can throw it back in Jules Verne's face. Theirs is a long-standing rivalry that would take more than eighty days to cover!

"I was surveying the competition, Sir," Violet remarks with a proud smile as she watches Enoch carry a large crate up the ramp. His big bulky arms wrapped around the wooden box carrying it with ease.

"Good show, my girl," the Doc says with a smile. "Now, all aboard. We'll be leaving shortly, and I can't leave my navigator behind, can I?"

"Definitely not, Sir," she says as she drops her hand and runs up the ramp onto the ship, nearly knocking Enoch over as she goes. Edison, ever the loyal creature, follows behind, but not before grabbing himself a bag, holding the strap between his teeth and carrying it with him up with the ramp.

Violet stands aboard the Queen Victoria, an airship with a large wooden base that looks as though it belongs sailing the high seas manned by a crew of bloodthirsty pirates. Instead, it's due to soar amongst the clouds, flying alongside the birds as it sails the atmosphere, floating in the air with its giant canvas gas-filled balloon. It certainly is a grand transport vessel and one of the biggest competing in *The Great Dirigible Race*. Any airship that is to be powered by a Queens dragon has to be a reasonable size, after all. Plus, the Doc doesn't do anything small!

She runs to the front of the ship and nestles herself within the small 'V' as she looks out over the park, viewing the spectacle from above. Edison trots over to her side, a large monocular in his mouth looking very much like a dog who's found himself a stick. Violet takes it from him with a scratch behind the ear as she raises it to her eye and looks out at the seventy-nine airships the Queen Victoria is competing against in this around the world adventure.

Edison jumps up, his front paws sitting on the rail alongside Violet as she looks from ship to ship, his head moving from side to side as hers does, taking a mental note of what they see. The designs are astounding, each one different from the next.

There's one with a black and white spiral striped balloon, looking like a circus big top, that looks to be powered by monkeys with top hats on penny farthings and a series of complicated gears and cogs. Another one has a balloon spiralled in the shape of a snail, and another is bright orange with feathers looking like something from another planet. There's one adorned with jewels, and it gleams as the first rays of sun hit it. If you could imagine it, it was there, and Violet was in awe.

"Doc?" she shouts over her shoulder, trying to gain his attention.

Everett glides towards her, travelling across the deck, his long brown coat flowing behind him in the cold winter breeze.

"What do your eyes spy upon the horizon?" he asks with humour in his voice as though they are pirates sailing the high seas… or skies.

"There, look," Violet says as she points to a particular ship in the far distance, one that has a balloon resembling a giant submarine. Handing her monocular over, she waits as the Doc spies her catch.

"Why that rotten ratbag!"

"Language Doc, young ears are present," she says with a smirk. It's usually the Doc who is telling her off for her potty mouth, at the ripe age of 12; it's pretty bad at times. But what can he expect from a little orphan who spent too many years alone on the less than desirable streets of London? Her parents died when she was but a young girl, too young to be left alone with no one in the world to care for her, especially at a time when London's population was overrun by the poor and oppressed.

She did everything she could to survive on her own on the dirty backstreets and alleyways. She rummaged through trash, stole from market stalls and pickpocketed when she could. She fought the bad men on the streets who tried to take her. The first few she bit and outrun by hiding in spots they couldn't reach. Until one day when she was trapped in a circle by big men who smelled like rotten fish, she thought that was it, at the age of 8 she was going to be taken somewhere by these bad men. She didn't know what they wanted with her, but she knew it wasn't anything good. Then Edison came into her life. He scared away the men with his loud bark and his vicious bite. Since that day, they have been inseparable. Since that day, she hasn't been alone.

Edison looked after her, kept her warm on cold nights, kept bad men at bay and stole the occasional loaf of bread from the local bakers. As well as a few pies from Mrs Lovett's pie shop, but Violet never ate those; they didn't smell quite right. Edison, however, gobbled them up with an abundance of drool dripping from his mouth as he licked his lips. She was pretty sure the filling was gone off dog food.

"I do apologise, young Madam. You are right. Such words should not reach ears as small as yours." She and the Doc had a rather amusing relationship. His eccentric personality, her independence, somehow it seems to work. It isn't like a father/daughter relationship. It's more like two lost souls who didn't realise how alone they were until someone else showed them. Violet was the little lost orphan with no one but a dog to love and care for her. A girl with no hope or prospects in life, doomed to spend the rest of her days living on the streets. Everett was one of the richest men in the city who spent his days lost in his inventions and shunned by his peers. He was a man stuck in his own head who needed to learn the art of adventure, and that was certainly something Violet has taught him over the past few years she has been living with him.

"Is it him?" she asks as she squints her eyes to the submarine looking design of an airship that she pointed out in the distance. He just had to go with that design!

"Oh yes! I know for a fact he had that design patented and copyrighted. Copyrighted, such hosh-tosh if you ask me. It's just his way of showing off. Typical Verne!" Everett huffs and puffs as he continues to stare ahead, eye refusing to move from the monocular. "It was *my* design, to begin with! The ratbag stole it from me and claimed it as his own. Just like Tesla did with that blinking electricity."

Violet rolls her eyes and watches as Edison does the same; he will never let that Nautilus issue go. The Doc is a nightmare when he gets started. This is especially true when it involves people who stole from him… and there are many those, according to him anyway.

"And then he went and gave the design to Frankenstein. Victor Frankenstein! People have the nerve to call me eccentric."

Violet left him to his mumblings as she moved away and watched Enoch pull the ramp-up and ready the moorings.

"Wait! Where's Thaddeus?" she asks, looking around the deck of their ship for the other member of their five-man troop; well, four-man and a dog. Or three men, one girl and a dog if you wanted to get technical.

"Below deck, prepping the dragon," Enoch says in his dull droning tone. He's definitely what would be considered 'the muscle' of their troop. The Doc is the brains and the wallet. Thaddeus is the pilot and navigator, and Violet, well, she's the one whose job is to keep them on track and monitor the competition. She knows just how side-tracked Everett can get! And Edison, he's her loyal steed and protector, always by her side.

"I want to go see," she says, the glee in her voice as clear as day. She starts to run off towards the small staircase leading below deck but stops when something catches her eye. Or more, someone.

On the next ship over, one entirely black in colour from its base to balloon, stands a man staring at her with a smirk on his face. He looks like a pirate captain who should be sailing the high seas searching for buried treasure rather than competing in an around the world race in a purpose-built dirigible to gain nothing more than a silly title. With his long curly black hair, handlebar moustache that stretches out past his cheeks and curls up at the ends, and the tricorne balancing on his head, he looks just like the pirates from the storybooks lining Everett's library.

There's something about this man that seems familiar. Something that sends alarm bells ringing inside Violet's head. She just can't pinpoint what it is.

She stares him down, Edison growling and baring his teeth at her side as he inches forward several paces to stand just ahead of her, his protective mode in full force. It seems she isn't the only one who can hear the alarm bell.

He stands there, straight-backed, the tricorne sat off-kilter on his head, standing underneath the tattered black balloon of his airship with skull and crossbones painted white on the side. She's so busy trying to work out where she seen him before, that she fails to hear the claxon. The one signalling lift-off. It isn't until she sees the moustached pirate bark orders and shift his gaze that she realises the race has begun. Edison barks at her side in excitement, jumping up and down on his gangly legs.

"Release the dragon!" the Doc cries, finally moving from the front of the ship where he hasn't stop sending Verne daggers.

Violet grips onto the outer railings, head thrown over the side as she watches ship after ship release their anchors and ascend into the sky, becoming one with the clouds while the Queen Victoria stays firmly planted on to the grassy knoll of Hyde Park.

"Doc?" she shouts as her head tips backwards, their competition moving higher and higher.

"Thaddeus?" Everett shouts, poking his head below deck. "Why isn't my dragon in the sky?"

Whoosh!

That'll be the dragon, Violet thinks as she scans the area to get her first glimpse. A large figure shoots out of a lower hatch in the ship and soars high above, its shadow looming over them. She looks up with her mouth agape at the red beast as it circles the ship with its wings spread out wide. Thaddeus guides it into a specially crafted harness designed with a complicated system of cogs and gears to use the dragon's wing power to fill the balloon with air.

The Queen Victoria rises, the last to touch off as the balloon finally fills with air and enters the competition. Eighty dirigibles in a race around the world.

The Rules

There are rules one has to follow when signed up to participate in an organised race, especially when that race involves sailing amongst the cloud and travelling around the world.

Rule One: Each contestant must be signed up officially with the race organiser.

Rule Two: Each contestant must start and end at the same place; Hyde Park, London, England.

Rule Three: Each contestant must start the race simultaneously; 09:00 am 5th May 1889.

Rule Four: Each contestant must travel around the world in a dirigible with a balloon contraption that can be powered by any means imagined.

Rule Five: No knocking other race contestants out of the sky.

Rule Six: Each dirigible can contain a MAXIMUM of 10 crew members; to include animals.

Rule Seven: Each dirigible MUST visit each destination on the map provided, collecting a token from a mystery point revealed with the collection of said token i.e. When you collect your first token, you will be given a clue as to the second token's location.

Rule Eight: The first dirigible to land back in Hyde Park with ALL tokens will be declared the winner.

Rules that Doc Everett took very seriously as they, Violet, Thaddeus, Enoch and Edison, stood around him looking at the rolled-up parchment in his hand, willing him to pull at the red ribbon holding it together and reveal their first destination.

"Come on! Open it," Thaddeus says, the excitement evident in his voice as it waivers slightly. He bobs up and down, resembling a child on Christmas morning, waiting to be told he can delve into the pile of presents waiting for him. Thaddeus was a funny little man, with his short skinny form and large spectacles perched on his angular face. His hair was always slicked back, and his tweed trousers sat several inches above his black leather shoes. If you asked him directly, he would claim he wanted to know which way to steer the Queen Victoria, but Violet could see that wasn't the only reason. This adventure must be beyond exciting to him; he got out of the lab less than Everett did, and that was saying something. Violet was sure this trip would do him some good; if anything, it could at least make his skin a little less ghostlike. A bit of colour in those cheeks would make him look **a lot** less like he had been scared to death and turned a ghostly shade of white.

"Yeah, come on, Doc," Violet chimed in, desperate to know where their first destination would take them. Would it lead to Egypt, where they could dig around amongst the Pharoah tombs? Or would it take them to Africa, where they would walk with the Elephants and dodge spears from the indigenous people? Or maybe they would head to Transylvania and battle an ancient vampire for a token?

'BARK!' Edison's bark broke through her day-dream.

Maybe she should start reading a little less, she thought; it was playing havoc with her imagination. But then, what fun would life be without a little bit of mind wandering on occasion?

Slowly, the Doc pulls on the ribbon. Violet watches with wide eyes, the anticipation building in her stomach as the parchment unravels, revealing their first destination in their round the world adventure.

PARIS.

Exposition Universelle

The French capital descended on them like a whirl-wind. It felt like they had barely set off from Hyde Park, the dragon moving at speed, its wings stretched wide as it pumped air into their canopy. Her excitement and exhil-aration that they were finally off on this adventure after months of planning and helping Everett build the Queen

Victoria, had helped the day pass in a blur as she moved around the ship like a wrecking ball. Paris emerged on the horizon as their ship dipped from the clear, darkening skies down towards the ground, skimming it like a pebble across a lake. The dragon kept them hovering above the city as bright lights began to twinkle like stars.

Violet hung her head over the railing taking mental pictures of a place she was unlikely to visit at a later date, and if she did, this was a sight she would never experience again. For this was the year that Paris hosted the Exposition Universelle. Her jaw hung open at the sight before her. The Doc had mentioned something about a giant tower being built in the heart of the city as a main attraction and spectacle for the millions due to descend on Paris in the coming months. And a spectacle it was indeed. Yards and yards of metal entwined and soldered together with four base legs moving inwards and upwards to join together, forming a point that sat high above the capital.

"I bet the views up there are something else," she mutters to herself as Edison nods his head in agreement.

"Nothing compared to the views from right here," the Doc's says as he moves to stand beside Violet, looking out over the railing. She smiles at him, one of her big smiles that is all full of shiny white teeth. Right, of course. They were sitting higher above the city than where the top of the tower stood. Their view was the better one, but not everyone was lucky enough to ride a dragon powered dirigible around the world; for some, the top of the tower was the best they would get for a bird's eye view of the Parisian city.

BANG!

Violet jumps out of her skin as a loud boom vibrates through the air. She ducks on instinct, Edison following her lead. Everett laughs as she looks up to see the sky alight with colour. Greens, reds, blues, yellows all accompany a barrage of loud bangs and whistles as fireworks fill the sky. Getting back to her feet, she hangs onto the Queen Victoria's railings as she tips her head back as far as it can go to watch the light show.

"Is this for us?" she asks dreamily in a whisper.

"This, my dear Violet, is to celebrate the official opening of Exposition Universelle," Everett says with a smile as he watches her continue to stare in awe at the firework display. He walks off, calling out to Thaddeus to bring them as close as possible to the metal tower. The instructions on the first parchment were clear; arrive in the great city of Paris, make your way to the new tower and hover a good several miles above, send at least one member to the ground. Once on the ground, the member or members of the competing airship must locate the race booth and get instructions on how to claim the first race token. Once the token had been claimed, they would receive the next parchment, which would reveal the location of the second token and so on, and so on. Until the world had been travelled and all tokens gained, the race to the finish line began.

Violet was tired; she has been awake since the early hours of the morning, her excitement for the start of the race too much for her. She had been bouncing off the walls all day at the sight of eighty very different airships crammed into Hyde Park. Then at the dragon and the sight of the Earth viewed from high above. Tired was definitely a good description of what she was, but her day wasn't over yet—she was being sent to the ground.

It had been discussed and decided during the flight to Paris that Violet would be the one to get the token, with Edison and Enoch as her companions. Edison never leaves her side anyway, and she would never go anywhere without him, not even to the toilet. But Enoch was a good muscle man, with his sizeable imposing stature and a face that rarely saw a smile grace its bulky features as it was fixed with a permanent scowl. Not many would dare to mess with her with a dog Edison's size by her side, but if they did, then that's where Enoch would come in. Violet was pretty sure he could lift their Queen one-handed if he tried – and that was saying something. Queen Victoria, the real one, was not known for being on the petite side. She would go, get the token, while the Doc stayed on board the ship with Thaddeus. She had tried to tell the Doc that he should go, but he refused to leave his ship, especially after seeing that Verne was competing in the race.

"I need to keep an eye on that ******," he said, another bad word coming out of his mouth, which Violet quickly pretended she didn't hear.

With a yawn, Violet climbs into a wicker basket built for two that was situated on the lower deck in the hold and sucked in a breath as Enoch squeezed in. Enoch had the build of two people.

"What about Edison?" Violet asks as the dog jumped up onto the edge and into the waiting arms of Enoch.

"Hold on tight," Thaddeus shouts as he pulled a lever that opened up a hatch in the floor. Violet screamed. Enoch screamed. Edison yelped and gripped onto Enoch's shoulder for dear life as the bottom dropped out from underneath them, and they began plummeting down to Earth. Violets knuckles turn white as she grips onto the sides of the basket, her hair upended to stick upright, going against gravity. Then with a small yelp, the falling comes to a stop with a jerk as the basket swings back and forth. She dares a glance over the edge to see they are already halfway down to the ground.

"Sorry!" she faintly hears yelled to them as she looks back up to see Thaddeus's head poking out the hatch they just fell through. It seems he forgot to tie the rope to the pulley.

That's a great start, Violet thinks as she watches them lower at a *much* slower and gentler pace the rest of the way to the ground. She can only hope that's the only hiccup they have. In reality, she knows that they will hit a few bumps in the road as the race goes on, especially when it involves passing through different time zones, different countries with different languages and cultures. But this is Paris, only a hop, skip and a jump—or a few hours dirigible flight by dragon—away from home, the bustling city of London. What could go wrong?

Violet looks around as they near the ground, the ants beginning to look like people. She sees others falling to earth too as dirigible after dirigible arrives at the French city and hover like a swarm of fancy-dressed locusts. But one particular craft catches her eye, it's not the craft itself but the man aboard. The pirate looking man with the handlebar moustache drops elegantly through the atmosphere. One hand gripped onto a smaller hand-held version of his airship, which he fills and releases gas using some sort of pumping motion. His fingers flex: clenching and unclenching onto something she cannot see as a balloon above his head fills to slow him down and empties to speed him up. She has to admit; it looks like a pretty fun way to travel.

The man catches her looking. She tries to divert her eyes, but it's too late. When she looks back for a brief moment, he sends her a wink and smirks before dropping rapidly out of her line of sight. She shivers, and not from the cold, as she peers over the edge to see the pirate land on his two feet, bending the knees slightly. He's the first one down to the ground. But he definitely wasn't the first to arrive; the Queen Victoria was—even after their delayed start.

Craft after craft pass them, each one a different form of getting to the ground, and all of them were faster than they were. It seems Thaddeus was taking things a little too slowly now. She looks up to signal 'faster' at him.

"Is that…?" she starts, momentarily distracted by a passing monkey with wings.

I don't think we're in Kansas anymore! Her thought is interrupted as Enoch jumps in the small space pushing the basket closer to the ground. A few jumps from the Enoch, with Edison clinging on tightly, his tail tucked between his legs, and they finally hit the ground with a jerk.

Violet attempts to push her way through the dense

crowd that has gathered fast. She can see her destination just up ahead, a little booth with a *'The Great Dirigible Race'* sign above it. She raises up on tiptoes, attempting to see over the crowd, but she's just too short. She wishes that Enoch had come with her and Edison, who bounces at her side, but he had to stay behind with their basket. There were way too many shady characters around, and she had seen more than a few eyeing up their way down from the Queen Victoria. Their little but large weaved basked designed for two when one of those two wasn't a man built like a giant.

They would be royally stuck if someone ran off with that or simply cut the rope. Their race would be tainted with no way back to the ship before it properly began. The airship wasn't allowed to ground during the entire race; it was to stay airborne throughout. How the race officials would know they touched the ground, she did not know, but they didn't want to risk it. You know what they say—there are spies everywhere.

Part of her wanted to put money on the pirate being a spy, the wink, the strange watchful demeanour he had, the fact that she had yet to spot any of his crew… but then she remembers that mop of thick curly hair and that ridiculously flamboyant baby blue suit. No spy would be caught dead looking like that.

So, they decided Enoch and his hulking form would stay with the basket and frighten off anyone who tried to play sabotage—leaving Violet to go for the token alone. Although that's the thing, Violet is never alone, thanks to Edison.

GGGRRRR. Violet almost jumps out of her skin

when she hears a threatening growl come from her dear, sweet boy. She looks at him, slightly shocked and ready to tell him off. But doesn't when the sea of people part, all seemingly terrified of the wild and rabid beast.

She takes the cue and runs through the gap, Edison following her with his teeth bared in a permanent scowl. People jump left, right and centre to scramble away, muttering angrily under their breathe. Violet doesn't care, though; she knows he would never hurt anyone, unless they hurt her. And especially because his act has led them on a path to the booth.

They come within steps of the small wooden booth, and Violet can see a little old man sat in a chair on the other side. He has small round glasses perched on the end of his nose and a thick mop of white-grey hair. He looks like an old scholar who would usually be found perched nestled within the racks of the great British library.

She skids to a halt as the pirate in blue steps in her path.

"I do not think so. You little brat," says a surprisingly high-pitched and sleazy voice with a hint of a European accent. But Violet isn't quite sure from where.

Edison growls, baring his teeth once more as his top lip quivers. The pirate whips out a small sabre, pointing it at the dog.

"Edison…" Violet says as she edges in front of him slightly. "Leave."

The snarling stops, but the look in Edison's eye is as ferocious as ever. Violet knows that if the pirate were to attempt to lay on hand on her, then Edison would bite his hand off, and she wouldn't be able to stop him.

"I am going to be first to the booth, and I WILL be first to the token," he says with a smarmy attitude. He turns with flair flinging his long black wavy hair behind his shoulder, and steps towards the booth.

"I think you mean you want to be the first one to *a* token. Not the token," Violet quips, planting an innocent smile on her face and flutters her eyelashes at him as he stops and turns towards her. She shrugs her shoulders and flutters a few more times, swinging from side to side, looking every bit like a sweet innocent little girl. The pirate glares before turning back and stepping up to the booth. The crowd gathers around him, blocking Violet's path once more. But she's used to be ignored and blocked out. And luckily, she's small enough to duck and dive, pushing in through the gaps of the crowd worming her way to the far side of the booth away from the baby blue-clad pirate. She listens closely, ear straining as she keeps out of sight hidden behind a rather large French fellow.

She listens as he explains in a hefty French accent, "I do not simply give token. One must earn token. In life, we do not get things for nothing." Violet glanced a look at the pirate's face and watched as he scrunched it up in anger and turned a deep shade of red which clashed with the blue of his chosen flamboyant jacket.

"To get a token, one must traverse new tower and solve puzzle at top." The old man in the booth says as he points to the top of the metal structure towering down over them. "Bring me answer to puzzle, and I will give token and clue to next destination in race."

The pirate points his sabre at the old man. "I do not have time for games, old man. Give me a token and the scroll."

Violet's eyes go wide, and she sucks in a breath as she watches the old man bring himself slowly to his feet and pushes his chest against the tip of the thin sword. "I have lived many years and seen many battles. A boy with curly hair, blue clothing and puny sword do not scare me."

She hides a snigger behind her hand, and she slinks away, pushing Edison back through the gaps in the crowd. It seems the frail old man isn't as frail as one may initially believe. She supposes there's a reason why they say to never judge a book by its cover; the same goes for people… and dogs.

"And no craft!" she suddenly hears bellowed out into the crowd. "The tower must be climbed by foot alone."

Violet screeches to a stop, her heels practically skidding on the ground when she hears that. She looks up at the giant metal structure, the new tower of Paris and baulks, her eyes popping out of her head at the thought of having to climb that on her two little feet. And after not much sleep and way too much excitement. Her eyes droop for a moment, but only a flicker of a second before she's rolling up her sleeves, planting a determined look on her face and starts marching towards the base of the tower with her arms swinging heavily front to back.

From London to Paris, the first leg of the race was pretty easy. She doesn't think the second leg—claiming the token—will be quite so. Especially not with a curly-haired pirate on her tail, one who seems to have anger issues as well as fashion ones. But she's not a girl who gives up or backs down easily. With Edison at her side, she can achieve anything. Even climbing a 1063ft (so a little sign next to the base announces) tower in order to solve a puzzle. And solve it, she will. The Doc is counting on her, and the race is on. If the pirate thinks he's going to win, he can think again. And so it begins. The race for the first token, to complete the first leg of *The Great Dirigible Race*.

The Eiffel Traverse

Violet reaches the Eiffel Tower and looks up at the giant structure of carefully entangled metal entwined to create a marvel unlike anything ever seen. Sucking in a breath, she strides towards the leg of one of the structures with an 'Enter Here/Entrer Ici' sign next to it. Stepping her foot up onto the metal step, her mission starts. Time to traverse the Eiffel Tower, make it to the top on foot and solve the puzzle to collect the token and the scroll to the next location on their great race.

She runs up the first few steps, Edison at her side, his long gangly legs quickly moving upwards. The steps up the leg are steep, and it isn't long before her legs burn and ache, and her lungs struggle to breathe. But she keeps ploughing forward; she can sleep once this is over.

Violet makes it to the first platform panting heavily as she bends over, hands on knees taking a moment. Edison does his awkward big dog sit, tongue hanging out of the side of his mouth as he too pants heavily.

"Stay here. I'll go the rest of the way," she says to Edison as she rubs his head. That place between the ears that dogs loved to have scratched.

Violets foot lands on the first step of the next flight right as Edison runs past her with a bark.

"You!" she hears coming from behind as she turns and sees the pirate in the blue powder suit standing on the platform—his black curly mop of hair looking a little dishevelled and his moustache all skew whiff.

"Run," she says to Edison as she urges her feet and legs to move, pounding up the steps moving higher and higher up the tower.

"Ah, ah, ah!" Violet looks to her side and sees a winged monkey that she'd seen descending one of the competing airships climbing the outer structure. There's no way she can beat a monkey to the top. She hopes that he'll be a bit puzzled when he gets to the puzzle. Assuming it's a he. Violet isn't quite sure how to tell a monkey gender, and she has no plans to figurc it out.

She keeps running, breathing getting harder and her legs burning. Stopping for a moment, she hangs onto the rail looking down and sees not only the pirate storming up the tower but hordes of others as well. It was to be expected; this is a race, after all.

"It's a marathon," Violet reminds herself under her breath. This is only the first leg of the race. A win now isn't required. All that matters is getting the token, even if she's the last to get it. Another monkey climbs past as she continues the ascent, slower this time as she tries to keep her breathing under control. Edison sticking to her side like glue. It only takes another flight before others begin to pass her, but she doesn't fret; she just keeps moving up. Another flight and several people now ahead of her, Violet feels a tug on the back of her coat, one which pulls a little too harshly.

"Ah!" she yells as she grabs onto the railing. Edison turns and growls at the mysterious figure trying to pull her down the stairs.

"I don't think so, you little…" The pirate… great!

Violet keeps a firm grip on the railing as she turns to see the mean man standing there with a snarl on his face and anger in her eyes. She would love to know why he has it in for her and what on earth she, at a mere 12 years old, did to offend him so.

"What you think doing?" says the deep voice of a large, strongman looking gentleman who speaks in broken English. He comes up behind the pirate and lifts him clean in the air by the scruff of his collar. Violet wants to giggle as the thug with the mop of curly black hair in the blue suit wiggles his feet in the air while being held up by a 7ft tall circus performer. "No bully girl. Girl is child."

She doesn't hang around to hear any more; she wants to, but more people pass, and she doesn't want to be the last one to the top.

Back on up the stairs, she starts. With a glance back and another giggle as she sees the strongman pushing the pirate down the stairs.

That'll teach him for picking on girls; she thinks as she focuses on her ascent to the top of the Eiffel Tower.

Violet reaches the second platform, legs burning now as she takes a moment to enjoy the view. The city is lit up like a Christmas tree; the sky is clear and bright, with hundreds of stars gleaming down upon them. Dirigibles of all shape and size float up in the sky, waiting for their token collectors to return and continue the journey onwards. She thought riding a dragon powered dirigible was magical, but there was something about this that was the epitome of the word. She always did love the twinkling bright lights of the city, usually London's, so it was nice to experience a different view for a change.

Moment over, she thinks as she takes in another deep breath and makes for the next and last flight, the one that will take her into the spire of the tower and up to that third platform, right at the apex.

Just as she places a foot on the first step, she sees something out of the corner of her eye. She moves into the centre of the spire, stepping onto a wooden platform where a rope dangles in the middle just above her head. There's a white sign with the words 'Tirez ici' written on it—the problem is that she doesn't speak French. Enoch does, but she left him on the ground. The dangling rope calls to her, and she is still technically a child, which means her ability to resist pulling the rope is low. Her little hand reaches above her head, grasping hold of the rope and she tugs.

Nothing happens as she pouts in disappointment. Violet reaches up with two hands to try again and pulls with all her might. The wooden board beneath her feet wobbles slightly, but not much else. She does think it a little odd that the boards would move when the rope is tugged, so she bends down and jumps up in the air, grabbing hold once more. The board lifts several inches off its platform.

"Woah!" she says in shock as she lets go and crashes back down with a small thump. Her mind whirs a hundred miles a second for a moment as she looks at Edison, and he looks back at her.

"Do you think?" she asks him as he nods in response. "In 3, 2, 1…" Together, both of them jump up in the air, reaching for the rope. Violet grasps it once more with both hands as Edison clenches his teeth around it locking his jaw. Their feet lift off the ground as the wooden platform shoots into the air. Violet lets out one of those laughter screams as they fly upwards, storming past the others puffing and panting on the stairs and straight up to that top third platform.

It takes less than a minute for them to reach the top, only to face a minor problem once there. She dangles over the shoot, hands cramping, legs wiggling as she tries to figure out how to get off the rope without plunging back down to her death. If only she could reach that platform. Edison starts to move, swinging his legs back and forth. Violet follows suit and begins to swing, both pushing themselves towards the platform. Edison's back legs take grip on the surface as he pulls the rope closer towards the edge.

"There!" Violet shouts as she wraps her legs around the rope and risks releasing one hand to point in the direction of a block of metal designed to anchor the rope in place. He twirls the rope around, tying it securely in place as Violet's feet touch the ground, and she pulls herself upright.

Edison dashes around the platform and hangs his

head over the railing letting out a loud, high-pitched bark. The others are gaining on them.

"Alright, where is it?" Violet wonders out loud as she looks around the space, searching for the puzzle they need to crack. She watches as Edison barks once more at the base of another small flight of stairs leading to one more platform above their heads. She looks up through the wire grate forming the space above and sees something sat up there. Dashing over to the steps, she climbs the few there to find herself face to face with a large chest upon which sits the first puzzle in the around the world race. And it's in French.

Enoch should have come; she thinks as she stares at the foreign language, which may as well be Latin to her. Her mind stares at it, panicking, the words jumbling even further, blurring before her eyes.

"You can do this," she whispers to herself as she focuses her eyes and looks at the words before her. Some of them she recognises, some are easy. Jules Verne. Destination. Those are fairly obvious to narrow down.

Le tour du monde en quatre-vingts jours. I know that, she thinks.

"Round the world in 80 days!" she shouts with glee. "Good job, the Doc isn't here."

Edison stands at the top of the platform, growling as another contestant closes in on them.

"Ok, ok. Jules Verne. Destination. Round the world in 80 days. Premiere… premiere. That rings a bell too. Come on, brain, think." Violet smiles one of those big bright smiles that shows teeth.

"What has you beaming, my girl?" Everett's voice

rings out as she turns to see him riding a bicycle in the night air, hovering alongside the tower's spire as he peddles away. Two large metal wings flap up and down as he powers them by foot.

"Doc!" Violet shouts with glee rushing to the railing. "What are you doing here?"

"I have come to assist you in your quest."

"Don't you trust me?" she suddenly asks sullen, thinking that maybe he doesn't trust her to complete the puzzle and gain the token on her own. Only she isn't on her own; she has her Edison.

"Of course, I do!" Everett says in that voice of his that makes her giggle, in other words, his normal voice. He has this way of speaking that lights her up and makes her feel happy, like a child beaming over praise from their father. Or, in this case, unofficial surrogate father figure. "But I can't let you have all the fun on this adventure of ours can I."

"What about Verne?" she asks, knowing the reason why he chose to stay on board the Queen Victoria was to keep an eye on his nemesis.

"Thaddeus is watching him like a hawk," Everett responds with a wink. "He has the dragon on standby if he needs singeing. So, hop on board and let's go get a token."

"They said on foot," Violet says sadly. After all those steps, her legs still hurt, even if she did get the 'lift' on the last section. At least going down will be easier.

"That was up. They never said anything about down," Everett replies with a gleam in his eye and a wink. "I checked." He nods his head, signalling towards the second seat on the bike.

Violet makes a quick decision and climbs over the platform's railing as the Doc edges the bike closer.

Don't look down, don't look down, she thinks as she stands there on the edge of the very top of the Eiffel Tower. If she were to fall now, she'd go ker-splat for sure.

"Don't worry, my girl, I'll catch you," Everett says as though he can read her mind. He reaches out his hand, and she reaches out hers clasping them together as she jumps, and he pulls. Violet flies through the air in the safe grasp of the Doc as she manoeuvres her body, so she lands clumsily on the seat behind him.

"But what about Edison?" Violet asks, looking at her faithful companion still standing on the platform.

Everett lowers the bike a little, so the large wings sit level with the railing.

"Jump on board, my boy. You can sit in the well between the wings. Only hurry up. I can't keep it here for long. We have places to be, a token to retrieve, a destination to reveal and a Jules to beat." Violet holds in a giggle at his pompous upper-class voice, and she thinks that about him in the kindest of ways, of course. After all, if it weren't for the Doc, she would still be living in street gutters with only Edison to keep her safe and warm. As safe as any child can be living on the streets. A shiver runs through her at the thought of the life she once lived, but she quickly pushes it to the back of her mind.

"Come on, Edison! You can do it!" she encourages her faithful pooch as he clambers over the railing with his four long gangly legs and leaps through the air, landing with a soft thump and a dip of the bicycle.

"Hang on, old chap!" Everett says as he pulls a pair of pilots goggles down over his eyes and passes a pair to Violet over his shoulder. "Safety first and all that."

She secures the goggles onto her face and tightly grips the handlebar in front of her as Edison grips the best her can to the wings, his little paws hanging over the edge as the whites of his eyes show in fear. The Doc reaches up and places a third pair of goggles onto the loyal beast.

"Now start peddling," Everett finishes as his feet begin to pedal the bicycle. Violet glances down briefly, quickly wishing she hadn't, as she notices just how high up they are and how far the ground is. She places her feet on the other set of peddles and joins the Doc as they ride the bicycle to the ground, the answer to the puzzle running around in her head.

They soar through the Parisian night sky, gliding down over the city, watching as the light-filled landscape flickers brightly. She watches as other race participants keep climbing towards the top of the Eiffel Tower, the new spectacle of France. And she can't help a giggle that escapes her lips as she sees the pirate, barely at the first platform, huffing and puffing away with bright red cheeks. It looks like that strongman who came to her rescue sent him back down to the ground. Good. He glances in their direction, and she sends him a little wave. She's pretty sure she just witnessed steam coming out of his ears.

Before she knows it, they are landing softly back on the ground. Edison is quick to jump down, shaking his body letting loose fur fly up in the air. Everett pulls off his goggles and pulls a little lever just under his seat. Violet ducks her head as the wings creak and groan with a woosh, folding themselves inwards and disappear out of sight into—what is no doubt—a complicated but intricately designed inner working of the Docs hand-crafted bicycle.

"Where to, young lady?"

Violet points over towards the little booth with the *'The Great Dirigible Race'* sign above it and the old man sitting behind. Everett begins to pedal once more, Violet joining in as they manoeuvre through the crowds standing at the base of the tower, watching those traversing the metal structure. He toots a horn, and Edison growls as he runs alongside, people jumping out of their way as they make for the booth.

Everett turns the bike as it smoothly slides to a halt alongside the length of the booth. Violet jumps off and steps up to the edge with a beaming bright smile on her face as she practically shakes in anticipation, desperate to see if she cracked the puzzle and have gained them their first token.

"I know the answer to the puzzle… I think," she says excitedly, barely able to contain herself.

"And what is your answer, young girl," the old man says in that thick French accent of his.

Violet leans forward towards the old man as she bends over the booth table. Her eyes dart from side to side to make sure there are no prying eyes or ears. Edison lifts his front paws up onto the table as he, too, leans over.

"Suez, Egypt," she whispers, hoping that she picked

up the couple of French words she recognised correctly.

The old man says nothing as she leans back and waits. Seconds feel like hours as she starts to fidget without thought. She squints, unsure whether or not she saw his head nod subtly. Then his wrinkled arthritic hand lands on the table in front of them, and he moves it towards her. Once his hand reaches the edge nearest her, he lifts it, revealing a shiny token beneath.

Violet's smile gets even wider as she grabs the token up in her little hands and bounces up and down in excitement. Edison, of course, bounces alongside, his big lanky body jumping up in the air.

"I knew you could do it, my girl," Everett says as he comes up behind her and places his hand on her shoulder. "Now, keep that safe. We don't want to lose our first token now, do we."

Violet places it inside her pocket, patting down the opening to stop it from escaping.

"Well done, girl," the old man reaches towards her once more with a rolled-up parchment bound with red ribbon in his hand and speaking in that broken English of his. "Wait till back on ship before open."

She turns, heading back towards the bike but stops when he speaks out for one final time.

"Extra gift for finish first." He hands her over another parchment, this one bound with gold ribbon. Violet reaches out and clasps the second scroll.

"Thank you," she says with a kind smile. The old man nods back that nod that is barely even there before he turns to another gentleman who steps up to the booth with an answer in his head.

"Come, my lady, the Queen Victoria awaits," Everett says as he perches on the saddle of his bike, goggles in hand, pulling them down over his eyes. Violet clambers aboard, securing herself in the seat and pulling her own goggles back down over her eyes.

They peddle on over to Enoch, who waits patiently at the woven basket used to bring them down to the ground. He climbs back inside with Edison in tow, signalling to Thaddeus to pull them back aboard their craft. They begin to their ascent back up to the skies as Everett pulls on the lever releasing the bicycles wings from their hiding place. Violet looks up in wonder as the giant metal wings stretch forth from the simple mode of transport.

"Hang on, dear girl, and peddle like you've never peddled before!" Everett cries as he begins to peddle, Violet following suit, and the bicycle begins to rise from the ground, lifting them into the air.

They peddle and climb, up and up and up to the heavens, back to their ship, their Queen Victoria, which hovers above the French capital safe in the capable hands of Thaddeus and the dragon they borrowed from the real Queen Victoria, the one who sits on the English throne.

It's still a marvel to young Violet that the Queen has pet dragons who spend their days guarding the royal jewels in the Tower of London. It's an even bigger marvel that the Doc could borrow one for their around the world adventure. And what an adventure it was turning out to be. Day one and she has travelled to Paris in an airship powered by a dragon, fell to the ground in a woven basket built for two, angered a pirate, traversed the Eiffel Tower, solved a puzzle in French and rode a bicycle with wings through the air.

Yes, it was certainly turning out to be an adventure. And already, she couldn't wait to get back to their ship and unravel the scroll to determine the second leg of their race. To see where they would travel to next, under the power of a giant canvas balloon powered by one of the Queens dragons.

This was turning out to be the best adventure of her life. One she knew she would never forget.

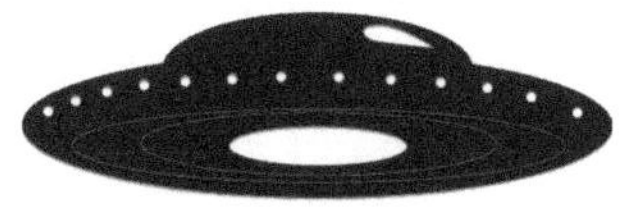

GRANDMA ASSASSINS IN OUTER SPACE

SHELLY JARVIS

When we colonized the moon in 2053, all the remaining wonder left the world. At least, that's what my
grandma says. She was just a girl then, nine or ten, but
she seems to remember it like it was yesterday.

"The moon, Vini," she says, staring up at the night
sky. "It used to be a thing of beauty and mystery! Now,
it's just another country."

She has said these words to me a hundred times—
twice this week—and I have my response ready for her,
like reading from a script. "What was it like, Nunu?"

"Oh, sweet girl, it was glorious. You could only
see it at night, mind you, but it glowed bright back then,
without those ridiculous lights that cover it now."

"You can see it all the time now. Isn't that better?"

She huffed, like always. "What good does that do

us, when we're still down here?"

She doesn't know how much it hurts to hear those words. I know she wouldn't say them if she did. I've told her before about the mission, about how I'm leaving tonight to fly to the dark side of the moon before I head off for the colony on Titan. I've even tearfully told her about how I probably won't see her again, about how I'm saying goodbye to everything and everyone and venturing off into the unknown, in the hopes of creating a future for the generations who come after me.

But she doesn't remember. Maybe it's better that way.

"You cold, Nunu?" I ask, watching goose pimples parade up the paper-thin flesh of her arms. "Want a blanket?"

"Pah," she says, as if it is an answer.

For her, I suppose it is. I've heard it so many times growing up, I know it means: "*Leave me alone and stop worrying, you little shit*." Or perhaps, "*I'm old, not incapable, you little shit*." Either way, "you little shit" is always implied.

I get her a blanket anyway, as well as her favorite brittle, and we sit cuddled up on her patio for another hour, watching the moon in silence. It might be too bright for her, but for me it shines with possibility.

When curfew nears in her retirement community—old hag confinement village, she calls it—I'm hesitant to go. I must, of course, and my brain knows that, but my heart aches at the thought. My grandmother dedicated her forties and fifties to raising a brat no one wanted. She spent her sixties and seventies cheering that same brat on as she made something of herself, a feat only achieved by the desire to make Nunu proud.

She kept my head on straight, showed me how to be a contributing member to the future of society, and saw through my shit when I tried to give it. I love her more than anyone else in the universe, and I'm leaving her to spend her final days in this place, alone.

Without thinking, I say, "Come on, Nunu. We're going on a trip."

She squints out from under what little eyebrows she has left. "Where are we going, Vin?"

"I'm breaking you out of here."

A smile creeps across her face, slow and steady and magnificent, before she says, "It's about damn time."

Nunu used to tell me stories about space. I don't know where she heard them, or if she made them up, but they were glorious. There was always a sassy lady pilot who bucked the system, or a foxy assassin with a heart of gold, or, in my favorite one, a ragtag group of space-pirates looking for the Davy Jones of the stars. Whatever the story, she made sure I could see myself in one of the characters, that I knew I could do anything. She's the reason I joined the planetary exploration unit.

And now, as I smuggle my eighty-year-old grandmother aboard a ship headed to the moon, she's likely the reason I'll be expelled from the P.E.U.

We cross through the first barrier with a flash of my smile—the guard has seen me every day for the last eight months and I'm pretty sure has a crush on me, without picking up on the fact that he is as far from my type as you can get. The second barrier checks my badge and rummages through my trunk for anything dangerous, but they don't seem to register the elderly woman in my passenger seat.

To say this surprises me would be an understatement. Nunu always says that old people become more like furniture as they age: invisible unless you run into it. This is the first time I've witnessed it. I don't know what I expected to happen when we rolled up to a government-run scientific facility with a white-haired sass machine who definitely was not on the guest list, but it wasn't this.

But this is exactly what she said would happen.

I tried to get her to hide in my duffel bag and she gave me a death glare. I suggested she lie on the backseat with a blanket over her and she "Pah'd" at me again. "I'll ride up front with you, Vini," she'd said.

"They won't let you pass," I'd tried to rebut.

"No one will stop us, dear. Trust your Nunu."

Since there wasn't another choice, I did what she said. Though I assumed they would end up calling my piece-o'-shit dad to come and take her back to the old folks' home when we tried to go through the first barrier, I drove on like she was exactly where she was supposed to be, and somehow she became just another piece of my luggage.

Now though, we're out of the car and in line at the final checkpoint that allows us into the facility. I have no idea how I'm going to get her past the last guard, and I only have as long as it takes them to check in the half a dozen people in front of us to figure it out.

My mind is drawing a blank as the line dwindles. I lean over and whisper, "I don't think we're going to make it, Nunu."

She pats my arm and says, "You need to have a little more faith in your grandma."

I grin, unable to help myself. Her confidence is ridiculous. I wish I could borrow a bit of it some time, since she's always been overflowing with it. Still, I've got no clue what to say to the guards, and whatever her plan is, she's keeping it to herself.

With two people left in front of us, Nunu takes hold of my left elbow and seems to dissolve into herself. Her perfect posture is now hunched, head bent, and she looks frail. My breath hitches in my throat. It's the first time I've looked at her and truly seen her eighty years, without her bravado backing her up. I don't like it.

"Present your wrist, please."

I catch eyes with the guard and step up, turning my wrist so he can scan in. It beeps an acceptance and I see the man's eyes widen ever so slightly as he sees my rank come up on his screen.

"Apologies, Major, I didn't recognize you."

"No reason you would, Guardian. I'm a civvy now."

A chuckle seems to rise in his throat, but he cuts it off. "Yeah, the one leading the Titan mission."

I smile as brightly as I can manage through my anxiety, but the young man hasn't seemed to notice my grandmother clinging to my arm. "Put in your time, Specialist. There will be plenty of opportunities for you once you're my age."

"Because of you, Major," he says, drawing his hand up in salute. "Thank you for your service."

I return the gesture and step past him, buoyed by the man's sincerity, and also by the fact that my grandma is some sort of sneaky ninja woman who can go wherever the hell she wants without anyone noticing her. She'd make a damn fine spy, were she so inclined.

Though I want to stop and celebrate with her, I don't, afraid to draw attention to her after such luck. Instead, we march through the facility like we own the place; with my pride nearly swallowing me whole and her constant unearned confidence, we pass a dozen more guards on walkabout as we head down the main corridor without batting an eye. We're unstoppable.

The ship taking us to the moon is a passenger ship. Somehow this surprises my grandmother, and as she walks circles around my small room, she continuously talks about the old combustion rockets that were used back in the old days.

"Nunu," I say, interrupting her third time telling me about how the payload fairing separates prior to orbital insertion, which is something she knows nothing about. "We haven't used those types of rockets for forty years."

She stops pacing and levels a "how dare you" look at me. "You think I don't know that? You were born the same day the first QI rocket launched. I was so thrilled, I would have named you 'Unruh,' after the radiation converted to thrust, if only your parents had been cool with it."

I smile as she starts her pacing again. Now that she's said it, I remember her calling me *little Unruh* when I was a kid. I didn't understand it then, so I would insist on my full name, Alvinia. Now that I've heard why she called me that, I'd kill to have her use it again.

A bell chimes overhead and the lights dim, coming back up with a red tint. A synthetic AI voice radiates from the speaker above the door, saying, *"Good evening, guests. This is your Captain speaking. Welcome aboard the* Falcon 76, *the smart choice for all your space-faring needs. Please secure yourself for initial takeoff which will take effect in four minutes."*

My eyes dart to Nunu, and I can see we're thinking the same thing: *shit.*

Considering that I'm in a single occupant room, with single occupant securing facilities, but there are actually two of us, the thought is concise, but accurate. She scurries about the room in the hopes that there's an emergency harness somewhere, but I know better. These may be passenger rockets, but they're not designed for comfort, and certainly not made with the expectation of stowaways.

"Two minutes," the AI Captain says.

"Strap in," Nunu says, pressing her hand against my stomach and pushing me against the wall.

"No way," I say. "You strap in and I'll climb in the closet with my bag."

"Don't be a fool. We're both using the straps." I feel my lips move into a fish-like pucker as she continues, "We barely make one good-sized man if we smoosh together. Get in the harness, then I'll get in, and all is well."

I do as she says. I don't know if this is a good idea, but we don't have time to argue. As I secure the harness around us, I feel an itch in the back of my brain, begging to berate me for the genius idea of bringing an elderly runaway onto the ship. I don't scratch the itch, hoping ignoring my stupidity will somehow make it go away. As I fasten the last buckle around Nunu's chest and wrap my arms around her, I'm fairly confident my foolishness will persist, as both a feature and a flaw.

We listen to the countdown, and if Nunu is as certain of our pending demise as I am, she doesn't say so. In fact, with her back pressed against my stomach, I'm fairly sure I can feel her humming.

The seconds tick by in what feels like an eternity of waiting, until finally we hear the engine burst into life and the shake of the ship rattles our teeth. Dimly I wonder if Nunu's dentures will fall out and the crew will find us hanging here tomorrow, my arms wrapped around a tiny old lady with no teeth.

Instead, in a very short time later, far shorter than I imagined even with my knowledge and preparation by the P.E.U., the turbulence ceases and the calm voice of the Captain says, *"We are now outside Earth's atmosphere and making our way towards the Independent Nation of the Moon. Our expected arrival time is in twelve hours. Feel free to release your harness and walk about your cabin. As always,* Falcon 76 *and all of SpaceX appreciates your dedication to safety."*

Before I can unhook the harness, Nunu has already pressed the release and extricated herself from the safety equipment. She looks back at me, a broad grin on her

face, and says, "Well, that certainly was anticlimactic."

The moon landing goes much the same. Aside from some mild turbulence as the craft settles down, it's an amazingly smooth ride. We disembark into the moonbase and make our way to the observation deck. I need to check in soon, but there's no way I'm going to pass up the chance to see my grandmother's face as she looks out over the place she's spent her life looking up to.

We stand by the railing, looking through the clear dome at the craggy surface of the moon. Nunu doesn't say anything, but she grips my elbow with a force that says she's happy, she's overwhelmed, she's trying not to cry. I swallow against my own emotion boiling up inside. This has been a long time coming.

After the newness of the visual spectacle has passed, we head off through the base in search of breakfast. Though the station we're in now was initially established as a scientific base, it now sprawls across the moon, branching into new housing developments, entertainment plazas, shopping markets, and tourist traps that give you the "real moon experience." I'd like to believe Nunu and I are both smart enough to avoid such places, but when you can get Neil Armstrong's famous moon pancakes AND a photo beside a piece of the original lander for the low, low price of ninety-nine credits, it's a no brainer.

While we're in line for our picture, Nunu sidles in close beside me and whispers, "Do not turn your head,"—at which point I immediately turn my head and she swats at me—"but there is a man back there in a black jacket who has been eyeing us since the observation deck."

I sigh. She had me worried for a second. "It's probably just another person who came up on the *Falcon*. Maybe he followed us because he wasn't sure where to go."

She purses her lips. "I get a bad vibe from him."

"You get a bad vibe from the postman."

"And I was right, too. That man was caught stealing packages."

"There's also the possibility that he recognizes me," I say, trying to keep my voice even. I hate the way it sounds like bragging to say such a thing, but it is possible. My face has been all over the newsfeeds for weeks leading up to the Titan mission.

Now it's her turn to roll her eyes. "Oh, right, because you're so important now."

"That's not what I—"

"He's moving away. He must've caught me watching him," she whispers.

"I'm sure that's it."

"Pah," she growls, and I'm certain I hear, "*Don't patronize me, you little shit.*"

After breakfast, I go to check into mission control. There's no way Nunu can get through security there, no matter how much she insists it's possible, so I hesitantly leave her inside a series of joined shops boasting to be the moon's largest outlet mall. I don't feel great about leaving her behind, but she assures me if anyone gives her trouble, she'll fake a heart attack and make a scene.

I kinda feel bad for anyone who might mess with her.

Check in is smooth. After we've all found our assigned areas and moved into our home for the next six months, I give a rousing speech to encourage the settlers. I harken back to the days when this same trip would've taken over three years. I speak of the names we all know—Neil Armstrong, Guion Bluford, Sally Ride, Mae Jemison, Ash Musk, Michael Yuen, Phạm Tuân—and then I read from the Titan's manifest the names the world will never forget. The assembly is full of excitement as I conclude, and I have to admit I'm pretty happy with myself as well.

We have two hours to tie up any loose ends before we ship off. For most people, it means a final call to their loved ones who stayed behind. For me, however, it means finishing what I put off before, what I dread to do: I have to say goodbye to my grandmother, for real this time.

As I head out of the mission area, I catch sight of a man lurking just outside the security perimeter. He's tall and brawny, with dark hair shaved to a stubble and eyes as black as the jacket he wears. Eyes that happen to be locked on me.

I offer a tentative smile that is not returned. I never saw the man Nunu was convinced was watching us, but I'm sure this can't be the same man. No, this is just some exploration enthusiast excitedly waiting for the launch. I will not subscribe to a paranoid story that says otherwise. Though really, the ideas would fit quite well with the adventure stories Nunu used to tell me.

I keep walking. If there's trouble to be had, I'm sure I'll find it. Accidentally, of course. But the guards will take care of any issues that arise. My priority right now has to be my last farewell.

As I make my way back to the mall, I'm struck with the skin-crawling feeling of someone watching me. I check my surroundings repeatedly, but nothing seems out of place. The man in the black jacket is gone or has at least blended in enough to avoid my detection. Though I try to shake off the feeling, it persists while I walk through the shops, searching for a tiny old woman who can't be seen if she's behind a rack of clothes.

The mall is bigger than I realized, and my paranoia is growing stronger every minute. I go to the information desk and have them page Ms. Eloise Harbinger, but she never comes.

When my time is nearly up and I've mentally beat myself up as much as humanly possible, I walk back to Titan headquarters to prepare for departure. I am completely broken up about what I've done. I have selfishly brought an octogenarian *to the freaking moon* without even the semblance of a plan, just because I felt guilty leaving her in her safe, comfortable home. And now I've lost her in a giant lunar mall.

Cool. Coo-uhl. Cool, cool, cool.

I'm on the settlement ship walking towards my room, my heart is so downtrodden, my mind so distracted, I barely notice the black-jacketed man standing in the corridor in front of me, along with two other unsavory characters. By the time I do give them my attention, noting with a frown that they aren't supposed to be aboard the ship, I know it's too late.

When I come to, it's the sound of things that draws my attention back to the land of the living. Or rather, the absence of sound. The darkness around me is unnaturally quiet. Tomblike. Then I realize my eyes are still closed.

I open them only a sliver, but it's too much. The light is far too bright, the room around me awash in sterile white and stainless silver, and in the back of my mind I wonder if I have a concussion. But I open them a tinge more and realize I'm where I'm supposed to be, inside a cryo-bed, on my way to…

No, that's no right. Cryo-beds were supposed to be used if there was danger. Put ourselves to sleep and wait for rescue. I must've been dreaming before. Taking Nunu to the moon, getting chased by men in black jackets—none of that could've been real. I scrub a hand over my face, wiping away the ice crystals clinging to my lashes.

I press the release on my cryo-bed as a figure approaches above. A rescue worker, probably, from whatever danger we were in. I smile and blink and them before I fully register who's in front of me: a short woman, white hair shaved on the sides and spiked on top. Though wrinkles cross her forehead and cause her thin lips to sag, her hazel eyes are vibrant and full of life. My Nunu, standing in front of me in a long grey duster with massive daggers strapped to her belts, looks like a fucking badass.

She reaches a hand over to help me out of the cryo-bed and says, "Come with me if you want to live."

I follow her to the door, pausing when she puts a hand up. In films, this means I should be quiet. While following a tough-looking old lady out of a creepy science lab, the vibe is pretty much the same.

A moment later, she flips her hand around and motions me to follow. We jog down the hall, the squeak of her combat boots on the floor the only indication of our presence. At the end of the hall, she stops us again, peeks around the corner, then darts across and into the adjacent room.

We're immediately met with the business end of a ray gun, though I'm not sure what sort this one is. I suppose the type of ray doesn't really matter when it's pointed in your face.

"Thank fuck," the woman holding it says as she lowers it to her side.

Without the thought of imminent death at her hands, I take a moment to get a good look at her. Her skin is dark, natural black and grey curls cropped short. Her face is fuller than my grandma's, less wrinkled, but I think she's nearly the same age. She's dressed similarly to Nunu, though her forest green jacket isn't as long and she only has the one knife tucked into her tall boot instead of two at her belt. She's rounder than my grandma, and a little taller; when she was young, I would almost guarantee people referred to her as voluptuous.

"Vini, I'd like to introduce you to the one and only Josephine Baker," Nunu says as Ms. Baker hooks an arm around my grandma's waist and pulls her close. She presses a kiss against Nunu's temple, and my grandmother practically melts. She turns back to me a second later and adds, "My wife."

I press a hand against my chest as surprise roils through me. "You're gay?"

Nunu smirks. "Did you think you were the only one?"

"What? No, of course not. It's just, you never said…"

"And you never asked."

"But you could've told me."

She shrugs. "Never seemed like the right time. Besides, until Josie, I never met a woman I wanted to be with for more than a night—"

"Nunu!"

Ms. Baker laughs. "While I am truly amused at this situation, we need to get moving."

"Wait, what exactly is going on?"

"Pah," Nunu says, meaning, *"Oh sure, now you ask. It wasn't exactly a priority question when you learned I was gay, you little shit."*

"The basic rundown," Ms. Baker says, "is that your mission was hijacked, they threw you and the other settlers into cryo-sleep, and they tried to ransom you for more money that the Earth has to give."

"It was never about the money," Nunu spits.

"That's your theory, baby," Ms. Baker says.

"So, wait, how long have I been asleep?"

Nunu puts a hand on my shoulder and squeezes. "Four years."

"Four...FOUR YEARS?"

"Shhh," they both hiss.

"I've been asleep for four years?" I hiss back.

Nunu nods. "It took our crew a long time to catch up to you, even longer to figure out how to rescue you."

"Speaking of the crew," Ms. Baker says, "Thelma and Regina are both late for check in."

"Gertie?"

"She's fine. She found a bank of frozen children passengers and she's awaiting further instructions."

The door behind me *whooshes* open. Before I can even turn around, Nunu has drawn one of the knives from her belt and thrown it across the room. It hits the man who'd just entered square in his eye, digging in deep with a squishy sound, and he falls forward into the room.

I look from my Nunu to the man, and back again. "What the fuck have you been doing for four years?"

"Knitting, mostly," she says, stepping over the body to retrieve her knife. "The assassin bit just sort of came back once I started doing it again, like muscle memory."

"Came back," I repeat.

She presses her lips into an almost smile. "You knew I worked for the government."

"Yeah, but like, I just thought you pushed papers, did your time, and got out, like everybody else."

"Remember when Uncle Sal would come pick me up in the middle of the night for hunting trips?" I nod and she says, "He was my handler."

"Holy shit," I mutter.

"I realize you may be in the middle of an existential crisis," Ms. Baker says, "but we need to figure out our next move. Bodies are starting to pile up."

"And who are these other women with you?" I ask, rudely ignoring my grandmother's wife.

"My knitting circle," Nunu says.

Ms. Baker shakes her head and says, "Ex-operatives, like your grandmother. The government called in a lot of us old folks when your ship was stolen, and their new agents had fuck all idea on what to do about it. Eloise picked out her own crew when she realized they weren't going to be able to save you, and you've had a bunch of grandma assassins chasing you through outer space."

Nunu shrugs. "If you think I'm going to let my precious girl go without a fight, you're out of your damn head."

I close the gap between us and crush her against me. Four years of her struggling and me sleeping are gone in an instant, and the unknown things between us become background, and it's just me hugging the woman who raised me, the woman who would chase me through space to make sure I'm safe.

When I step back from her, my head is clear and I'm all business. "Where are we now?"

"Between the Kuiper Belt and Jupiter."

"Fuel should've expired ages ago."

"They stole a refinery ship. There's enough fuel to keep them going indefinitely."

"Any other ships?"

"A warship. We're not sure who they stole it from,

because no one will own up to creating a death machine when we're supposed to have a universal peace treaty," Ms. Baker says.

"Any other hostages, besides this ship?"

Nunu winces. "Not that we know of. There have been reports of smaller crafts going missing, but nothing concrete."

"And we have no idea what these people want?"

Nunu and Ms. Baker share a look that seems to convey an argument they've had at least a dozen times. Pretty sure Nunu's stare wins, because she says, "I don't think they're people."

I look between the two women before asking, "I'm sorry, what?"

"Not Earthlings, anyway. I think they're from Saturn, or maybe Titan itself, and they're trying to keep us from taking over their world."

"But the outer planets are uninhabitable without terraforming," I say. "There's no way they've lived there without our detection."

"Or that's what they want us to believe."

"If that's true—and that's a BIG if—couldn't we just talk to them? We can tell them we mean no harm, try to work things out. I mean, that would be a huge discovery for us and could propel us forward by hundreds of years," I say, getting excited.

"We've tried talking to them," Nunu says. "Whether they're Earthlings or something else, they're completely hostile."

"Not completely. They put us in cryo rather than killing us."

"That's what I *been* saying," Ms. Baker mutters.

The door *whooshes* again. Nunu's hand flies to her belt but stills when a little old waif of a woman comes through. Her voice is shaky with both age and emotion as she says, "They got Thelma."

Ms. Baker releases a string of curse words in combinations I've never heard before. Then she asks, "Dead?"

The woman, who I assume is the missing Regina they'd discussed earlier, shakes her head and says, "She was alive, last I saw her. They were taking her to the bridge."

"Should I tell Henry?" Ms. Baker asks.

"No," Nunu says. "He'll come in hot, and we need him in our cruiser, ready to take off if things get too dicey. Better to keep him in the dark until we know what's what."

"How many of them are running the ship?" I ask.

"More than a dozen, less than twenty," Regina says.

I nod. "Okay then. If we're going to save Thelma and the other passengers, we need to take them out. We should stick together, remove them one by one."

Nunu says, "You need to find a quiet place and hole up. Better yet, I'll get you to Henry and the getaway ship. We can handle this."

"I know this ship better than any of you. And I might not be a trained assassin, but I know enough to handle myself."

She draws in a sharp breath, gives a terse nod, and says, "Okay then, let's do this."

We sneak through the ship with a stealth I never imagined a herd of grannies could have. One at a time, the soldiers go down. Whether they're human or alien, I don't stop to look. They've been holding my crew as prisoners for the last four years, robbing children of the chance to grow up, so whatever they are, they're the bad guys. With the help of my grandma's knitting group, they're the dead guys.

We scour the corridors until we're certain none are left and find Gertie to fill her in on the plan. We've only killed nine in the halls, so there's a chance we're heading to the bridge outgunned two to one. None of these firecrackers seem to care one bit.

The doors part before us. Before the baddies can take in the fullness of the elderly onslaught, the women are on them. From the corner of my eye, I watch Ms. Baker do a flying kick into the face of one of the men. Tiny Regina kicks a knee so hard the crunch echoes around us. Gertie, the baby of the group at seventy-two, has shot two of them before any of theirs has even drawn a weapon.

Then there's Nunu, running around the place like a bat out of hell. Her blades slash before her like extensions of her hands. I've never seen her like this before. In all the years I've known her, maybe this is the first time I'm actually *seeing* her.

I fight my own baddies, but there's nothing exciting about it. There's the usual adrenaline surge, the rush of endorphins at victory, but I don't have a special move like these old ladies who might as well be videogame characters.

Still, it feels good when I look up and see they're all safe, all well, and all standing above a bad guy who won't hurt anyone again.

Ms. Baker steps to the controls at the front of the ship—the ship I should have led to a settlement on Saturn four years ago—and presses the call button. "Marta, Lolly: anyone read me?"

"Loud and clear, Jojo," someone answers. "The warship is ours."

"Refinery copies, safe and secure, one casualty," another voice answers.

Nunu laces her fingers through mine and we stand there in silence, listening to the radio chatter as the women report back their victories. There's a narrow window at the front of the ship and outside I can see a couple of the moons of Jupiter orbiting the gas giant.

"You know, this isn't what I expected when I busted you out of that nursing home. Space-faring grannies wielding knives, kicking ass, and taking no prisoners? Never in my wildest dreams."

"Really?" she asks. "Because it's exactly what I thought."

She squeezes my hand and we stare off together, watching the moons, imagining the next adventure to come.

DIRK DANGER AND THE DIAMOND OF DAYS

L. T. EMERY

Danger Diary 19 – Entry 1

Goddam broads. I knew they'd be the end of me.

I don't usually write these until I'm home, but I'm starting to worry I may not make it out of this one.

Here I am, soaked through to my skin, twenty feet up a tree, in the middle of a jungle, hiding from a bloody tyrannosaurus rex! A real, living, breathing, jaw-snapping tyrannosaurus rex!

But I'm getting ahead of myself.

Let's catch you up while I wait for this glorified iguana to make like a tree.

The name on my office door is Dirk Danger. Under that is written 'Private Investigator.' It's not really what

I do, but I can't exactly put 'Adventurer for Hire' now, can I? I'm an archaeologist by training; a gun-toting, risk-taking, pilot during the war, and a bourbon-drinking lady-man by night. But what I really excel at is finding things.

And that's what I usually get hired to do. You need something found no questions ask; my number's in the book, give me a call.

A week ago, I was awoken but the shrill ring of the phone. It was around 4 pm; I'd had a few too many at lunch and passed out on my desk. What can I say? It was a slow day.

I answered with a grunt.

"Please hold."

"Hold what?" I asked, looking around, eyes still blurry.

"Mr Danger?" a voice cooed. It was soft and posh, and damn if it didn't rev my engine. It woke me up in an instant.

"Speaking, doll."

The dame scoffed in disgust. I can only assume she didn't like being called 'doll'. Hey, I'm comfortable in my skin; I like what I like and say what I say. Sue me!

"If you look out your window, you should see a car waiting for you. Go with my man, if you please. I'll provide details on the job and pay in person."

"Who is-" I started, but the line was already dead. Who the hell did this broad think she was, throwing her orders at me? For all I knew, she was some dumb Dora wasting my time.

I stuck my fingers through the closed blinds of the

office window, looked down to the street below. And nearly fell over.

Waiting down on the street for me was a goddam limousine. A Lanchester no less. I was intrigued, and the broad clearly had some moolah, so I grabbed my coat and fedora off the rack and slammed the door shut behind me.

I was shown to the drawing-room in this huge stately home. I'd seen some up-market homes in my day, but this one took the biscuit. It seemed everywhere I looked, it was all leather, mahogany and silver.

A sweet young thing entered the room, head held high. She had that look like someone had smeared dog muck on her upper lip, and now all she could smell was shit. She can't have been more than twenty, I'd have guessed. But she was a looker, that was for sure. Tight ass, perky tits. Mmm-mm.

"Can I interest you in some tea, Mr Danger?"

"How about a cup of joe?" I should mention, I picked up a lot of American mannerisms and colloquialisms thanks to my time over there after the war with a good friend, goes by the name of Barnum Brown. We dug up the most monstrous dinosaur skeleton you could ever imagine. You guessed it, a bloody T-rex. I like them much better when they're bones in the ground and not trying to eat me.

The bugger is still sniffing around my tree, by the way. You should see the size of its teeth!

"A cup of what?"

"A cup of joe. Coffee."

"Oh. Well, I'll see what I can do."

"You do that, and while you're at it, be a good girl and send in your husband. We need to talk business."

"Excuse me?"

"Your husband?" I said. "No, wait? You? You want to talk business, darlin'?" I asked. "I thought your purring voice was just bait to get me here. Well, isn't this a turn up for the books!"

"Do you have no respect at all, Mr Danger?"

"I mean no disrespect, ma'am. It's just, I like my woman with a little up here," I said, pointing to her head. "And a little more down here." I continued, pointing to her not inconsiderable chest.

She gasped in horror. "Mr Danger! How dare you!"

I gave her a sideways glance and rolled my eyes. Broads these days can take things the wrong ways sometimes.

"I mean no disrespect, ma'am. I just thought a beautiful girl like you would have a husband to conduct her business. My apologies."

She gave me a look that said she couldn't trust me as far as she could throw me but nodded, nevertheless. She needed my services, and we both knew it.

"And please, call me Dirk."

"Well, Dirk. I suppose you may call me Elizabeth."

"Liz it is."

She frowned at me, but I'll be damned if I didn't see the edges of her lips rise just the tiniest bit.

"So, how can I be of service?" I asked.

"You must understand that I'm only here in London

visiting a friend. Your business is a happy coincidence."

I'd heard it all before. No one wants to hire me until they need to hire me because all other options have failed them. Either way, I humoured her and twirled my finger, urging her to get to the point.

"I used to help out in a convalescent home for wounded soldiers. My ancestral home was converted to be so after the war. I realise you fought in the war, and this must seem like a small act, but for me, it was all I could do at my age."

"On the contrary," I said. "It's a noble thing to help others. We each do what we can."

She nodded and continued. "I became close to one of the men I helped look after. We became good friends. You'll be interested to know he was an American. I notice you favour the use of some pretty vulgar Americanisms."

I smirked. On the inside, of course. Outside I was all professionalism now.

"The soldier had horrendous injuries, and I regret to say he passed away. But before he did, he told me a story. One I assumed was just that. A story. But after he passed, something told me to do some reading on the matter, and the more I read, the more I thought his story had some truth."

"Liz. Please, I have a friend waiting for me back in the office. Get to your point," I said. My good chum Jack Daniels was waiting for me. The hangover was starting to kick in, and I wanted Jack to take the edge off.

"I'm sorry," Liz said. "He spoke to me of a diamond, deep within the forests of South America. It was said that any who laid eyes on the diamond would lose days from staring at its beauty."

"The Diamond of Days," I whispered. My mother once told me stories about it. I thought it was a myth.

"Yes," she said, looking impressed. "My friend says he saw it once. He, too, was a pilot."

This broad was starting to impress me, she'd done her research on me.

"He'd seen it once; had flown through a storm and spotted it atop a pyramid, deep in the Andes jungle. He told me how to get there."

She paused then, a tear spilled over her eye and down her cheek.

"I still remember his last words. He said, 'You're more beautiful than the Diamond of Days. I've lost weeks and months staring into your eyes. You should be hung, drawn, and quartered. Hung in diamonds, drawn in a coach and four, and quartered in the best house in the land.'"

I passed her a handkerchief, and she wiped the underside of her eyes. She thanked me, told me why she was really in London and what she wanted the diamond for.

I think old Rexy has finally moved on. I'm drying out now, thank God. But I'll just finish catching you up before I leave the safety of my tree and move on.

A week after meeting Liz, I'd packed everything I needed and spent five days aboard a liner sailing from Southampton to New York. This was where things got specific. I was to sail to Bermuda first, where I'd have a plane waiting for me. I was then to fly in a west-south-west direction toward Cancun, Mexico.

When I arrived in Bermuda, I won't lie, I didn't want to leave. Paradise on earth there— and the women, you should have seen what they were wearing!

Anyway, my want to travel returned when I saw what was waiting for me. A plane I was very familiar with. A Sopwith Camel biplane. The very same I used to fly in the war. My baby, I called her Tallulah, had got me through many a scrape in the war, and this one too was an absolute beaut. Restored from the war, Tallulah 2 was ready to go.

Liz had told me what was awaiting me in Bermuda, and I had already asked her all the obvious questions about my flight; the most pressing of which was, how would a plane with a range of around 300 miles get me the 1500 miles required to land me in Cancun? I wasn't too confident with her answer of 'trust me'. Even with the money she'd paid upfront, and promised to pay me upon delivery, I still wasn't sure. The broad got me though, when she said, 'I thought you're an adventurer, Mr Danger, not a coward?'.

Sometimes I damn my thick-headedness, and obviously, I agreed, and that's when the real adventure started.

The purr of Tallulah 2's Bentley engine was music to my ears as we cruised over the deep blue waters of the Atlantic Ocean. My reverie was short-lived as the sky darkened, a storm seemingly brewing from thin air.

The winds picked up and keeping the biplane on

point was becoming tough. Soon the rain started. Big, fat splotches started to ding of the twin wings, and I started having to wipe off my goggles with increased frequency. It was nothing I couldn't handle, though.

The skies darkened so that it seemed that day had turned to night.

The first crack of thunder nearly made me mess my britches. It lit the sky for an instant, revealing nothing but the white peaks of waves and angry black storm clouds.

I needed to get out of the storm; Tallulah 2 was a bloody lightning rod. I started to swerve her back and forth and dove as low as I dared over the ocean in an effort to make myself not so attractive to lightning and sure death. The lightning boomed time and time again, lighting the sky.

I was desperate to see land but knew there was none to be had. Or so I thought. Another crack revealed an island dead ahead.

"Land-ho!!!" I screamed to nobody and pushed my plucky little plane to its limits; I needed to land asap and didn't even consider how it had sprung up where no land had any right to be.

"You're not getting me today!" I bellowed to the skies, laughing. This was scary, but damn if it wasn't a rush I'd not felt since the dog fights during the war.

In an instant, I was blinded and deafened as another lightning bolt came down. It hit my wing this time, ripped a hole straight through both the upper and lower right wings.

Tallulah 2 veered right and bombed.

Without any sight or hearing, I had only my touch

and intimate knowledge of piloting to save me. I pulled up and compensated for the loss of lift on my right. The tell-tale vibration of the engine had ceased too, and I knew it was out. I was gliding blind.

I kept my eyes closed, knowing they needed time to recover from the blinding bolt of lightning. My hearing started to return and along with the cacophony of the storm. It sounded like machine-gun fire; such was the frequency of strikes.

My intuition was all I had. I corrected my course and hoped I was headed toward land. On the inside, I was readying myself for the next life.

By some miracle, I wasn't hit again, and just like that, the world went silent once more.

I assumed another bolt had deafened me again. I tentatively cracked my eyes open, letting in the light once more.

My sight was returning, and I opened my eyes to beautiful sunshine. I blinked over and over, thinking I'd died and gone to heaven. The island was dead ahead. It was stunning. White sandy beaches ran all around. Thick green jungle seemed to run right to the centre of the island, where a steaming volcano sat. Dotted all through the jungle were breaks in the canopies and reaching into the skies at each was a pyramid. Step pyramids and the more traditional Egyptian-style pyramids too. But dead ahead at the base of the volcano was what caught my eye. Atop one particular pyramid, a shining light. Could it be? The Diamond of Days?

I managed to pull my eyes away from it to dare a look behind and saw the storm fading into the distance.

Joy overtook me for just a moment until I realised, I was gliding just feet over the ocean, my propeller nowhere in sight. With all my might, I pulled up, giving myself a little more height. I pulled more and more in a last-ditch attempt to make it the last few hundred feet to the beach.

I screamed and my muscles screamed right along with me, giving it everything. Then the bloody flight stick ripped off into my hand. I was done for.

I hit the water about a hundred yards from land. Tallulah 2 saved my life then. The wheels sheared off on impact, cartwheeling into the water. The belly came down next and bounced back up off the ocean. We came in like a skipping stone, bouncing over the suddenly calm water.

Until finally, the nose caught, and the Sopwith Camel abruptly dived about twenty yards from shore. It threw me forward, and I saw stars as my head cracked off the dashboard. It was a fight to stay conscious as the plane started to sink but the cool water pulled me back to reality.

I managed to get out of the plane with my trusty satchel in tow and swam to the shore, where I promptly collapsed, falling into darkness.

When I awoke it was still daytime, I had no idea how long I'd been out, but it can't have been long, as I was still wet from my swim. It seemed to be mid-afternoon by my reckoning. My head thumped where I'd bashed it. When I tentatively prodded at it with a shaky finger, it came back caked with drying blood.

While my senses were returning, I felt a rumble in

the ground but chalked it up to the exhaustion and trauma on my crash.

An inhuman roar made me sit bolt upright in terror. I looked to my left in time to see a tyrannosaurus rex crash through the jungle that hugged the golden sands of the beach.

For a moment, I was paralysed, assuming I was still asleep. The booming footsteps and another warning roar told me otherwise. Without further thought, I was up running the opposite way down the beach.

Rexy was bloody quick though for something so huge. It stood as tall as a house and was all muscle and power. He gained ground on me, so I darted into the jungle seeking refuge amongst the hulking trees.

As he crashed through the foliage next to the beach, I ran deeper and deeper into the jungle until I found my temporary home—this tree.

It's thick and old and sturdy. Rexy gave it a couple of testing headbutts, but the tree didn't budge. Thank God.

That brings you up to now. I'm stranded on an island in the middle of the Atlantic with no food.

All I have on me is my satchel. In it, I have my gun; a Smith and Wesson Triple Lock—my sidearm from the war—a canteen of water, a compass and this journal and pencil—how none of this got wet, I'll never know—and that's about it.

Great.

I guess I'll head north and hope that pyramid and

the diamond atop it has some sort of help there.

Danger Diary 19 – Entry 2

Seriously. Broads. They're going to be the end of me.

I'm in prison. Amazon prison.

Let's rewind a few hours. Rexy's gone, and I'm finally getting out of the tree. I lifted my hand to rearrange my fedora, only to find it missing. I very nearly screamed 'goddammit' at the top of my lungs but managed to hold back for fear of attracting Rexy back. That was my favourite hat.

"Oh no!" I said to myself, patting down my coat; my veins ran cold as fear coursed through them.

No, no, no!

Oh, wait. Thank God. I found it. In my inside pocket. My hipflask of Jack. Phew!

I popped the lid and took a deep, well-earned, and much-needed swig. It burnt the whole way down, filling me with the warmth of happiness.

Although the light was still good, I was convinced night was soon coming, so wanted to move fast. I pulled out my compass to get a heading—I needed to go north, toward the pyramid—but the point just spun on its axis, round and round at an incredible speed. No matter how much I bashed it against the tree it wouldn't stop. So, I threw the compass back in my satchel in frustration.

With that, I descended the tree and started making my way through the undergrowth.

Squeaks and squawks rang out from around the jungle. The noises of the animals were none I'd ever heard. I've been to enough places to know these were not your usual animals.

The going was slow, as I had to ascend a tree every couple of hundred yards to make sure I was heading the right way.

My water was drained pretty quickly thanks to the baking heat of the jungle, and I felt myself start to weaken.

I decided to climb one last tree before taking the risk of pushing on in the same direction in the hope of conserving some energy.

Before I started to climb though, I heard the shouts and cries of a woman. My ears pricked up—a damsel in distress. The diamond could wait.

I ran in the direction of the screams, sticking my hand into my satchel to pull out my gun as I went.

I cleared the trees only to see a woman locked in battle with a scorpion the size of a Saint Bernard. It had razor-sharp claws and a stinger the size of a football, that had a drop of yellowish poison seeping from its tip.

You'd think the scorpion would have shocked me or put me off my stride. You'd be wrong. The dame was my height—six-feet tall. Long blonde, shimmering locks of hair ran to the small of her back. She had not an ounce of fat on her; in fact, she looked strong, all of her muscles rippling in the sunlight. And she was buxom, so very buxom, wearing only the tatters of a bikini, made from some sort of animal hide. My luck was in. I think I may have even drooled a little.

In her hands was a spear topped with a razor-sharp

flint that reflected the light with a green hue.

The scorpion rushed the dame, claws snapping for her ankles. She screamed. I couldn't watch someone as beautiful and helpless as that in what was clearly a losing battle.

I rushed from the jungle's edge, gun in hand.

"Fear not, my lady, I'll rescue you from the grips of this most horrendous beast."

She seemed more surprised to see me than she was by the giant bloody scorpion.

I pointed my gun at the scorpion and pulled the trigger, once into its abdomen. It screeched and reared around toward me. I shot again, this time aiming nearer its head, and yet it came, scuttling across the twenty or so yards between us.

I started to panic—on the inside only, of course. I had a dame to impress—and short four more times, emptying my cylinder. The last two shots hit its head, pasting white (what I can only describe as) goo all over the ground, and fell down dead.

"Haha!" I laughed. "Another monstrous creature dispatched."

The dame looked at me like I was a bloody alien. A little gratitude would have been nice, but I didn't let it get to me.

I strolled over to her, trying my best to keep eyes off of her bubs, and said, "Dirk Danger at your service."

I took her hand and gently kissed it.

Her confused look started to turn to one of happiness. A smile spread across her face.

"My hero," she said.

"Oh please, it was nothing. A man's job is to protect a lady, such as yourself."

"Please, you must come with me, back to my village. You will be handsomely... rewarded," she said raising an eyebrow.

I like rewards.

"And please," she continued. "Called me Stella."

I followed Stella back to her village, all thoughts of exhaustion forgotten. It wasn't far. But as we walked, she told me she lived in an all-woman village.

Jackpot.

The village sat in the middle of a huge opening in the jungle. I could see another pyramid sat at its centre—not the one with my diamond on. It was surrounded on all sides by a high wall of sharp-pointed and weaved together logs.

A manned—womanned—gate opened as we walked toward it. The guards wore a similar outfit to Stella. Again, all beautiful and all strong.

One guard shouted something to Stella in a language I didn't understand. It may have been an ancient Greek dialect, but I didn't hear enough to be sure.

Stella shouted something in response and the guard disappeared.

"What did she say?" I asked.

"Oh, nothing. Just a greeting."

We walked through the gates and into the village. I looked around and saw many buildings made of mottled red mud bricks and mortar and topped with grass-weaved roofs. It was quite pretty.

The doors crashed shut behind us, and I turned to

see another guard lock the gate with a wooden stop that looked as large as a tree. The woman looked quite big too, but I just waved it off.

When I turned back, shock grabbed me. A dozen or so woman had come out to see my arrival. Stella was my height. Big for a dame. But the rest of the women here stood at least 8-feet tall. I was amongst the mythical Amazons.

I looked at Stella, and she smiled back at me. It was an 'I'm sorry' smile. I realised she must be young, real young for this tribe of Amazons; she was not yet fully grown.

I felt the rippling of fear course through my body, and goose bumps erupted all over my body. I didn't let any of this show, though. I had saved one of their own and had to keep up the bravado.

I strutted through their main street, shouting, "It's okay now, ladies. A man has arrived. I will look after you all. You needn't be scared anymore."

I shouted that at least two or three times, I think, as I walked, aiming for the pyramid at the village's centre. Stella was just behind me, and more and more Amazon's followed.

I turned to Stella. "Can they understand me?" I whispered through the side of my mouth.

"Oh, they can understand alright."

"Good," I whispered back. "I have saved Stella here from an evil, giant scorpion. I will save you all from the horrors of this island."

Finally, I made it to the base of the pyramid. It was another step pyramid but of a slightly different design.

On each level, there was a large entrance into the pyramid.

Stella said, "Wait here." Her voice had a hint of menace in it, daring me to challenge her. Then walked off up the steps of the pyramid.

I looked over my shoulder to the looming Amazons that leered at me, their expressions a mix of anger and, I may be going crazy, but was that lust I sensed? I gave them a glimpse of my most winning and, may I say, alluring smile.

When I turned back Stella was coming back down the steps, her face the very picture of childish sulking, mumbling something I couldn't hear.

"Follow me," she said, passed me, and carried on walking. Before I even had a chance to move, she growled, "Now."

"What's happened?"

"You happened. Today was meant to be my coming of age. But you killed the creature with that loud, banger object."

"My gun?"

She ignored my question. "Now I have to wait and go out into the wilds for a month and start again. I hate it here; that was my ticket to freedom. To do what I want! To leave this village and set out on my own, do something for myself."

"You should just leave. What's the worst that could happen?"

"Argh!" she cried in frustration.

"Where are we going?" I asked.

"You're our guest. I'm showing you to your residence for the duration of your stay."

"Oh, how lovely. I hope I'll have a lovely maid, like you?"

She shot me a mildly disgusted glare, "You'll have the pleasure of meeting our queen a little later on today."

Queen? I thought, *I could be their King! If I can't get off this island, I could rule these broads. What a life of luxury that would be.*

"I can't wait to meet her."

We came to the entrance of a large building, built in the same fashion as the rest of the village.

"Here," Stella said, holding out her hand. "Let me see your bag?"

I handed it over whilst thinking about laying face-down on a palm tree leaf bed, being fanned with a palm tree frond, whilst being fed grapes by one Amazon beauty and massaged by another. I coughed and rearranged my trousers as Stella shoved my bag back in my hands.

She led me inside. It was dark and cool, a nice change from the scorching heat outside. We walked down a corridor, and she waved me through a door and into a large room.

I walked around the room; a small table sat in one corner had a lit candle on top, radiating a warm glow.

"No window?" I asked, looking around. The room was sparse; an upside-down stool sat in another corner, while a small bed was in the next. And in the last corner... a toilet?

"What's going on h-" I started but was cut off by the bang of the door being slammed shut.

I ran to the door to try and open it, but there was

no handle on my side. So, I banged on it with my fists. "What's the meaning of this?" I demanded.

Stella opened a small hatch in the door and peeped through. "Relax, Dirk. All will be revealed later by the queen."

"Am I your prisoner?"

She tilted her head from side-to-side thinking. "You'll see."

"What have I done wrong?"

"You've got a couple of coconuts and a... sapling between your legs."

With that, she was gone.

"Can I at least get some water?" I shouted to no-body.

Damn broads.

Danger Diary 19 – Entry 3

THEY'RE GOING TO NOOKIE ME TO DEATH!!!

Danger Diary 19 – Entry 4

Sorry about that.

I've composed myself now.

After writing my second entry in my Danger Diary, I kept shouting for a drink. I kept shouting about I'd saved the life of one of their own. How I was a man and how I could help civilize the village.

It seemed I was shouting to no one at all until I damn near jumped out of my skin when a raspy, choked voice shouted at me from a room next to mine. "Would you keep it down?"

"Ahh!" I screamed. Then, "Who's there?"

"The King of the Amazon's. Ahh ha ha ha!" The man sounded half insane.

"Why are you here? What's going to happen to us?"

"I am the father of all Amazon's. The Chief Seed! You better not be trying to take my job! I'll kill you, boy!"

Yeah, the man is insane.

"I can assure you, my good fellow; I do not want your job. How did you get here?"

"Good! If you even think about it, I'll gut you like a fish, boy."

I didn't really understand what the hell this man was talking about, but he sure sounded like he'd lost his mind.

The next second he was talking like a normal human being, though. "I was stranded here when my ship got wrecked during a storm. I was the only survivor. I washed up alone in a life raft on the eastern shore. The Amazon's found me, then locked me in here," rasped the old man, then he broke out in a dry cough.

"And I thought I need a drink," I muttered.

"I've been here for what feels like years. What year is it?"

"1920."

"Damn it. I've been here less than a year then. Every day is the same here. A small breakfast, and then the tea. Then it's to work."

"Work? What work?"

He flipped back to insane mode then, "I've told you, boy! I'm the King of the Amazon's! Ahh. Ha ha ha. The

Chief Seed! My first offspring should be born very soon. I service the ladies every day. It's my job! I think I'm in heaven."

Like I said... they're going to nookie me to death.

I need to get out of here.

Danger Diary 19 – Entry 5

You won't believe what happened. I'll jump straight into it.

A little while after the King settled down next door, Stella returned.

"Please take a seat facing the wall. You will not disrespect the queen by laying your eyes on her?"

"Seriously?"

"Now."

"Geez, I liked you better when you were being nice."

I complied. I needed to come up with something to get me out of there. I needed to create an opportunity to run from these people and find some way of getting off this blasted island. In the past, my charm and wit has always come to my rescue, so why not here too?

There was silence for a moment, but then I heard the whine of a stool being dragged over the stone floor as someone sat outside my cell.

"Queen?" I said. "Hello?"

There was no answer, but I heard her clear her throat, so I just dove right on in.

"Your highness. Your Majesty. Queen of the Amazons," I started. "My most humble of thanks to you for gracing me with your presence. I want you to understand that I am a gentleman, and as a man, it is my duty to protect you and every woman here. You are in no danger from me or my presence here. In fact, when I saw Stella in distress, I ran to her aid. Killing the monster who was terrorizing her."

Still nothing.

"I propose a union," I continued. "I would like to offer you my hand in marriage. I would become your King. But as your King, I offer all the perks that come with having a husband such as myself. I will teach you how to protect yourselves in a fight. I will teach you the latest techniques in gathering. I may even be able to teach you a little in way of cooking and cleaning," I chuckled, looking around this dirty old room. "That will come naturally to you, I'm sure. But most of all I will teach the ways in becoming civilized, so you no longer need to live in this squalor. In short, I will turn you into ladies."

"Are you done?" came a voice. It sounded strained as if spoken between gritted teeth.

"I am. And please, take your time, consider my offer carefully. But I'm sure you'll see the sense in it."

"Good, I can't take that drivel any longer," said the queen, unlocking the door and kicking it open.

"I should just feed you to the dinosaurs now, you chauvinist pig."

I heard the queen step into the room and turned around, expecting to see another 8-foot giant of a dame walk through the entrance. But what I saw in front of me sent me to my knees in shock.

The queen was smaller than me. She wasn't much more than five feet tall. Her face was red with anger as she stormed toward me. All thoughts of becoming King fled.

"Mummy?"

She stopped in her tracks. Anger changed to confusion on her face.

"Excuse me?" she said.

I didn't know what else to say. I hadn't seen my mother for thirty years, and here she was. Right in front of me, and she hadn't aged a day—in fact, she looked ten years younger than me.

I spluttered nonsense for a while until her confusion started to switch back to anger.

I held up a finger and ran to my satchel on the bed. I dug through the contents. "Where's my gun?" I said aloud to myself.

"Excuse me?" my mother, the queen, said.

"Nothing," I said and pulled out this very book. Showing it to her. Like it held all the answers. And in a way it did.

I flipped to the back page and grabbed the one and only photo I had of my mother. She was sat in a white blouse and large black dress, popular of the time. On her lap was a little baby, me. She held me tenderly, looking down at me with nothing but love in her eyes and a smile spreading the width of her face.

I held the photo out to her. She took it and looked. A moment later, she fell to her knees in tears, pressing her face into the photo she cradled in her lap.

She stood up, red-eyed, and looked me in the eyes. Then slapped me across the face.

Stars erupted in my vision, and the hearing in my

left ear became a high whine.

"You stupid boy. Do you think I would have raised you to be a male chauvinistic pig?" Then she grabbed me and hugged me so hard it hurt.

I lapped it up and hugged her back just as hard. We were both crying.

"How...? What...? When..." I started over and over.

We spoke for a while then about her and my past. I became an adventurer because of my mother. She was probably the first lady of her ilk. As soft and loving as she was tough and adventurous. She was an archaeologist on her way to the Andes, part of the race to discover Machu Picchu first. It was found the year after her disappearance.

She told me of how her plane went down in a storm. How she was washed ashore on this island and was taken in by the Amazon's.

She told of how she had missed and thought of me every day since the accident. How she'd tried and failed to get back to the real world and me, but fate or the island had always prevented her.

Instead, she tried to make the island home. She told me of how she leaned the Amazon's language. How she'd not only won their trust but their hearts and confidence as a leader too. How she had to beat the last queen in non-fatal combat—they don't kill their own.

Silence then gripped us. I was in awe of my mother, her bravery, and her gumption to not only make a life for herself here but to thrive. But there was still one question in my mind that needed answering.

"Why haven't you aged?"

"Honestly, I don't know," she said. "But I think it has something to do with the diamond."

"The Diamond of Days?"

She laughed. "You remember the stories?"

"Of course, I do. You're the one that made me want to do this job."

"I used to love telling you those stories as a child."

"I loved hearing them," I said and laughed. "Too bad they were all wrong. It seems you don't lose days to the diamond. You gain them."

"I know. I've studied it a little in my time here and it seems to be some sort of power source for the island. It's stopped me from ageing. There are bloody dinosaurs and all sorts of other extinct or giant-sized animals running around. And have you noticed how it never gets dark here?"

"I was beginning to wonder. I thought it might be night-time now."

"I think it keeps this island running somchow."

And I needed to take it.

"Mummy let's get off this island. Let's go home."

She gave me a mournful smile and cradled my cheek in her palm. "It's been too long for me. There would be too many questions. People would come looking for the diamond. It would be a death warrant for the island."

Way to guilt me, Mummy, I thought.

"But it's not too late for you. I'll get you out of here. Get yourself off the island. Go home, forget about this place and live. I'm sorry I left you, I'm sorry I've missed out on so much. But know that I love you, and I always will, Norman."

"I love you too, Mummy," I said. "But my name is Dirk Danger now."

She smiled at me, it was a smile of pure and comical pity. We hugged each other again and she kissed me on the cheek. She told me how to get out of the village and then she pulled out my gun from somewhere—I have no idea where she was hiding it—and handed it to me.

I cocked my head; surprised Stella had taken it without me noticing. I took it, walked to my satchel, and stashed it away. By the time I turned back, my Mummy was gone.

It seems the time is right now that I've finished writing this diary entry.

I'll see you on the other side.

I hope.

Danger Diary 19 – Entry 6

I almost got out of the village without getting caught. As I was walking away from the Amazon's, from my mother, I stumbled across a familiar face.

"So, you're Queen Tallulah's son?" Stella said, hunched above me in a tree.

"Jesus! Do you jump out on everyone like that?"

"Only escaping prisoners," she said and let it hang in the air with raised eyebrows.

"What do you want?"

"I want you to take me with you. I want to get off this island."

"How old even are you?"

"I'm eighteen," she said, full of that smugness only

a teenager who thinks they know everything but really know nothing has.

I laughed. "You won't like it where I'm heading, kid."

"It'll be better than putting up with this place, scared that I'll be eaten or killed every day by some huge beast. Besides, if you don't take me, I'll scream."

Damn it. She had me.

"Fine, but do what I tell you," I said, and we carried on walking deeper into the jungle.

I had two stops to make. First, I had to get to the centre of the island. Get that diamond. Then, head east to the shore, with any luck, the Chief Seed's boat would still be there, and I might have a chance of getting off the island.

"What do you think would happen if someone took that diamond? The one on top of the pyramid?" I asked Stella.

"Who knows? Who cares?"

It was nice to know teens were the same every-where, even on this mythical island.

"You don't think the island would blow up or any-thing like that do you? I mean, taking the diamond isn't going to kill the island, is it?"

Stella raised an eyebrow in thought. "I doubt it," she said. Then a few seconds later she said, "Maybe, but if we're getting off the island, then who really cares."

I shook my head; she was of no use.

"Which way is it?" I asked.

Stella took stock of her surroundings, figuring out which way we needed to go when she tilted her head.

Alarm spread across her beautiful features.

"What is it?"

"Shhhh."

There was a crack of wood somewhere behind us, and we turned toward it. Before Stella was able to answer, a roar and crash came from the same direction. I looked to see the jungle parting.

A triceratops was charging us. Trees toppled like dominos thanks to its enormous weight and size.

As I turned to run, I saw it wasn't charging me, but instead was fleeing Rexy. That bloody overgrown iguana was back.

I turned and legged it. Stella was already in full flight beside me. I followed her as best I could, but she had experience in this terrain. She was getting further ahead of me with every step. Branches smacked off my face and ripped at my clothes and skin. I could've cared less. When you have several tons of extinct animal running for you, a scratch here and there is not a big worry.

The ground rumbled under feet as the beasts neared. My heart raced so fast I thought it might explode. But still had sight of Stella, so I kept running.

Before I knew it, I was in an opening, and the pyramid was right ahead of me. It was framed by the smoking volcano that stood directly behind it. Stella stood at the pyramids base waving me in her direction.

"Come on!" she shouted and started to climb the pyramid.

I saw now it was a step pyramid, in the fashion of the Maya. The diamond sat atop its peak and was blindingly bright. Thanks to the way volcano stood behind it, it looked like the diamond was smoking, giving off a strange, but alluring aura.

In another ten yards of running, I came to the pyramid. Five levels, each at least twenty feet high, stood in front of me. In the centre of the face was a series of more manageable steps to the peak—thank god.

I ascended about twenty steps, fumbling inside my satchel for my gun. At the second time of asking, I gripped the handle and pulled the gun, swivelling on my feet to face the beasts. I pulled the trigger before I'd even managed to turn my face to see what I was shooting at. All I got was a dull click.

Stella had taken the bloody bullets when she confiscated the gun. That, or I was out of bullets anyway.

When I got my eyes up though, I saw Rexy and the triceratops standing side by side at the clearing's edge. They both looked agitated, nervous somehow.

I looked around to see no other animals in the clearing. In fact, the grass even yellowed and died as it got closer to the pyramid, so it was just bare, dusty land at its base.

Rexy and the triceratops gave each other a confused look and turned back into the jungle.

I sat on the steps and started laughing then. Whether it was exhaustion or adrenaline or finding my destination, I laughed loud and deep from my belly.

"What's so funny?" Stella said.

"Honestly, I don't know," I said. All I knew was I was exhausted. I hadn't slept in I don't know how long. I put my hand back into the satchel and pulled out my trusty flask. I gave it a shake and there was still some

Jack left. I popped the lid and held it out to Stella.

"Here, give this a go."

She took it, sniffed, and scrunched up her face. I jerk my head up, insisting she give it a go. She swigged, and promptly spat it all out.

I burst out laughing. "That'll teach you to threaten me." She scowled at me, and I chuckled again. "Go on, take another swig. I promise. It grows on you."

She did and seemed to enjoy it a bit more this time, but still grimaced as it went down.

She handed it back, and I took a swig. Well, I tried to, but it was bloody empty now. I looked to Stella to see her giving me a sarcastic smile. I laughed again. "You're okay, kid. You know that?" and with that I laid down on my back and fell into a deep sleep.

I've been thinking about this adventure a lot since I got home.

Usually, in these Danger Diaries I keep, there's a real-life villain. Be it the Hun, or an arms dealer, or a slave trader, or this new communist party in Germany that seems to be getting big just lately. But in this diary, there wasn't one.

It was only then, I realised it was me. I was the villain. I was a sexist and, on a path to being a mass murderer and maybe even a genocider.

It took getting slapped by my Mummy to realise my actions all that time were abhorrent. I know now that I need to be a better, more respectful, more open-minded man. I want to be someone my Mummy would be proud of.

I hope that my actions henceforth are those of an honourable man. A real man.

I stood atop the pyramid after my nap looking at the Diamond of Days. I could feel the power pouring from it. Being so close to it filled me with confidence and strength. It filled me with a drive to take. To keep it for myself and to sod Liz. I would have all the power in the world with this diamond.

But I thought back to my Mummy's words, *'go home, forget about this place and live'* and I knew that if I took this diamond, there would be death for me and many more.

Instead, I looked east to the shore. And even from a distance, I could see the life raft on the beach.

I grabbed Stella's hand, and we ran down the pyramid, two steps at a time.

I was laughing again, this time at the weight that seemed to be lifted from my shoulders.

We got to the boat, and although the going was incredibly tough, we got off the island. We made it home. And somehow, I have become the surrogate father to a giant of a woman. But she's a delight. She's bright and tough, just like my Mummy. Stella and I have become a bit of a duo now and we will be going on adventures together. She loves the world, but she misses the island too. It had its charms, which she tells me about. Most of the stories she tells me involve my Mummy, and I listen to them rapt.

I hope to teach her everything about the world. I want to give her the tools to make her own decision on what to do with her life.

But before all of that, I had to pay somebody a visit.

"I'm very sorry, ma'am, but the search for the Diamond of Days was a washout," I said to Liz, in the same luxurious room we had previously met in. Stella wasn't with me; that would've just raised more questions than I needed. "I hate to tell you this, but your soldier friend's directions were nothing more than the mad ramblings of a dying man."

Liz nodded, clearly upset.

"I'm also sorry for the way I spoke to you before. I can see now that the way I spoke to you was totally unacceptable, as was my notions of women. I'm working on being a better man."

"Well, good for you, Mr Danger. You have a lot of work to do."

I chuckled, "I know. And please, call me, Norman."

"Norman Cottonwood. Much better."

I raised my eyebrows; how did she know my name.

"I do my homework before hiring someone, Norman. It's nice to see you've taken up your original name again," Liz said.

I gave her a warm smile. "Only to friends and family. As far as the general public know, I'm still Dirk Danger, adventurer extraordinaire!"

We both laughed.

"Then please, call me Elizabeth."

"Thank you, Elizabeth," I said and turned to leave, but before I did, I could see this young lady was in turmoil over my failure to return the diamond. "Oh, and Elizabeth. I too do my homework before I take any job."

"Oh?"

"Yes, and I want to assure you, you're a fine, bright, capable, and beautiful young lady. I know you wanted that diamond to be a gift, but Prince George will be lucky to have you. You and just you. You'll be the jewel in his crown."

"Thank you, Norman."

"Not that he'll ever become king, but you know what I mean, nonetheless. Not that you wouldn't make a fine queen, and him king. But it's just that Edward... I'm sorry, I'm rambling."

Elizabeth chuckled. I gave her a very charming smile and wished her a good day.

I had an appointment to keep. Stella and I would be meeting the curator of the British Museum, to discuss an expedition to find the ancient relic, known only as, Excalibur.

THE DIAMOND CAPER

DECLAN FLETCHER

Harry's muscles ached. He'd had hangovers before, but nothing like this. His body felt like he'd wrestled a bear all night. He tried to blink the sleep out of his eyes without much success. How much did he drink last night? He was fully dressed, shoes too, not a good sign. He hadn't fallen asleep with his clothes on since University. Thinking back, he could only remember 2 drinks and then everything went black. Had there been a girl? Maybe. He reached over to grab his phone from the bedside table, but it wasn't there, no phone, no bedside table. What the hell?

This wasn't Harry's room, so, where was he? He looked around, nondescript furniture, functional but not comfortable. A kettle on a desk, sugar, tea and UHT milk. A hotel room and not an upmarket one. How did he get here?

The room had no distinguishing features. The desk had a single chair. Relief flooded through Harry when he saw his jacket slung casually over the back of the chair.

Rolling out of bed, he cleared the room to his jacket in 2 strides. His hand dropped to the pocket. He felt the reassuring lump of his phone. His bag sat underneath the desk, the zip open. Looks like this will just be a funny story for me to tell at work on Monday. He straightened up and froze, the light caught a gun in his bag. Why was there a gun? Was it his?

Oh God. Not just a gun, a small black bag of some kind of velvety material. He'd seen enough TV to guess what would be inside, but his fingers trembled as he pulled the drawstrings. Sure enough, inside glittering against the black velvet were diamonds, a lot of diamonds. At least he assumed they were diamonds. They looked like the real deal, but if he didn't know much about guns, he knew even less about diamonds. For all he knew these were worthless, but he could be holding a small fortune.

The sudden blare of his phone snapped him out of his reverie. Who would be calling him, nobody he knew had phoned anyone in years? Unknown number, probably a call centre. When you wake up in a strange hotel room with no memory of the night before, you can't take that chance. He picked up the phone.

"Hello?" he asked.

"Hello Harry," a woman's voice, Harry struggled to place the accent. Harry thought English but with a lilting quality.

"Who is this, how do you know my name?" he demanded.

"Call me Madelyn, we don't have a lot of time Harry. I'm trying to help you, but you're going to have to trust me," her voice was calm but the words a little too fast. "There's £150,000 worth of diamonds in your bag right now, and a gun that the police will link back to the robbery. Who knows how many other crimes as well?"

"What, are you insane?" he gasped.

"Please Harry, the police are on their way. The same people who planted the evidence called them."

Harry didn't respond. This was all too outlandish. Who would put this much effort into playing a prank on him? Even if they put the effort in, who'd be able to pull this off?

"I can help you Harry. I assure you this is all real. There is a fire escape just outside your window. You'll have to jump but it's that or spending the next 10 years in prison," she said.

"Why would I listen to you?" Harry asked, the sound of sirens now audible in the distance. "I've done nothing wrong, jumping out a hotel window isn't going to get me out of this. The police don't arrest innocent men…"

"How adorable," she laughed, a short, sharp yet musical sound. "Someone has watched too much television. No Harry, the people setting you up know what they're doing. You have the stolen goods, the weapon and no alibi. They've given the police everything, they'll be so relieved to wrap this up in a neat little package they'll never stop to question it."

Harry wished he had a good answer to that, but it

had the cold ring of truth. How did she know he had no alibi? Who was this woman?

"Harry, you're going to have to make a choice. You need to believe I'm on your side. Get out of the hotel and we can meet, I'll explain everything. Please Harry, I'm just asking you to trust me for now and hear me out when we can meet somewhere safe," she pleaded. Harry heard an undertone in Madelyn's voice. A faint echo of what Harry thought might be desperation.

The line went dead, and Harry lowered the phone. What now? He didn't have long to decide. The sirens were louder than ever, and it sounded like they'd stopped moving. He had minutes at most. It all fit together just a little too well. How could the police know where he was and that he had the diamonds? It didn't seem possible; he didn't even know where he was. He was being framed, that much seemed clear. If he was being framed, then he couldn't take his chances with the police. Picking up his bag, he ran to the window, his muscles screaming in protest.

Harry pushed the window up as far as it would go, wincing at the screeching sound of the warped wood.

He'd moved just in time. At the same moment he climbed out of the window, the room filled with the boom of someone banging on the door.

"Police. Open up!" a voice blared through the door.

Harry looked down, the fire escape looked a long way, Five metres maybe? He wasn't good with distances, but long enough that this was going to hurt. He had no choice now, throwing his bag first before leaping himself. Pain flared through his shins. At least he'd made it.

One of the police officers' head and shoulders were out the window. His gun trained on Harry. Harry dropped to the ground and sprinted. He had to get away. Glancing back, he saw the second police officer grab the gun pointed at Harry.

"Not here," his voice faint over Harry's feet pounding the ground as he ran "Too many questions. Let's go."

He needed to keep moving. The police might have a description of him, he had no way to be sure. Everything happened so fast maybe they just had the room. Either way he couldn't stay around here, but he couldn't draw attention to himself. The fire escape led into an alley between buildings. No way to know if the police are watching it. As he prepared himself, his phone chimed.

Remember running attracts attention, try to stay calm and act natural. Tube station, 200m south – M.

Good advice he thought, although he had no idea which way was South. Shouldering his bag, he started walking away from the hotel, his heart hammering like he was sprinting as fast as he could. The morning road was peaceful, with minimal traffic and a stillness in the air. Harry felt like a trespasser in a strange land. He needed to stay calm. What could be more natural than talking on the phone? Taking his phone out, he realised it wasn't his. It looked similar, and he'd been too stressed to notice, but there were differences. Most notably, none of his contacts were there. Well, that explained how this Madelyn got his number.

Harry lifted his arm to dash the phone against the floor in frustration. If he'd just been able to call someone, talk this through. He felt like a rat in a maze, scurrying around for the amusement of some larger power. He didn't know the rules of the game he was playing. He felt blind. Taking a moment to steady himself, he put the phone away. If nothing else, he might be able to use it as proof that he'd been set up.

As he approached tube station, he took in the scene. It had a small car park that was deserted, not surprising this early in the day. There were police cars, some kind of stop and search? Like a checkpoint. Had they put out an APB on him? Were those even real things or more stuff he'd seen on TV? He wasn't sure. There didn't seem to be many people on the station platform.

It'd be damn suspicious to turn around now, so he took a moment to steady his breathing and kept walking. There were only a couple of police officers and they were talking amongst themselves. The thrill of getting through hit Harry like a drug. He felt alive. Every sense seemed to b maximum. His shirt clung to him, damp with his own sweat. He ducked into the bathroom to collect himself. He took deep breaths to steady himself, looking in the mirror his pupils were dilated but he seemed to be getting back to normal. His phone chimed again.

Astoria Cafe, 1 hour – M.

He knew Astoria Cafe; it was around the corner from where he worked. He had been having drinks in the same area last night. Was this Madelyn local as well? Maybe he'd seen her there before or vice versa? Only one way to find out…

The café was a throwback, red and white tablecloths

and dark wooden chairs. Harry slumped into a seat at the first empty table after the door. His body still aching as he leaned back, but at least it was a bit darker in here. It felt good to close his eyes for a second. Why was it so bright outside? He should get a coffee, that would help make him feel better, but it wasn't like he could pay in diamonds. Where even was his wallet, he checked the pocket in the bag but nothing.

"Looking for this, Harry?" a woman's voice interrupted Harry's search.

Lifting his head, he took in the woman in front of him. She couldn't be more than medium height, with dark hair, but her eyes had an almost magnetic pull. Light blue contrasting with such dark hair, but it was more than that. A mischievous light danced behind them, as though she were thinking faster than you were talking. A man could trip over himself trying to keep up with those eyes, Harry thought.

Tearing his gaze from those bewitching eyes, Harry finally saw the wallet she held loosely in her hand. Some relief at last, his missing wallet had been low down on his list of priorities but sometimes you have to take whatever positives you can.

"Thanks, but who are you and why do you have my wallet?" he asked.

"I told you, call me Madelyn. Come on, I have coffee," she gestured to one of the other tables, steam rising from the two cups of coffee. Harry picked up his bag and they moved to Madelyn's table. She had chosen her table with much more care than Harry. In one of the darker corners of the café it gave a clear view of the counter, the door and most of the other tables. Plus, while sat there, you wouldn't be seen from outside.

"I need some answers, what the hell is going on? Who are you and how are you involved in this? How did you know where I was?" Harry fought hard to keep the rising note of panic out of his voice.

"Harry, keep your voice down, there's not many people here but we don't want to be overheard," she breathed.

Harry hadn't really taken stock of the café when he'd come in. Having a look around now there were eight or so tables, most of them empty. By the window sat a middle-aged looking man. A few pounds shy of overweight, he wore a high viz jacket and read a paper while picking at his breakfast. Probably a builder, Harry thought. The only other person, sat by the counter, looked like a woman on her way to or from the gym. Harry could only see the back of her, but he dismissed her. She looked wrapped up in her own world.

"Look Madelyn, I need answers now or I'm going to the police and letting them sort it out," he said.

"That's why I brought you here, have you ever heard of Tommy Evans?" her voice dropped to almost a whisper when she said the name, as if it were dangerous to say out loud.

"Has he got something to do with these diamonds?" He asked.

"He's a criminal, gangster I suppose you'd say," she said. "Part of his business is smuggling. Those diamonds you have are the tip of the iceberg. He's about to smuggle millions of pounds' worth of stolen diamonds out of the country."

"Why plant…"

"Diamonds on you? To give the police a fall guy. A nice easy target for them to parade in front of the press. Then while the police are busy patting each other on the back he's free to move the diamonds. Sleight of hand, just like a magician."

"So, he called in the tip to the police, that's how they knew where I was. Why me though?" Harry took a sip of the coffee. It tasted terrible. He'd always thought you could tell the quality of a café by its tea and coffee. He would not be ordering food here.

"Just in the wrong bar at the wrong time," Madelyn looked down at the table, a slight colour visible in her cheeks.

"Wait… it was you! You were at the bar. You slipped me something, didn't you?" he demanded.

"You have to understand, I had no choice. My dad: he owes Tommy money. A lot of money," Madclyn was unable to quite meet his eye. "I've never done anything like this before, but I had no choice."

"No choice…" he said, his voice rising as he got out of the chair.

"Harry wait," Madelyn grabbed the sleeve of his jacket. "I couldn't do it, I've barely slept. That's why I called you, I couldn't live with sending an innocent man to jail."

Harry brushed her hand off his arm and heaved the bag onto his shoulder. He stopped himself from shouting. The other customers were trying to look like they weren't watching them. Harry couldn't afford to make a scene.

"I can still help Harry," Madelyn's eyes darted between Harry and the door. "You need to be careful; I know which police we can trust. Harry, don't go…"

But he had already left, her words fading into the background noise as the door swung closed behind him. What had Harry been thinking? Why would he trust a voice on the end of the phone? The whole situation was so surreal that for a minute he'd almost been caught up in the current of it. His head was clear now though. Time to let the professionals deal with this.

A faint whistle caught his attention but before he could turn his head pain exploded in the base of his neck. He stumbled to the ground, but arms hooked underneath him, and he felt himself being dragged. The world spun: he was going to be sick. He felt the arms let go, and he dropped to the floor, cold concrete rough beneath his hands. The world went black…

Harry did not know how long he had been unconscious, but it didn't feel like long. His vision still swam. The world mostly a big light blur. The back of his head throbbed in time with his pulse. Nausea was held at bay for the minute but lurking patiently below the surface.

"Looks like he was going to the cops," a deep male voice said.

"The Good Samaritan routine. I'll tell the cops I scared off some kid, but I wasn't in time to save this one," the voice again.

Harry could make out the figure of a man now. He hung up a phone call. One mystery solved, at least. The man squatted down next to where he had propped Harry up against a wall. Harry tried to size him up. Average looking for the most part, but he had a definite air about him. A set of the shoulders and flat look in the eye that spoke of violence ready to be unleashed. The kind of man you'd step carefully around if you met him in a pub, although you couldn't quite put your finger on why.

Harry's face stung. He hadn't seen the slap coming, but it did bring him somewhat back to his senses. On instinct, Harry looked around for his bag. There, in the alley behind the ogre, overlooked for the moment.

"Wakey wakey boy," he rumbled. "I've got some questions for you."

"Are you Tommy Evans?" Harry asked.

"If a man like Tommy Evans wants something doing, he doesn't do it himself," the man laughed. "How did you know about the police?"

"I don't know what…" Harry babbled.

"You want another slap boy?" the man questioned. "You start answering my questions or things are gonna get unpleasant."

"I don't know…"

Another slap cut Harry off, harder this time. Did Harry catch a flicker of movement down the alley or was that effects of the blow?

"Next time I break a finger, you got that boy?"

Harry tried desperately to think of any way out of this situation. What could he actually tell this guy? He could tell him about Madelyn, but as soon as he did, he then feared he'd be left in this alley on a rather permanent basis. He needed some way to convince him he was useful alive.

Lost in thought, Harry almost missed the faint popping sound. It took a few seconds before he connected it in his head with the red patch spreading over the man's chest. He fell to the floor like his strings had been cut. Behind him stood Madelyn. She looked as though she had been shot herself. Her ashen face frozen between anger and a scream of terror, the gun itself slipping from her gloved hands and bouncing on the concrete. All Harry could think was dropping the gun sounded louder than the shot. How had Madelyn done that?

The tableau lasted for what felt like hours until Madelyn snapped out of her trance and rushed over to him. She knelt down by his side and took his head in her hands, feeling around the bruise on his neck, taking care to not press to the point of pain.

"Oh my God Harry are you okay," she ejaculated. "I'm so sorry, I tried to warn you but you left so quickly."

"Thank you." Harry couldn't think of anything else to say. Words couldn't seem to express the gratitude he felt. His voice raspy but stronger than he would've expected.

"I knew they'd come after you," Madelyn's voice was breathy as if she'd run a mile. "I couldn't just leave you, not after what I did."

"Now what?" Harry's eyes still fixed on the motionless man. "We can't stay here."

"True," Madelyn's eyes never went to the man on the floor. "Just give me a few minutes to catch my wits. I've never even held a gun before."

"Well lucky for me you started today," Harry tried to reassure Madelyn. He had no idea what to do next and he needed her not to fall apart. "I heard him on the phone, I think he planned to kill me."

"He's one of Tommy's thugs," Madelyn said as she picked up Harry's bag. "Killing you wouldn't have phased him. We need to go. I know a detective we can call, he'll help, but we can't tell him about this."

"I should've trusted you from the start," Harry said. "You saved my life."

"You're welcome," Madelyn grinned almost despite herself. A glimpse of mischief trying to crack the grim visage of the last few minutes "Now if we want you to stay saved, we have to move. Can you put the gun back in the bag? I just can't,"

"You don't need to explain, let me get it." Harry hurried over to where the gun lay. Taking care, he dropped the gun into his back and zipped it up. He breathed a sigh of relief.

"We don't have time to hide the body, so maybe just put some of this cardboard over it?" Madelyn sounded unsure of herself for the first time, but Harry supposed that was to be expected under the circumstances. "While you rest up for a minute, I'll phone the detective."

"Will he be able to help us?"

"He has to; we've got nowhere else to go…"

Detective Parker was not at all what Harry had expected. He looked to be in his early forties and had the bearing of a man of action, the kind of person who doesn't waste time second guessing himself. Harry had been expecting an air of world weariness, the man in the pub who's seen it all and can tell you a thing or two. In a way this made more sense, Parker seemed like the guy you'd go to for help if you needed it. Explaining the situation took longer than Harry had imagined. Parker asked questions, but the right questions, extracting details Harry would have disregarded. By the end, Harry felt certain Parker understood the situation better than he did.

They'd met in a park, outdoors where nobody could sneak up on them or listen in. Tall trees casting long shadows on the ground. Late in the day, the park nearly empty, they were stood by a gazebo. Surprisingly well kept, the white and green paint still catching the last of the evening light. A popular spot during the day, it stood at almost the centre of the park. The perfect place for their meeting.

"Quite a story Harry," Parker said his expression unreadable. "You're not looking at jail time, long term there's no motive and you'd alibi out. Evans must've known that. You'd buy him maybe a week or two, that'll probably be enough."

"Thank God," said Harry.

"I won't lie to you though Harry, running from the police don't look good," Parker said. Harry and Madelyn had decided not to include the man in the alley. Parker was a good man as far as Madelyn knew, but dead bodies had a way of complicating matters.

"He just panicked. Anyone would do the same, they can't hold that against him," Madelyn's fingers clutched a bench, the knuckles white.

"I believe you," Parker soothed her. "More importantly, a jury most likely would too."

"So what now, do we come into the station?" Harry asked.

"Odds are if we play this by the book, you both spend a month or so clearing your name and Tommy gives us the slip in the meantime," Parker said.

"That bastard, I'll make him pay I swear," Madelyn said, the bench creaking under her grip.

"I just want this to be over," Harry muttered.

"After today he's going to be coming for you Harry," Parker said. "But we can kill 2 birds with 1 stone."

"What are you talking about?" Harry knew in his heart the detective was right. He'd already had one experience of this Evans' way of dealing with loose ends.

"We have the diamonds; we can set up a meet with Tommy. He'll want to compare them to his stones, so we just need to track them and he'll lead us right to the rest of the stolen diamonds. We arrest him in possession, plus conspiracy to smuggle. He goes away for a long time so you're in the clear. Everybody wins."

"Everybody except the guy who gets beaten to death with a baseball bat or whatever this guy uses." Harry said.

"Don't worry, we'll be monitoring; you won't be in any danger," Parker made a reassuring gesture with his hands.

"What do you mean me? I'll give you the diamonds and you can set this up with an actual police officer. Leave me out of it," Harry declared.

"That's not going to work. Obviously, he's expecting you to have the diamonds Harry," Madelyn's expression became thoughtful. Harry could almost see her turning the idea around in her mind.

"This is insane; I've never even been in a fight before today," Harry said.

"It's our best chance Harry…" Madelyn squeezed Harry's shoulder.

"Plus, you'll be getting one of England's most dangerous men off the streets," Parker said.

"Is that a good thing though, I like my legs as they are: unbroken," Harry met Madelyn's eyes. Her face held a touch of sadness, but Harry saw the determination there as well. She'd saved his life. He'd trust her judgement on this.

"He already thinks you've stolen his diamonds. Trust me Harry you're safer with him in jail," Parker said.

"Fine, how do we set this up?" Harry nodded his head in resignation.

"I'll get in touch through one of his guys. He's going to be suspicious, so we need to be careful, I'll tell him you're interested in selling the diamonds back to him," Madelyn said.

"But if he's trying to frame me, why would he want the diamonds back at all?" Harry asked.

"If he thinks that you're just some greedy kid who's trying to get rich quick, he'll take the meeting. He's had to give up over 100k in diamonds. We'll dangle getting those back and still having a scapegoat for the police in front of his nose," Madelyn explained.

"As long as he thinks he's smarter than you, Harry, he won't see the danger until it's too late," Parker grinned. "The only worry is him sensing something amiss when you contact him Madelyn."

"Don't you worry about that detective," laughed

Madelyn. "He'd never suspect a woman. I won't be contacting him directly. A man like Tommy has ways the public can contact him. He likes to think of himself as a modern-day Robin Hood, helping the downtrodden. Keeping the streets safe like the Krays. It's all bullshit but I can make it work for us."

"Okay, Harry, you come with me and we'll get you set up with a tracker," Parker said.

"I'll let you know once the meeting is set up." Madelyn's words hung in the air as they left in opposite directions.

Harry found himself having trouble standing in one spot. He'd walked the few steps between the warehouse door and the end of the alley at least twenty times in the last ten minutes. Leaning against the wall, shifting his weight from one foot to the other and flicking his fingers against his leg. He checked the time, any minute now. He adjusted his belt for what felt like the thousandth time, all too aware of the tracker concealed in the buckle.

An arctic night wind blew a host of unpleasant smells from the alley. It was the kind of place any sane person would avoid at this time of night. The back of a warehouse in an industrial district. Illuminated only by what light that could be had from the streetlights on the main road. The little of it that crept between the buildings deepening the shadows of the alley.

Light swept across the alley. He had to shield his eyes for a second. They weren't as sensitive as they had been, but the car headlights were a stark contrast to the late evening gloom. As his eyes adjusted, he saw a dark saloon car, hard to tell the colour in the low light, but he suspected probably black. Taking a deep breath, he walked toward the car. As he got near, the world suddenly went dark…

Harry's head jerked back. He felt water running down his face onto his shirt. Not a civilised way to be woken up, but certainly effective. Attempting to lift his hands to wipe his face he felt the rough bite of rope around his wrists. He appeared to be in a storage room of some kind. The room could be any of a million storage rooms in a million warehouses. It had a depressing grey uniformity, cracking paint and empty shelves. No windows, the light coming from a single light bulb suspended over his head. They had tied him to a sturdy wooden chair, the only other furniture a rickety table and some folding chairs propped against the wall.

The sound of the door opening behind him broke the monotony.

"Tell Stevens to keep watch at the main door…"

A man Harry guessed to be in his fifties walked around the table and took a chair. Well groomed, hands manicured and hair a perfectly styled widow's peak. Touches of grey at the temples making him look if anything more distinguished. He opened the chair and set it opposite Harry, straightening his suit before sitting down.

"Can I assume you know who I am, Mr Sullivan?" his voice far more urbane than Harry expected.

"Tommy Evans?" Harry guessed.

"Correct. You look surprised, Mr Sullivan." Tommy continued, "Allow me to guess: you were expecting some crass East-end thug?"

"Well…"

"Occupational hazard unfortunately," Tommy laughed. "I assure you, Mr. Sullivan, I am no thug. Merely a businessman."

"A businessman who knocks people out and ties them up for meetings?" Harry saw no harm in dragging this out. The longer he could stall Tommy the more time the police had to get him out of here.

"A precaution," Tommy smiled. "My only interest is in securing my assets."

"Joke's on you Tommy," Harry spat. "The police are going to be here any minute."

Tommy's eyes hardened but his smile never wavered.

"You refer to the tracker in your belt?" Tommy said.

Harry's insides seemed to simultaneously freeze and churn. A weight settled on his chest, breathing seemed to be getting harder. Without thinking, his eyes flicked around the room again, but he could see no escape, no way out of this situation at all.

"Or perhaps the tracker in the diamond bag?" Tommy continued. "No matter, both are taken care of. We are, I assure you, in the last place anyone will think to look. You understand your position now, do you not?"

Harry could only nod, his shoulders slumped.

"Good. Now on to business," Tommy 's tone was soft, almost concilatory. "You seem a reasonable man Mr. Sullivan, unfortunately you are responsible for the death of my associate and such a transgression must be punished in kind."

Harry felt a trickle of cold sweat run from the nape

of his neck to the base of his spine. He suppressed a shiver. He would not give this man the satisfaction of seeing his fear.

"Purely business, you understand," Tommy smiled. "I cannot have people believing they can trifle in my affairs with impunity. What remains to be seen Mr. Sullivan is the how…"

"Does this Hannibal Lecter shtick impress people?" Harry snorted.

"Do not test my patience," Tommy's smile slipped for once "We know the diamonds you brought are fakes. Where are my diamonds, Mr. Sullivan?"

"What?" Harry didn't have to feign bafflement. Was this a trick? Tommy must have the diamonds; Harry had been carrying them when he was knocked unconscious.

"Your friend Madelyn works for me, Mr. Sullivan," Tommy's smile was back. "She warned us about the trackers and suggested this locale for our chat. A most astute woman. She alerted us to the fake diamonds. A simple appraisal proved her correct."

"No that doesn't make sense…" Harry's mind whirled. Madelyn hadn't said anything about fake diamonds…

"This is your last chance, Mr. Sullivan." Tommy's voice rose an octave. "Tell me where the diamonds are!"

"You have them," Harry said. "I had them with me."

"Obviously I was wrong; you are not a reasonable man after all," Tommy resumed his cultured manner. "I had hoped we could handle this as businessmen, but you force me to employ more straightforward methods."

"For God's sake I don't know anything!" Harry

shouted, "I can't help you!"

"It was a good plan, Mr. Sullivan," Tommy said "If it were not for your friend you may even have managed to abscond with my merchandise, but alas…"

Tommy left the room and returned not long after carrying a small bag. With his back to Harry, he set the bag on the table. Harry couldn't quite see what he was doing, but the bag seemed to open out flat on the table.

"Please remember, Mr. Sullivan," Tommy stepped to one side allowing Harry to see the tools on the table. "I tried to save you from this…"

Lying on the table were two small saws, a pair of pincers, various knives and a collection of implements Harry couldn't even identify. Strange, hooked objects and something that looked like over-sized scissors. Harry's mind went blank, panic shutting down almost all brain function. He couldn't take his eyes off the torture tools.

"Now, Mr. Sullivan," Tommy picked up the pincers turning them other in his hands and making quite a show of inspecting them. "Shall we discuss the location of my diamonds?"

Harry screamed. A wordless emotional howl. Please God no, he thought. This was all a mistake.

Tommy's head whipped round as the door slammed open. "Police hands up!" a voice shouted from behind Harry. Euphoria swept over him in a wave. The gruff voice was the most beautiful thing he had ever heard.

Harry had spent the night at the police station answering questions, asking a lot of his own, filling out forms and finally sleeping. He finally after everything returned home. Stepping out of the taxi into the morning sun, he paused for a moment to enjoy the warmth on his face. He walked across the shared lawn, enjoying the feel of the grass beneath his feet. The grey of the flat block looming above the lawn, the 60s relic had never felt so welcoming.

Stepping into the foyer, he checked his mailbox out of habit. To his surprise, he saw a large jiffy bag with just the word Harry written on the front. Tearing it open, he spilt the contents onto a table, his phone tumbled out. He'd forgotten about it in all the excitement, but seeing it there gave him a shot of relief like caffeine. Picking it up, he checked for damage, it seemed to be in one piece. He tried the power button, but nothing happened. Not surprising, batteries only last for so long. It took him a few seconds to notice the note. It must be from her…

Harry,

I don't know if you can understand, but a life lived under the thumb of a man like Evans is no life at all.

Escape was all I thought or cared about for so long.

I regret that I had to use you, but I am free now.

As I'm sure you have guessed I took the diamonds and thanks to you, and Parker, Tommy will not be coming after me. Tommy would've found the trackers himself, so I told him about them. The fool trusted me implicitly after that. I suggested using the warehouse you met at to interrogate you. The police would assume you'd been taken in the car and only do a cursory check of the area.

I watched to make sure they took you inside. I knew Tommy would wait a couple of hours for the police to disperse and so I called them when he arrived.

You are a good man Harry, I apologise for putting you through this but you were simply in the wrong place at the wrong time.

Do not try to find me.

"Madelyn"

PS I have hidden the gun, your fingerprints on it could still incriminate you for the shooting in the alley. Not to worry though, nobody but me knows where it is.

Harry smiled; he didn't know how he felt about Madelyn. She'd used him for her own ends, but she had also saved his life. Who could say how she really felt? All Harry knew was that he'd miss her.

"Good for her."

THE KYTHIRA MECHANISM

CHRIS HEWITT

Aegean Sea, 83BC

Aegeus braced himself as another wave crashed over the deck of the trireme, panicked shouts confirming the chaos below as oarsmen chose between bailing and rowing to safety. The tempest unleashed its full fury on the bedevilled vessel, the tattered sail lashing at the deck as fork lightning arced across angry dark skies.

"Believe me now, Aegeus?" yelled Kryillos, clinging to the rudder. "Even the gods want these accursed devices destroyed and us with them."

"Stay your course. It's just a storm. We've survived worse."

"We were kids back then, brother."

Aegeus laughed. "A lot younger."

A week out of Rhodes and a day short of the safe port

of Kythira, the captain cursed his luck as he stared across the swirling maelstrom at Theron's ship. His cousin's trireme sat high in the water, weathering the worst of the storm. That's when Aegeus knew that his avarice would be his undoing, not some cursed orrery. When General Sulla wanted his loot shipped back to Rome, Aegeus had argued for the most valuable and heaviest items to be placed onboard his ship for a bigger share of the profits. The bronze statues, heavy ceramics and countless other spoils of Greece would be his downfall.

Even as the storm approached, he'd refused his brother's council to lighten their load, knowing the General's love of the games would likely see their end in the Colosseum, in the jaws of god knew what.

The sight of a monstrous wave rolling over the bow, dragged Aegeus from his regrets and as he hung on, a sickening crack reverberated along the structure. Hearing the death throes of the ship, half-drowned oarsmen scrambled onto the deck, to lash themselves to anything that might float. Aegeus had long given up barking orders. It was everyman for himself. He turned to find his brother gone, the rudder rattling back and forth, lifeless. He searched the ship and the sea, hoping to see his brother but finding only the racing white horses of the wave that would send him and his ship to the bottom of the Mediterranean.

Indian Ocean, 2021AD
The hissing plasma torch bathed the container's interior in a blinding white light. Ed shielded his eyes,

watching darting shadows dance about the detritus that had been their home for the last week. Three sleeping bags buried under discarded bottles and packages blanketed the small eight-foot square cell, the rest of the shipping container, packed high with chintzy Japanese imports.

In the corner, beyond a clutter of unboxed waving lucky golden cats, sat the putrid horror that had changed their plans, forcing them from their hidey-hole two days early. Ed doubted he'd ever forget the smell of the overflowing bucket. Maybe if there hadn't been a storm, maybe if they'd not been so terribly seasick, things might have been different. But right now, the *plan* could go to hell, they needed out. With a deafening clang, a section of the container door fell free, releasing the promise of fresh sea air.

"Well, so much for stealth," said Kira, picking up a waving kitty and tucking it into her ruck sack. "That'll save some time at the airport."

Ed shook his head. Kira's niece would likely take one sniff of her gift and bin it.

"Ladies, first," said Yerik, bowing.

Kira didn't hesitate, squeezing past the big Russian and out through the smouldering hole.

He found Kira, eyes closed, head up, breathing in the fresh air as they stood in a narrow canyon between stacked shipping containers. Overhead a slither of sky blazed from sunset orange through cobalt to black, chasing away the last of the twinkling stars.

"Fuck's sake, Yerik," cried Kira as the ex-sailor re-lit a stinking cigar, he'd tucked into his dirty Mariner's cap days earlier. The stench bought back the worst of their ordeal, making Kira gag.

"Calm Kiska, breath in that fresh ocean air," mocked Yerik, taking a long drag on his glowing cigar. He'd not used her name once, preferring the derogatory feline nickname, a nod to her occupation. Something about the term cat burglar had tickled Yerik, a man more familiar with armed robbery than cracking safes. The idea of taking anything without violence had probably never occurred to the thug.

Kira slipped him the bird, making the Russian chuckle.

"Shall we get on with it?" said Ed.

"It's your party, Professor," said Yerik, bowing as Kira and Ed passed.

"How are we getting out of here? We're two days early for the rendezvous and there's no way I'm going back in that box," asked Kira.

"Relax, Kiska, I can pull the Somalis in early."

Kira snapped, pushing the big man hard against a container. "Tell me to relax one more time and you'll find out this kitty's got claws."

A flash of steel and the tip of Yerik's cigar bounced across the deck. The big man spat out the butt, grinning at Kira, before glancing down to where a large combat knife threatened her navel. He raised an eyebrow.

Kira grinned back at him. "Meow!"

Yerik winked as she let him go.

Ed rubbed his neck. "Will you two stop dicking around? We've got a container to find."

Volume 3

Ed stared along another long row of stacked containers, wishing they'd persevered with the original plan of tagging the container. Although calling the mobile vault, a container was to ignore the electronic and mechanical gizmos that secured their prize. Not that any of that mattered, when they couldn't even find the needle on the titanic haystack. The container ship ran for several football fields, nigh on twenty thousand containers stacked in rows that towered to the sky as they descended into the depths of the hull. It had all been so easy on paper.

"You'd think, finding a fifty-foot-long orange box would be easy," said Kira as if reading his mind.

"Told you to tag it," growled Yerik.

"We've been over this. The container's electronic security would detect any tracker, durak. At least we know it's above deck, towards the bow."

That had been a work of genius, Kira hacking into the Tokyo traffic system to ensure the container arrived at the port late. They might not be able to tag it, but that didn't stop them narrowing the odds.

Ed reached the end of the row and stared out over the vast azure expanse of the Indian Ocean. They'd checked less than a quarter of the ship's containers in the last hour and by his calculation it would take several more hours and with each pass they got a little nearer to the crew quarters and the chance….

"Hey!"

Ed spun around to see a confused crew hand starting at him. "Hey! You wouldn't happen to have seen a big orange…"

Yerik knife burst through the man's chest and in one swift movement the Russian hoisted the gurgling sailor over the side, to vanish with a distant splash.

"What the fuck?" cried Kira, staring over the side. "No one was meant to get killed. That was the deal. You could have…"

"Deal just changed," said Yerik, his bloodlust clear to see.

Ed held Kira back. "Leave it. It won't be long before he's missed. If the alarm is raised, this gig is over. There won't be any second chances."

Kira pushed passed Ed and stalked off down the next row of containers.

Yerik fixed Ed with piercing blue eyes, wiping the blood from his knife. "You're right there, Professor. Vicili, don't do second chances."

Ed's hands balled into tight fists as a piercing whistle broke the tension and the men followed its source to find Kira leaning against a large orange container. "Can we get this shit show on the road?"

"Whoa, numb nuts," cried Kira as Yerik fired up the oxy-acetylene cutter. She rummaged in her rucksack to retrieve four small black discs and threw two to Ed. "Shove them on the other end at the corners, green is on and you-" she said pointing at Yerik, "don't move a muscle."

Ed placed the small devices as instructed and returned to find Kira, fingers dancing over a data pad. "Right, that outta do it. Hulk can smash now, without alerting half the planet. I need this whole side off, big boy."

Yerik flicked down his goggles and set to cutting through the exterior of the container.

Ten minutes later the end fell with a gust of wind and a muted thud, thanks to the airbags Kira had strategically positioned. Her planning for the job stood out in stark contrast to Yerik's cavalier bull in a china shop approach. Not that Ed had a choice in muscle. Victor Vicili had called Yerik 'insurance', one of two policies he'd taken out to ensure Ed delivered what lay within the container.

"Right, then let's see what we're up against," said Kira as the swirling smoke cleared to reveal a shiny onyx wall. She tapped the glass-like surface with a tuning fork she'd magicked from one of her many pockets. "Okay. Pretty much what I expected. Apart from the C4."

"The what?" asked Ed.

"Yeah, bit of determent for amateurs who might break out the thermite. It also makes one hell of a statement."

Ed rubbed his chin. "A statement?"

"Mine or no ones," said Yerik.

"Bingo, big boy. Maybe there is a brain behind those vacant blue eyes. Mr Mikami ain't sharing. Whatever is in there, he's willing to destroy rather than let anyone else have it. So, before I bust this thing open, it's time for truth or dare."

Both men stared at the arch-thief, confused.

"I need the truth about what's in there, or you can have a crack at opening it yourselves, if you dare, as it seems the deal is up for renegotiation."

Kira turned at the click of the desert eagle's safety being removed and stared down the barrel before sighing. Ed stepped forward, lowering Yerik's arm and pulling Kira aside.

"I think we got a real workplace romance going on," said Kira, grinning back at the Russian.

"Stop fucking about. There's too much at stake," hissed Ed.

"That's what I'm worried about. This ain't no diamond heist. What's in the fucking box, Ed."

Ed rolled his eyes and stared up at the tower block of containers. A stark contrast to the night he'd stumbled over Kira, literally, in the Louvre. He'd been cataloguing Egyptian antiquities. She'd been shopping for a wealthy collector. That night she went home disappointed, but free, and he went home with a new friend. Their paths had crossed many times in the years since, and he'd never once called in that favour, until a fortnight ago.

"You remember the Antikythera mechanism?"

Kira stared at him; mouth open. "No! Really? I'm risking my life for some fucking national geographic rusty arse advent calendar. I can't believe this. I should have guessed."

She stormed away, only to return, pounding her finger into Ed's chest. "Fuck, Ed, how does a professor of antiquities end up partnering with the Russian mafia, to steal from the fucking Yakuza. What dusty journal is that getting written up in? I told you this obsession would get you killed, but I didn't expect it to get us both killed."

"I haven't got a choice."

"Tell that to Eliz-"

Kira stopped mid-sentence as Ed's chin slumped onto his chest. She lifted his head until she could see his welling eyes.

Through a faltering smile he repeated. "I haven't got a choice."

"Fuck, Ed."

Ed nodded. Vicili held his daughter, Elizabeth, the ultimate insurance policy. He'd seen her a month ago, in Cairo. Vicili had kept his part of the bargain, treating her like a princess, ensuring she longed for nothing. But that arrangement depended on Ed, keeping up his side of the bargain.

"But why, Ed. What's so important about a load of rusty old cogs?"

"The Antikythera mechanism, sunk in a storm in 85BC. That incomplete rusted artefact sits in the National Archaeological Museum in Athens. The Kythira mechanism on the other hand…"

"The what?"

"There were two. The one that sunk off the coast of Antikythera and the one that made it to the island of Kythera to be unearthed by a goat herder back in two-thousand and seven."

"Why haven't I heard of this?"

"Few have. The device never made it into academic circles. I heard rumours of it passing between dealers and, well, it's no surprise it found its way into Miki Mikami's collection."

"So what? You've blundered into the middle of a billionaire's pissing competition?"

"No, Mikami and Vicili answer to people too," said Ed, shaking his head and pointing a finger upwards. "Interest in the device goes beyond far beyond the crime gangs."

"Why?"

"It isn't just an orrery, or astrological calendar, Kira. It's a key to unlocking something else, something we've misunderstood. That's why everyone wants it. That's why they took her, and that's why I need it."

Kira stared at him for the longest moment, shaking her head. "Well, I hope you've got a plan. Cause the moment Yerik gets what his master wants, we're going to find ourselves surplus to requirements."

Yerik finished cleaning his desert eagle, loading the clip and cocking the gun with a satisfying clunk.

"Shush," hissed Kira. Two hours she'd probed and drilled the secure container, a cobweb of wires interconnecting sensors and primed micro-explosives. "If I miss just one of these dead bolts."

Yerik stubbed out his cigar, holstering the weapon and blowing the last of the stinking smoke at Kira as he resumed his patrol.

"Arsehole," hissed Kira.

"How long?" whispered Ed, watching the big Russian walk away.

"I'm pretty much there."

"Good. Yerik can't kill me until I've verified the artefact's authenticity. Make sure I'm between you and him and be ready."

"You've got a plan?"

Ed nodded. "If this is the Kythera mechanism, there might be a way out. But we'll need to move fast."

Kira double checked her handiwork, following the rat tail of wires back to a black box sitting on the deck. She flipped a switch and a series of LEDs blinked from red to green. "Right, were in business."

Yerik wandered back to stare down at Kira. "About time. I hope for your sake this works."

Kira grinned, raising her hand to reveal a detonator. She winked and pressed the button. What started as a dull hum, built in frequency and volume until the noise stopped, replaced by several muted pops. Smoke emanated from the holes, but the container remained closed.

Yerik wasted no time pulling his handgun and pointing it at Kira's head. "Too bad, Kiska."

"Wait!" barked Ed as cracks spread across the onyx surface. A second later the front of the container shattered to reveal a large empty container. Empty but for a table.

Yerik waved his gun. "You're up, Professor."

Ed looked across at Kira. "Is it safe?"

"Let me check," she said, stepping ahead of him.

Ed was quick to squeeze in behind her as they moved towards the table. Under Perspex he could see a copper device, unlike any artifact he'd ever seen, its metallic cogs and contrivances showing no sign of rust.

"Don't look like an antique," growled Yerik, stepping behind them, gun still levelled.

"Is that your professional opinion," said Ed, running his hands over the panel. "I'm gonna need a hand here, Kira."

She checked the table, before pulling out a small bottle of liquid and tracing a circle. The liquid bubbled and fizzed before the panel fell free. Ed retrieved the contraption, trembling fingers wrapping around his life's pursuit.

From the moment he held it, he knew it to be authentic. The device had no weight. What looked like copper gears on closer inspection were far more intricate gyroscopic elements, allowing every cog to rotate and engage with the other gears in complex patterns.

"Well?" Prompted Yerik.

"Well, if it's a copy, it's an excellent copy. There's only one way to be sure," said Ed, turning to Kira. "You got a spare power pack?"

Kira rummaged into her backpack to pull a palm sized battery, complete with cable. "What you need USB-A, B, C?"

"Err yeah, well something a bit more B.C." said Ed, pointing at two contacts on the device.

"Right," said Kira, pulling a knife and splicing the cable. "Old school, positive and negative coming up."

Ed scrutinised the contraption, the largest outer ring, featured a range of symbols, most of which he couldn't recognise. Two hieroglyphs, however, stood out. "Akhet Khufu."

"What?" said Yerik.

"The Horizon of Khufu," Ed added, manipulating

the contraption until all the other cogs aligned on the selected symbols. He lay the contraption on the table as Kira handed him the battery.

Yerik raised the gun. "You better start making sense, Professor. Is it the real deal or not?"

Ed wrapped the negative wire around one contact, and then attaching the other wire, stood back.

"Well?" barked Yerik.

Ed's heart sunk. He'd expected some kind of re-action, at least something to distract the big Russian. Instead, the device simply sat unmoving as it had for countless centuries. Even if he could cover the distance, he doubted he could disarm the thug, not before he'd put a bullet in his and Kira's heads.

"Look," said Kira, pointing at the smoking power pack, the green LEDs indicating battery charge blinking off one after another until the battery burst in flames.

Yerik fired his gun behind him, the deafening crack of the desert eagle in an enclosed space causing Ed and Kira to duck.

"Enough, bullshit," said Yerik, taking aim at Kira. "Yes or No, Professor. Last chance."

Ed raised his hands. "It's—"

The Kythira mechanism floated into the air, cogs beginning to spin as a low bass hum reverberated through the container. They all watched the device as the mechanism's intricate gears began to glow blue.

"Authentic," gasped Ed as one of the cogs appeared to lock into place, sending out a pulse of energy that made the hairs on his neck stand on end.

"Okay, Professor. I believe you," shouted Yerik over

the growing din. "Vicili, wanted you to know he'll take care of your daughter."

The big Russian aimed the gun at Ed's head and pulled the trigger and missed, the bullet ricocheting off the wall. Another cog locked into place, the static build-up creating arcs of electricity between the device and the container's sides. Yerik fired again, his bullet finding the back wall. A third cog locked into position on the contraption, and Yerik's third shot went into orbit around the device, slowing as if caught in some terrible gravity.

"Err, Ed," said Kira as the fourth cog clicked into place and the world slowed. Ed wrapped his hand around Kira's as the world stopped. For a heartbeat everything froze, the arcing electricity, the contraptions spinning gears and gyroscopes, even Yerik and his next bullet.

In the next heartbeat, the world resumed with the sound of thunder, a rumbling cacophony of screaming steel, as they were thrown to the shaking floor. The walls buckled with the weight of the containers above and Ed glanced at the exit to see the tower of containers opposite slide pass, straight down, like poker chips.

Yerik scrabbled to the open end of the container and Kira followed. Ed picked up the device, a vicious bite of cold forcing him to wrap his sleeve around the largest cog to carry it. He joined the others, steadying himself against the groaning metal walls to stare out over a sunrise like no other. A spectacular desert, a sea of orange sand stretched to a sprawling city, half lost in morning mist.

"My god, the stories were true."

Ed looked down one hundred and thirty-nine meters to the see the last of the shipping containers cascade down the side of the Pyramid of Khufu. Several hundred containers had transported with them, many torn open on the Great Pyramid, their contents scattered across the sands below. The worst excesses of consumerism buried the pyramid's base.

He'd been here countless times in his career; a Mecca for all who studied antiquities. Well, not here, not precariously balanced in a shipping container on the pyramid's peak.

"Are we dead?" asked Kira.

Yerik answered her, seizing Kira by the neck and pinning her to the wall, feet dangling as he forced the barrel of the gun into her mouth. On instinct, Ed swung the Kythira contraption at the Russian's head. Now, a hefty ball of condensing ice it connected with bone with a sickening crunch, dropping the thug instantly. Kira followed, collapsing to the floor, gasping.

Ed helped Kira to her feet, as the walls buckled, and the container's ceiling dropped a foot, the metal wailing like a banshee. He looped the device through his belt, ignoring the thought of frostbite in his nether regions as they lowered themselves from the container, swinging under and dropping onto the limestone blocks as the container moaned and shook. Kira landed like a cat. Ed did not, hitting the stone blocks hard as the weight of the containers above crushed the compromised vault.

"Serves him right," spat Kira, staring up at the crimson waterfall dripping from the flattened end of the container. Ed took one glance and scrambled from under the creaking, swaying stack.

"What fucking stories?"

"What?"

"You said the stories are true. What stories? How the hell did we get here, Ed?"

They climbed down the pyramid, picking their way through the debris, careful to remain parallel with the teetering containers above as the sun climbed above the horizon, bringing the promise of wilting heat.

"The mechanism is the key to a technology that predates even the Sumerian's. I've got a pretty good idea, now, why so many civilisations built pyramids."

"Aliens!" said Kira, kicking a rubber duck. One of thousands of battered fake fowl scattered down the side of the pyramid, along with toasters, bikes, cars and of course an army of unlucky waving plastic cats.

"What?"

"It's got to be aliens, right? I saw this-"

"It's not aliens!"

"They landed their mother-ship on the-"

"It's not bloody aliens," cried Ed, stumbling over a kitchen sink.

Kira threw her hands in the air. "Not, aliens! Ten minutes ago, we were in the middle of the Indian Ocean, three thousand miles away, and now I'm staring at downtown Cairo. Not to mention, the last time I checked 7-Eleven hadn't opened a store on top of the greatest wonder of the ancient world. If it isn't aliens, Ed, then what?"

"Mycenaean, Minoan maybe?"

"Maybe? Ed, look around you. That clockwork contraption just turned our world upside down. That's one hell of a high-water mark for Bronze Age forging."

As they neared the base of the pyramid, they climbed over broken containers, carving a route around the worst of the chaos. High above, they could hear the thrum of the first helicopters arriving as thousands of people emerged onto the sands to investigate the impossible sight.

Kira lost Ed as he ducked around an up-ended blue container. "Ed, hold up!"

"We don't have time."

"What's the big hurry?"

She turned the corner to find him pointing to the circling chopper and to the approaching wave of people. "That. Them. It'll already be splashed all over the news."

"Good," said Kira, tying her jacket around her waist. "It should be. This is biggest archaeological find since… well, ever."

"No! Don't you understand. Vicili will take one look at this and put two and two together, and when he does…"

"Shit, Elizabeth. That's why you picked this pyramid."

Ed nodded.

"Do you know where she is?"

"I've got an idea. But she'll be heavily guarded."

Kira grinned, nodding to the device on his belt.

"Well, just as well we can move heaven and earth then."

By the time they reached the base of the pyramid, half the locals scavenged the boon of goods, eager for souvenirs of the day the Great Pyramid became a shopping mall. It was easy to merge with the preoccupied looters and as they hailed a taxi, Ed looked back at the Pyramid of Khufu sporting its top hat of four containers. That would be the image on every screen around the globe right now.

***

"Here!" said Ed, thumping the back of the driver's seat. The taxi pulled across the traffic, stopping outside the Cairo Opera house, and they climbed out. Ed patted his pockets, searching for his wallet.

"I've got it," said Kira, producing a fifty dollar note. The taxi driver sped away before change could be discussed. "I'm adding that to my bill. Is Vicili the phantom of the opera?"

"No, he has a compound on the other side of the park," said Ed, running into the early morning rush hour traffic, honking horns and angry Arabic insults hinting at the commuters' displeasure. In the park, he stopped at a bench to remove the Kythira mechanism from his belt. The device still felt icy cold, but enough of the ice had melted, to allow the various cogs to swing.

"Are you trying to get yourself killed?" gasped Kira, catching up.

"Have you got any more power packs?"

"Kira, have you got this, have you got that" she mumbled, rummaging into her backpack. She pulled out two more palm sized packs. "That's the lot, and that one is only at forty per cent."

"Probably for the best," said Ed, taking the battery. "Can you do the honours?"

Kira pulled out her knife and spliced another USB cable. "You think the power controls the size of the effect?"

Ed smiled. It wasn't the first time Kira's problem-solving skills had caught him out. "Yeah, it stands to reason."

He scanned the symbols on the side of the device, looking for something other than Akhet Khufu that made sense. It didn't require a Professor of antiquities to spot influences from several ancient language systems. Maybe if he had access to a library and a month, he might decode the set, but standing in a park he was at a loss. His finger rested on an odd symbol, almost an emoji. "What does that look like to you?"

Kira looked closer. "A cat? An unhappy cat?"

Ed sighed. They'd need to take a chance. He locked in the cat symbol and aligned the aligned the rest of the cogs.

Kira took the device and worked her magic. "There you go," she said, handing back the augmented contraption, the power back duct taped to the outer cog. He could see the wires wrapped around the contacts.

"Don't worry," said Kira, holding the detonator trigger she'd used earlier. "When you're ready to party. Press that."

"Thank you, Kira. I'll take it from here on in."

"Right! No disrespect but you're no Indiana Jones, Professor," laughed Kira, swiping the trigger from his hand and strolling away across the park.

"Kira. This is different, this is dangerous."

"Right! Let me be the judge of that. Are you coming?"

Ed chased after her, cursing.

"Compound? It's a bloody mansion," said Kira, staring through the fence. The immaculate green gardens of Vicili's home stretched down to the Blue Nile, where a luxury superyacht sat moored. Beside it a modern mansion, an architectural wonder of its own, screamed ill-gotten wealth, multiple sweeping tiered verandas mirroring the lines of the expensive boat.

"How are we going to find her in there?"

Ed extended a finger to point to the second tier, where a noisy party appeared to be in full flow, at ten o'clock in the morning. A single bikini-clad figure danced on a table.

Kira stifled a laugh. "Well, I see Lizzy has err… grown up. You must be so proud."

Ed ground his teeth as his daughter fell from the table into a group of laughing revellers. Up until now, he'd only imagined how Vicili's hospitality might corrupt his little girl. Little girl? She'd long stopped being that. Somewhere between burning down his study and declaring she was going to travel the world. From what he could see, she was no nearer to finding herself. Not unless it involved the lap of an Arabian Adonis.

"Are you sure she needs rescuing?"

"Even more so, now. Vicili will know the mechanism works, and he'll stop at nothing to get it. Right now, he has one bargaining chip."

"Well, let's give him three," said Kira, landing on the other side of the fence. The sound of distant alarms ringing out as an army of security guards appeared across the grounds. "What? You thought we'd be sneaking in?"

Kira put her empty hands in the air and knelt on the grass. He could only imagine where she'd hidden the trigger.

Ed landed beside her and joined her kneeling, mechanism held above his head. "Well, I thought you were a cat burglar?"

"I am, but sometimes it's easier to go through the front door."

The first guards reached them, assault rifles flickering red laser targets across their faces.

"Hi, there," beamed Kira. "Is Victor home? I imagine he's expecting us."

"Ah, my guests. Let them in," crackled the guard's radios.

"Ah, Professor and the delightful, Ms Ellis," said Vicili, arms held wide as if greeting long-lost friends. "Now, aren't you two meant to be on an all-expenses paid cruise in the Indian Ocean?"

The guards had led them through the grounds to a large living space that provided a commanding open view of the Nile and Vicili's pride and joy, his yacht. A guard jammed his AK47 into Ed's ribs as another pushed Kira onto a long white sofa.

Vicili slumped onto the sofa opposite and poured three glasses of orange juice. "Come now, we're all friends here. Lower your arms and let's have a grown-up chat about your new discovery."

With little choice, Ed slumped onto the sofa beside Kira and placed the Kythira mechanism on the glass table as Vicili slid over two full glasses.

"Now that's better," he said, gulping back the fresh orange juice and switching on a large video screen that stretched across the length of one wall. It showed an Al Jazeera news feed from a helicopter circling the stacked containers sitting on top of the pyramid. Far below, a military cordon deterred any further would-be looters. The display switched to showing a different helicopter feed, hovering over another scene. A container ship, a humongous hole in its deck, like someone had taken an enormous ice-cream scoop to the vessel.

"They were lucky. Another forty feet and it'll have compromised the hull. Amazing, really, only one crew member missing. Any chance you've seen him?"

Ed and Kira looked at each other, shaking their heads.

"And Yerik?"

"He had a pressing engagement," offered Kira.

Vicili nodded. "Shame. His mother will take it hard."

"Dad?" said Elizabeth, bursting into the room, still dressed for the beach. "What are you doing here?"

Ed rushed over to his daughter and hugged her tight.

"What? What's wrong?"

"Have they hurt you?"

"Hurt me?" said Elizabeth, pushing him to plonk herself down beside Vicili and pour herself a glass of juice. "Are you mad? Victor has been the consummate host."

Ed returned to his seat, listening to the rush of blood, as his heart cried out. It was bad enough that she hated him, but that she didn't see through this monster's charade. He thought he'd prepared her for the realities of the world.

"So, Professor. It appears we've both delivered on the deal," grinned Vicili, hand patting Elizabeth's leg. Ed's fingers gripped the sofa, nails digging into the leather as he nodded, and Vicili reached out a hand to take the mechanism.

Ed snatched the device back. "I've just got one question."

Vicili rolled his eyes, his hand tightening on Elizabeth's thigh. "Now that wasn't part of the deal, was it?"

"And neither was this," said Elizabeth, smashing her glass into the side of Vicili's temple, in an explosion of orange juice.

"Elizabeth!" cried Ed, seeing his daughter snatching a grapefruit spoon from the table and jamming the slender handle into Vicili's ear.

With blood and orange juice dripping from his face, Elizabeth held the Russian crime lord in a headlock, pushing home the utensil every time he threatened to move. "Dad, we don't have time. The guards will be here in sixty seconds, and we will not want to be here."

"CIA?" said Kira, leaping to her feet and teasing the hidden trigger from her hair.

Elizabeth laughed, shaking her blood-spattered head. "More Lambeth than Langley. Now if you'd like to, you know, get us the fuck out of here."

Kira pressed the trigger and half the LEDs on the battery pack blinked on. Ed stared at his daughter, mouth agape, trying to pinpoint just when she'd become a spy and a killer. Only the rapidly heating device, pulled him back to reality, and he launched it towards the gaping opening, the device landing on the grass as the last of the LED's blinked out and the power pack melted.

"Move," cried Kira, running towards the device. Ed and Elizabeth followed, leaving Vicili clutching the spoon sticking out of his ear. The first gun shots rang out as they reached the device, cogs and gears spinning as it rose into the air.

The first cog locked as the guards burst into the room. Two running at them, another checking on a raging Vicili. The crime lord snatching the assault rifle from the guard and bringing to bare as the second cog locked into place.

Ed wrapped himself around his daughter, turning his back to the gunfire that peppered the perfect lawn. Kira stood smiling; middle finger held up as several more guards surrounded them unleashing a hail of bullets. The third cog locked, and the bullets formed a slowly spinning tornado of lead as lightning arced across the chaotic scene.

Ed spun back around, to look into the vengeful eyes of his nemesis.

When the fourth cog fell into place, the world stopped, and Ed hugged Elizabeth close. His only thought, that he knew nothing about his daughter.

For a split second, Ed, thought the device had failed as all around him the guards, Vicili, and his home remained. But as he watched that world fell away, collapsing like a house of cards. The crime lord's flailing arms and legs swallowed by a sea of green. Anything further than six feet from the now frozen device, cascaded down a steep pyramid, into the clutches of a hungry jungle far below.

"Whoa," said Kira, dropping the trigger she'd held so tightly in her hand.

Ed stared into his daughter's eyes, as she looked around the endless vista of foliage. "I've got questions."

"You've got questions!" Ed gasped.

"Hey, hey, can we figure out where we are before, you two get into the whole daddy issues thing."

"Guatemala," said Elizabeth, staring over the edge. "La Danta."

Ed stared at her in disbelief. "How do you know that?"

"I didn't lie about travelling the world."

"Just the whole spy thing?"

"Well, technically, I didn't lie about that either."

Kira laughed. "So, I'm guessing that cat symbol, is probably a Mayan Jaguar."

"Of course," said Ed, removing his jacket and wrapping it around his daughter's bare shoulders. "So, what now? You're going to hand the mechanism over to British Intelligence?"

Elizabeth pulled the jacket tight "Are you kidding? No government should control this. Can you imagine? No, we need to make sure no one gets it, starting, with getting the hell out of here."

"My turn to pick," grinned Kira.

THE ROYAL BLOOD

GORDON LINZNER

Too late, Rayun bolted from his horse's stall in the Numali common stables. In seconds, the youth lay flat on his back, the rough dirt floor digging into his shoulders, staring up into the darkened rafters.

The speed of Jakor's attack stunned the lad more than the fall. More painful than his impact on the hay-strewn earth was the harsh laughter of the stable hands. Most of whom were but a few summers short of Rayun's own eighteen years. Only the dull throbbing in his jaw, which had tortured him for days, distracted him from this ignominy.

Jakor, grizzled hero of the seven kingdoms, was not content with publicly tripping his young charge. His knee pinned Rayun's chest. A violent expulsion of air opened the lad's mouth wide. That orifice was quickly filled with thick, probing fingers. Rayun considered biting his mentor's hand when a white-hot lance of pain sheared through the right side of his skull.

Agony washed over his brain. He lay dazed. Sticky warmth crawled down the side of his face. A damp rag was pressed into his right hand, and that hand was then lifted against his lips until he could hold the cloth in place without help.

"Here, sprig," came a stranger's voice. "Drink this. It'll ease the swelling and kill the pain."

A thick, strong hand pressed against Rayun's shoulders, helping the lad upright until he could brace himself on one elbow. His brown eyes opened took in the goatskin nipple approaching his lips. Suddenly thirsty, the lad gulped the offered potable.

The liquid burned Rayun's mouth. He spat out his first taste. The nipple remained in place. He could scarcely breathe without drinking in more warm, bitter wine.

After the first shock, he decided it was not so bad, after all.

When he could drink no more, Rayun pushed the goatskin away. His benefactor, satisfied the lad could now fend for himself, joined the crowd surrounding Jakor. The short-lived scuffle had attracted an audience of eight or nine Numalians, in addition to the stable hands.

Gripping the rag against his mouth, the young man shakily rose. His cheeks burned with tears and blood and wine and anger; his sea-green blouse was streaked with stable filth and wine. He leaned against a stall to study the bloody scrap of cloth in his hand. Fresh drops were becoming fewer.

Rayun brushed at his clothes, picking bits of straw from smoke-gray trousers as he glared at Jakor. His mentor stood proudly in the center of the crowd, one hand resting on his paunch, the other displaying a tiny white object.

"Observe," the dragon-slayer said, "this most insidious of Chaos' representatives. This object alone put my apprentice, a slayer of demons who did not so much as whimper at a broken limb, into such paroxysms of agony that strong men wept to hear him suffer!"

Mulish laughter greeted the hero's speech. Jakor spun in a slow, tight circle, so all could see the infected tooth he had yanked, root and all, from his apprentice's jaw. Turning, he spotted Rayun stalking away with heavy tread, his thick brown hair tossing angrily. Jakor raised a hand to dismiss his audience, then pushed through the group to reach the youth's side.

"This way, lad." He grasped Rayun by the shoulder. "Let's see if this town has a decent salt merchant. That's the best thing for the soreness."

"Take your blood-stained hand off me!" Rayun spat.

Jakor's deep gray eyes widened. He drew his hand away. "What in the seven kingdoms has gotten into you, boy?"

"Don't take me for a fool as well as a buffoon, old man. You had no excuse for treating me so poorly in front of all these...these peasants! You deliberately humiliated me!"

Rayun tossed his bloodied rag at Jakor's feet and again stalked off. He'd gone no more than five paces when a powerful grip spun him around. Jakor glared at him.

"You think you're the first person in the seven kingdoms who's ever suffered a toothache?"

Unnoticed by either of them, a figure draped in a cowled, rust-colored cloak separated from the dispersing crowd to move nearer the arguers. This stranger paused to retrieve the discarded scrap of cloth. His hand was thin and yellow, with a great wart on the knuckle of the little finger. The stranger drew the scrap into his line of sight, for closer examination. The motion caused the cowl to slip back a centimeter, providing a glimpse of a face that could barely be considered human.

Numali was a frontier town, near the furthest border of the seven kingdoms. It was not civilized enough to completely ostracize the neighboring community of swamp people. The townsfolk were unwilling to have much social contact with them, due to certain unsavory rumors – and an equal distaste on the part of the swamp people to mingle with Numalians – but they were content to trade for certain herbs and foodstuffs only found deep within the Great Swamp, which true men entered only at their peril. There had never been any unpleasant incidents, at least not serious, involving Numalians, and the swamp people were amenable to wearing long cloaks on even the hottest days to disguise their disturbing, unhealthy appearance.

The average Numalian might have proved less tolerant of the look in this swamp man's round, watery eyes as he lifted the rag to his nostril slits. A thin forked tongue flicked in a lipless mouth, passing over double rows of tiny, needle-sharp teeth. The swamp man drew his cowl forward again, then slipped into an empty stall, where he could eavesdrop on the quarrel without being observed.

"You might have told me what you were up to!" Rayun retorted.

"It was no more than I'd been promising to do these last three days, every time you started whining. Do you think I enjoyed listening to your moans, from dusk to dawn? Would you rather I'd pulled it in our rooms at the Sleeping Dog? Don't think that wouldn't have drawn a fine crowd, and half the Numalian guard as well!"

Rayun continued to rant. "To think that I considered you the greatest living person in the seven kingdoms! Riding alongside the fearless Jakor, fighting side by side against evils, human and not, was the best thing that ever happened to me. Now I see you're no better than anyone else, including my overbearing father."

"I never claimed to be," Jakor replied quietly.

"Telling me what to do, what's good for me. I'm fed up with it all!"

"All right, my lad, that tears it! You invited yourself along on my journeys, as I recall. Since our first meeting, you've dragged me into one hare-brained adventure after the other, just to keep yourself from growing bored. If you dislike the way I teach the hero business, you're free to go!"

"Don't think I won't!"

This time it was Jakor who turned to march angrily from the stables, leaving his apprentice to fume.

Pompous old fool! Rayun thought. The lad cursed

himself for ever believing Jakor deserved his respect. What a child he'd been, not to see the situation sooner! His foot lashed out at a nearby bucket; its muffled clattering across the hay-strewn floor echoed through the stable.

"Young man." The deep, soft whisper issued from a nearby stall.

"What do you...Great Chaos!" The lad's anger drained as the swamp man lowered his cowl, revealing subhuman features.

"Young man," the stranger repeated, "might I ask if you hail from the kingdom of Pellnor?"

"Aye," Rayun answered warily. "I'm a native of Kalimar."

"Ah. I thought as much. And of high birth, I'll wager. Your father is an influential man?"

"My father?" Rayun had given little thought to the man who raised him since they'd parted on poor terms at Kalimar's gates. He had, in fact, completely renounced his progenitor, transferring his allegiance to Jakor. However, now that the dragon-slayer had also betrayed the lad's trust, he saw no reason not to acknowledge his true parent.

"Naturally," he replied proudly.

"As I suspected. You have that unmistakable bearing. Please forgive my addressing you so casually. My name is Solon, of the swamp people. If I may be candid, these Numalians are a coarse lot. You saw yourself how readily they...made light of your suffering. They are quite ignorant on matters of rank and breeding." Solon waved a warty hand at the space the spectators occupied moments ago.

"Quite might be understating it," Rayun agreed.

"We swamp people, on the other hand, have a long and treasured sense of tradition dating back almost to the time of Chaos. Although things have gone poorly for us in the decades, nay, centuries since, and we live roughly, our people retain our sense of decorum. In short, young sir, I beg to have the honor of extending to you an invitation, on behalf of all my people, to share a few of your precious days with us, and partake of our humble hospitality."

Rayun hesitated. "I'm not sure. My mare needs to rest, and I've paid for her feed and boarding a week in advance."

"My village is not far. I often walk the distance twice a day. It would please me to share your company along the way."

Rayun hesitated only a fraction of a second longer.

"Sure. Why not? Just allow me time to pick up my things at The Sleeping Dog."

"As you see best, young master. Shall we meet at, say, the southern gate, in half an hour?"

Neva, ruler of the swamp people, peered uneasily from the doorway of her mud-and-twig hut. Unaware of her scrutiny, the young human sat, patient and wide-eyed, on an overturned cooking pot in the square that served as the village's hub.

"You had better have a good explanation for your actions, Solon," she warned the hut's sole other occupant. "We forbid our villages to humans for good reason. They suffer us when we are useful yet fear us because we are different. Should that fear ever turn to hate, only secrecy can protect us."

"Of this, I am well aware, my sister. Take this rag. It will explain all."

Neva accepted the stiffening brown cloth. Her watery eyes studied it in puzzlement; her yellow fingers ran along its coarse edge. She raised it to her nostril slits.

"By the golden finger of Aa!" she exclaimed, blinking. "Can it be...?"

"There can be no mistaking it," Solon replied. "The scent was even fresher when I came across it. Our inborn perceptions cannot be denied."

"The royal blood! Not for a century has the scent been detected this far south." Neva crumpled the rag in a withered hand. "We must be cautious, Solon. The desire was too much for our ancestors. The last subject to come our way perished before provision could be made for an alternate supply."

"I considered as much. I have already arranged for our late sister's child, Kael, to entertain him tonight."

Neva's lipless mouth pressed tight in a mockery of a smile. "You always think ahead, Solon, always have a plan. I often wonder if you should not have been born female; you take to the necessities of leadership so much better than I."

"I merely anticipate my sister's wishes, and put them into action," Solon answered humbly. He had no desire to take responsibility for the dozen and more villages scattered throughout the Great Swamp. As his sister's advisor, Solon already commanded more power than he felt comfortable wielding.

"We'll not keep our guest waiting any longer, then. Show him in, so I may properly greet him. And see that runners are dispatched to all villages to announce a celebration tonight."

Solon scratched his neck scales. "Is that not premature?"

"Not a full-scale celebration, of course," Neva amended. "Our usual monthly get-together, just pushed up a few days."

"I shall attend to it at once, sister." Solon bowed lowas he backed out of the ruler's hut.

Neva raised the blood-stained rag to her nostril slits again. The scent was palpable. She had never smelt royal blood before; none of her people's present generation had the opportunity. Yet she recognized it instinctively.

Neva expelled a hiss of pleasure. Her tongue shot out to lick at the cloth; she pulled back before it could touch. As her people's ruler, she needed to set an example of restraint; there would be time enough to indulge once a steady supply was assured. Then, should another error be made in the heat of the moment, at least the results would not be disastrous.

She stuffed the rag into her waist-pouch as Solon returned with the human. "Neva, ruler of the people of the swamp," Solon announced officially, "I herewith present to you Rayun, of the roy...of noble parentage."

Rayun's nose wrinkled at the ophidian stench within the hut, far more pervasive than in the open square. He privately hoped whichever hut he was to sleep in would prove to be well ventilated. His faux pas seemed to go unnoticed. Neva had lowered her eyes in respectful salutation, and Solon had already departed to dispatch the runners.

"This is a most rare...honor, Rayun," the ruler greeted.

"I hear drums."

Jakor addressed a dark-haired wench named Aleen, with whom he'd retired to his room at The Sleeping Dog shortly after dusk. He'd been unable to find his usual solace in the taproom's offerings. Now he gratefully paused in his mechanical responses to the woman's caresses, to wonder aloud at the thrumming sound that nagged at the back of his mind.

"That's my heartbeat," Aleen responded. "To show how thrilled I am to be bedding a legendary hero." Her fingers continued their busy work.

Jakor grasped her right hand, squeezing hard. "Don't take me for a fool, wench," he warned. "I know the difference between a whore's heart and a drum. The latter is less hollow."

Aleen pulled free, nursing her fingers. "You've no need to hurt me or get nasty."

"Is there a drum, or isn't there?"

She cocked her head to one side, straining to listen. "It's faint, but yes, I definitely hear a drumbeat. Nothing to worry about. The swamp people are having one of their parties. The wind must be from the south, for you to hear it at all."

216

Jakor grunted. "In the frosty climes near Menthal-one, drums always precede an attack by mountain bandits. That town has a quite effective relay warning system."

"There's no need for that here," Aleen replied. "We mind our business, and the slimies mind theirs. We get along fine."

Jakor grunted again, shifting his weight on the straw bed. The woman turned onto her side, shifting her breasts into a more comfortable position. Her free hand combed through the hairs on the warrior's chest, wandering near to, but not touching, his pot belly. She'd learned earlier how he disliked reminders of his excess baggage.

"Is something bothering you, love?" Aleen asked. "You've acted sullen all evening. I can't even get a rise out of you, and I'm the best Numali has to offer. Surely the famous dragon slayer is adept at wielding more than one kind of sword?"

"I apologize for my outburst. I'm concerned for my apprentice's safety."

"You mean the laddie who checked out this afternoon?"

Jakor nodded. "We had a stupid argument. He can take care of himself, I'm sure, but he's still my responsibility. I feel I've let him down."

"Oh?"

"It's a childish pique, of course. He'll soon realize I have his best interests at heart. Still...I've had enough experiences to fill ten lifetimes, and never have I felt the way I do now. I've gotten used to having him around."

"I see." Aleena sat up to perch on the edge of the

bed as she reached to the floor for her gown.

"You needn't leave. Talking about it seems to help."

"We can talk, if that's all you want to do. But..."

"I'll pay you double to stay."

"That's sweet of you, Jakor, but you needn't pretend. We get all kinds in this border town. Your secret is safe with me."

"Secret?"

"If it's boys you prefer, I know a lad in the stables willing to do service."

"What!" The warrior roared, sitting upright. "I'll have you know that you slur not only myself, but also the son of Kalimar's High Councilor! To imply that I would even think to take advantage of such a lad, one decades younger than myself! Or that he would allow himself to fall prey! Were we back in Pellnor, you would be whipped and dragged through the streets for such baseless slanders!"

Aleen's eyes widened, reflecting the moonlight that seeped through the slatted window. "Then why...? Oh, I see. Hmmm. I would never have taken you for impotent."

"Impotent!" Jakor grasped Aleen's arm and dragged her down beside him. "You've gone too far now, wench. Never let it be said that Jakor failed to rise to a challenge."

She smiled inwardly. Her goading worked, and he proved as good as his word.

Rayun did not need to ask about the drums; the

sound was so loud, so persistent, he could hear little else.

He occupied a seat of honor, he was told, to the right of Neva's roughly hewn throne. Solon, on this occasion, occupied a lesser place at Neva's left. None of the villagers, not even the ruler, wore more than a belted loincloth and pouch, and many not even that. Their long cloaks, kept in communal storage, were used exclusively for dealings with Numali.

Rayun looked to his right, toward Solon's niece. Kael was lovely by swamp people's standards. Still, were her small breasts not exposed, gleaming golden in the moonlight, Rayun could not have distinguished her from the males. Kael had been appointed Rayun's guide and interpreter; Solon and Neva had other duties in connection with the celebration, and so could not themselves make the stranger as welcome as he deserved. Kael explained in detail the symbolism of the dance before them, but its subtleties were lost on the youth. He could barely distinguish the dancers' whirling bodies and ever more frenzied beating of the drums.

He reached into the wooden bowl on his lap and pulled out a roasted slug. When Kael first handed him the swamp fare, he accepted it courteously, vowing silently to dump the contents in the excrement pit at his first opportunity. The odor of roast slug, fried worm and snake innards was foul enough to make him gag; he planned to afterwards eat some dried beef from his pack.

Now, however, entranced by the eerie dancing, Rayun unconsciously dipped into the bowl, barely noticing the rancid smell as the slug went past his nose, or the taste reminiscent of burnt bear fat. He nodded approval as the flesh cracked against his teeth. Kael's lipless mouth seemed to form a smile.

The moon rose higher, illuminating the scene, its only source of light. Swamp people eschewed torches. They had a natural distaste for fire, using it sparingly, primarily for cooking purposes. They also feared the smoke might one day reveal their location.

Those villagers who'd been sitting in a large circle around the dancers now joined in. They leapt high in the air, circling a huge rock carved roughly in the shape of a serpent's head. Rayun felt blood pound in his temples, matching the rhythm of the drumbeats. He fought an urge to also leap up; permission to witness this ceremony was concession enough to a human visitor. He sucked snake membranes from between his teeth, unaware of what he chewed – unaware of anything, in fact, save the dancers.

The drums stopped abruptly. Their echoes faded away over the malodorous marshes. Dancers froze where they stood, in various awkward postures, save for a single male who, completely naked, writhed and moaned on the flat table formed by the serpent head stone.

Rayun's heart skipped a beat; he feared he'd made some unforgiveable gaff. The entire village seemed to be staring at him. Then he realized it was Neva, not himself, who commanded this attention. He expelled a pent-up breath.

The lad glanced at the ruler of the swamp; Neva returned the gaze and, for the first time, Rayun understood the phrase 'hungry eyes.' He felt like a particularly attractive bit of worm. His empty bowl dropped from his lap to the ground as he watched Neva run her tongue over pointed teeth.

A tug at her elbow distracted the ruler. Solon, his mien full of reproach, pointed to the figure on the table. Her subjects grew restless. Some struggled, clumsily adjusting their frozen postures to retain their balance. Neva nodded gratefully to her brother, then rose majestically from her rough throne. In a trice, she threw off her loin cloth and joined the writhing male.

At this signal, the dancers joyfully embraced one another, and the orgy was in full sway. Rayun knew then he had been right to hold himself in check. He gladly let Kael take his hand to lead him from the scene. Once the two were well on their way to Rayun's hut, Solon abandoned his own seat to join the mass mating.

The pair passed hut after hut. The lad stumbled several times. Now that he was moving again, he felt weak, almost as weak as when that time a demon-inflicted wound became infected. His eyesight was usually keen but, even with the moon nearly full in a cloudless sky, he could not see more than two meters ahead. Kael supported his weight more often than not, leading him gently into his hut, then settling him onto the thin-worn Numalian blanket laid out for his bedding.

"Whew," Rayun muttered. The hut spun about him. "Now I know how Jakor feels after one of his bouts." Yet the lad wasn't inebriated; after his first sip of the slimy, fermented brew Solon called swamp beer, he'd drunk only water from his goatskin.

Kael bent over him. Her thin fingers swiftly undid the ivory buttons of his blouse. Rayun felt her hardened, scaly knuckles rasp against his chest, but was too enervated to shudder with the revulsion he felt.

"I'm fine," he promised, gesturing for Kael to stop. She brushed his hand aside. His palms turned clammy as he felt his trousers being drawn down past his knees. Her weight pressed against on his exposed thighs. In the darkened hut, with only moonlight streaming through the open doorway for illumination, the look on Kael's face was unreadable; nonetheless, Rayun knew what it must mean.

Her scales rubbed against his skin. A cool, moist hand crawled up his inner thigh toward his crotch. He responded against his will. He reached out to stop her. Too late. Rough, squamous flesh surrounded his own; his hips churned of their own volition.

Rayun quickly grew inured to the harsh scraping, but the final moment of release held more pain than pleasure for him. He blacked out, and so did not feel Kael disengage, although she did so almost immediately.

Kael stretched out on her back on the dirt floor, resting, a full meter from Rayun's body, until her breath no longer came in short, sharp gasps. She shuddered, smoothed her leg scales, and knelt to face the youth again. Exposed as he was, Rayun looked ridiculously vulnerable.

Kael started to pull the lad's trousers back into position. A shock ran through her as her fingers touched his pale flesh. Instead, she raised a corner of the blanket and doubled it over him. Then she fled the hut, toward the muddy stream that flowed past the western edge of the village. She felt an urge to bathe thoroughly before returning to her own hut.

Sleep would not come easily for her tonight.

One week to the day after his display of dentistry, Jakor led Aleen to a weapons shop near Numali's southern gate. For the past seven days, the woman had been well paid to jolly the hero out of his morose moods, and to be silent when no words were called for.

"This represents your finest work, Claven?" Jakor asked. The weaponeer was a stocky man with sinewy arms.

"It's a labor of love," Claven answered proudly.

"You're fickle, then. The blade is bent."

Claven clapped his meaty hands to his bald pate. "Is it, now! If Bleese has ruined another sword with his clumsy handling I'll skin his arse. Why, I see where you mean, sir. A small imperfection, easily repaired."

"But hardly, in that case, worthy of your finest efforts," Jakor countered.

"I have several others on display..."

"So I saw. None looked promising."

"...but, of course, those are designed for the rabble of this town, and you are obviously an experienced, well-travelled swordsman. Bleese! Fetch me the special inventory!"

A gangling youth stepped from the back room, bearing a rolled-up faded rug. He unfurled it on Claven's worktable, revealing half a dozen swords. The weaponeer snatched one away.

"Not this one, Bleese, you idiot!" the merchant cried.

He turned to Jakor. "My apologies, sir. An inferior bit of goods, placed with the quality items by mistake."

"But, sir," began the apprentice, "you told me..."

"Bleese," the merchant warned, "how often must I remind you not to discuss shop while there's a customer to be attended to?"

"That blade looks fair enough to me," Jakor intruded. He plucked it from Claven's fingers. "In fact, I've taken a sudden fancy to it. Make up my bill of sale; I've made my choice."

"Now see what you've done!" the weaponeer hissed, shaking a fist at his apprentice. Bleese cringed. Claven then turned back to his customer, offering an apologetic smile.

"The truth is, sir, this blade is of a special design, at the request of Numali's governor. It should never have been brought out. It... ah...it's not for sale."

"Aye, but, as you say, the rabble in these parts cannot appreciate your artistry as I do. Make your governor another."

"But, sir, all that detailed filigree in the hilt! You're a man of action; would you not prefer something less... ostentatious?"

"For myself, yes; but I'm purchasing this for my own apprentice, who lost his blade pulling me out of a mudhole."

"Perhaps your apprentice should choose for himself?"

Jakor shook his head. "That would spoil the surprise. Besides, he's...on leave for a few days. I expect him back soon, however, and sorely wish to gift him with this sword at that time."

"I wouldn't hold my breath," Bleese muttered.

"What?" Jakor turned to the nervous apprentice, his voice taking on a hard edge.

Claven winced. "Again, I apologize for Bleese's ill manners, sir. It's difficult to get good help in the outlands."

"Still your tongue," Jakor spat. He took Bleese's arm in a crushing grip. "Continue wagging yours."

"Meaning no offense, sir," Bleese stammered. "But if your apprentice is the lad I saw you with at the stables, I doubt you'll hear from him again."

"Explain yourself, whelp!"

"I saw that lad a week ago, leaving the city by the southern gate."

"Don't bore the customers, Bleese," Claven put in. "People come and go. They leave Numali, by either gate; if so inclined, they return the same way. If you're talking in circles merely to avoid your duties, I'll take a strap to you!"

"Honest, sir, I saw him go! He was with a swamp person!"

Jakor turned to Aleena. Her face had turned ash white. "Those drums we heard that night..."

"Don't upset yourself, sir," Claven put in. "The slimies are harmless folk. I've done business with them myself. No weapons, of course, just occasional decorative metal work."

Jakor shook Bleese like a kitten, to make his point. "Then why does your apprentice think that mine won't return?"

Claven spread his thick palms out before him. "I regret to say the slimies can't resist plying a little con artistry now and then. Many strangers have been led into the swamps; most return unharmed, save for being cheated out of everything they owned. Undoubtedly, those who did not come back were too embarrassed. We have never had reason to believe foul play was involved."

"And you permit this in your town?"

"Why not? No Numalian is foolish enough to fall for their obvious tricks. It's a good joke on gullible travelers."

"You have a poor sense of humor," Jakor concluded grimly. He laid a fistful of coins on the table. "For the sword."

"But sir!" Claven protested in dismay. "The finest steel went into that blade!"

"Exactly why I want it. Good day, gentlemen."

In the narrow street outside the weaponeer's shop, Aleen hurried to keep pace.

"Jakor!" she called. "Wait!"

"Not now, Aleena," the warrior growled. "B'or's balls! The boy should have come to his senses by now, left to his own devices. But if he's been tricked or cheated, I'll wager he's still sulking out there, chewing roots and berries. He's too proud to crawl back like a dog with its tail between its legs."

Aleena worried her lower lip. "He may also be dead."

The hero halted mid-step, turned to stare into Aleena's earnest green eyes. "By the Blessed Blue Boar," he muttered, balling his fists. "It may be second nature for a shopkeeper to lie, but if he's played false about this, I'll give him more than a taste of his wares!"

"No! No, what Claven told you is true enough. But you told me Rayun was the son of Kalimar's High Councilor."

"Yes. So?"

"According to legend, the swamp people are descended from a degenerate strain of the Pellnoran royal family. As more powerful rulers emerged after the time of Chaos, the slimies were pushed further and further south, and have become so well adapted to the climate of the Great Swamp they can no longer bear the cooler lands of Pellnor. Nonetheless, it is their belief that, if enough royal blood can be fed into their own veins, they may once more become true men."

"Chaos! The Kalimar Council is selected from its nobility, all of whom are descended from kings of Pellnor!"

Jakor's purse had been growing uncomfortably light of late, but he nonetheless drew out a gold coin and pressed it into the woman's palm.

"You've already paid..." she protested slightly.

"A bonus, for your information. Take tonight off. I must get to the stables and see how quickly they can ready my horse!"

On completion of her examination, the aged swamp woman patted Kael's belly, rose, and stepped out of her hut.

Neva paced in a tight circle before the entrance.

Solon shuffled mud between the claws of long, flexing toes. At the crone's appearance, the swamp people's ruler came to a halt and rubbed her hands together with a slithery sound, torn between anxiety and the respect due the village's medical authority.

The old woman first met Neva's eyes, then Solon's, before allowing the siblings the satisfaction of a brief nod.

"You're sure?" Neva blurted out.

The medicine woman drew a sharp breath in disdain. As if she, Adda, could err on such a matter!

"Forgive me, revered one," Neva muttered hastily, kneeling in supplication. "I meant no offense. It was a meaningless expression."

With an impatient hand wave, Adda bade the ruler stand. Kael stood waiting in the entranceway, braced against a strut. The young woman's nostril slits flared as she sucked in the fetid air of the surrounding swamp. It smelled soothingly refreshing after the stifling scents of herbs and fungi that permeated the medicine woman's hut. Solon gently took her arm.

"Congratulations, niece. You perform a great service for our village; nay, for all the villagers in the Great Swamp."

Kael nodded emotionlessly. Adding the royal blood line to the village gene pool was no doubt a good thing, though she feared what sort of monster might come of the union of swamp woman and true human. Still, Adda seemed content, almost smiling as she collected her fee from Neva before hobbling back inside her hut.

"A celebration tonight, Solon!" Neva chortled. "A

real celebration, this time, such as our village has not known in over a century."

"I would still advise caution, my sister," Solon responded solemnly. "Our niece is healthy and strong, but there is always the chance of an accident. I suggest we recruit a few more volunteers among the younger females."

"An excellent suggestion, brother. I leave the details to you. Ah, if only I were still of child-bearing age! Still, that celebration is called for. Although I have never known the tang of royal blood, my throat aches for it. My thirst has been growing ever since you brought the lad here. I must have a taste; just one taste!"

Solon scratched his earhole thoughtfully. "I ache for as well, sister, but the risk is great. The human is extremely weak from the herbs we fed him; even Adda, aged though she is, might find it difficult to stop. Once that blood is tasted..."

"I know, I know, Solon. I will content myself with a mere drop. I must be a model of restraint for my people."

Solon's tongue flicked nervously as Neva strode off. He himself would have trouble struggling with the temptation. His sister was far more impulsive. If he could only manage to keep the human alive for one more week!

"Uncle?" Kael pointed toward the sinking sun. "It is time for Rayun's dinner."

Solon nodded. "You overheard my discussion with your aunt?"

"And your unspoken words. I shall not add the hypnagogic herbs to his meal this time."

"You are as clever as your late mother, Kael," Solon acknowledged. "The lad will still be as feeble as a newborn rat, but at least he'll be capable of facing tonight's celebration. I just hope he's strong enough to survive it."

Rayun lost track of how often his head had been propped up and food forced down his throat. Unlike the vaguely cloying meals he'd come to expect, this fare tasted bitter, almost rancid. When he tried forcing it out with his tongue, a scaly hand clamped over his mouth, remaining in place until he chewed and swallowed. Then more food was shoved between his lips.

The lad could see now, though in a partial blur. His eyes rolled around of their own accord. From time to time he caught a glimpse of the swamp woman feeding him. Kael? It was hard to tell the individuals apart. Whoever she was, she inspired memories of his first night in this village, now seeming so very long ago. Had he really been seduced by such a creature?

Another mouthful of food stifled his groan.

With dinner done, Rayun's head was laid back gently. He saw the world whirl before his eyes, caught a final glimpse of his nurse as she left the hut. Soon enough would come the stuporous sleep that followed every meal.

Oddly, it did not happen this time.

After an hour, Rayun grew aware of a nauseating, unclean feeling. He sat up and saw why. His trousers were down past his knees, and the blanket on which he lay – which half-covered his nakedness – was fouled by his own excrement.

A tin of muddy water lay nearby; he'd plunged his face into it whenever the ravages of thirst overcame his lethargy. Rayun rolled away from the soiled portion of blanket and dampened a clean corner. Half an hour – it felt like half a day – passed while he worked the kinks out of disused muscles, cleaned himself as well as he could, and pulled up his pants.

Rayun wanted to stand. The challenge proved too much. The best he could do was crawl on his hands and knees. In the hut's dim light he spotted his pack in a corner, and moved toward it.

His dirk was missing; he'd expected as much. He patted the goatskin; it was nearly empty. Rayun gulped the stale liquid anyway, then tossed the skin aside. His food packets were gone; dried beef would be a rare delicacy in the swamp people's diets. Still, his clothing seemed intact, including his traveling cloak. There must be some way he could use that to form an escape plan. What would Jakor have done?

His head ached too much to allow clear thinking. His eyes burned. Indigestion bloated his stomach. Slowly, Rayun slid onto his side on the hard mud floor. He needed to rest again. Just for a minute.

They came for him at sunset.

Jakor wrestled with a disloyal thought.

The warrior wished for a younger, faster horse between his legs. This warhorse had served him well for over a decade, but age took its toll. The animal's back swayed, its coat ran to mange, its movements required increasingly careful deliberation. The beast was hardly the ideal steed for riding to a rescue on.

To be fair, though, the thick mud they sloshed through would have slowed even the swiftest horse in the seven kingdoms.

Jakor peered up at the moon, his only guide, and a poor one at that. Swamp vegetation blocked his view; clouds periodically obscured the satellite. A clammy dankness charged the air, making the warrior's bones ache. Yet Jakor forbore drawing his cloak tighter; he might need speedy access to the sword at his side and the dagger in his belt.

The fetid odor of composting vegetation filled his nostrils. He tried to scan each tree as his horse picked its cautious way along a narrow, long-disused footpath, but could only make out walls of black. In younger days, he recalled, his night vision could rival an owl's.

Rushing into the swamp at so late an hour had been a mistake, Jakor realized. He ran a grave risk of getting lost; even now, he was unsure he could find his way back to Numali.

He snorted; here he was, acting as foolishly impulsive as Rayun. If his apprentice lived — and Jakor felt certain the lad still breathed, he dared not believe otherwise – surely the few hours before dawn's light would make little difference.

His horse had been progressing so slowly that Jakor did not at first realize the beast had stopped. The warrior leaned forward as far as his belly allowed, peering into the gloom ahead. The path they'd been following had disappeared.

"That's it, then, old boy," he sighed, patting the animal's neck. "We must have missed a side trail, assuming there even is a path to the swamp people's village. Might as well turn back. We'll try afresh in the morning."

The horse snorted as Jakor reined it around on the narrow tract of mud. Regret gnawed at him. In giving up so easily, he was not exactly living up to his reputation as the foremost living hero in all the seven kingdoms. He knew Rayun would never permit him to do so, if the lad rode at his side. Yet the aging swordsman saw no other option.

Until he heard the drums.

Under the full influence of soporific drugs, Rayun could be handled by Kael alone. Without them, Solon was reluctant to chances. The apprentice was a strong youth. Adda claimed a minimum of a day was required to shake off the effects, but a swamp man's constitution was no match for that of a true human.

Half a dozen of his fellows now entered the hut to haul Rayun to his feet. Awake and standing, the lad was pleased to discover he could now remain upright on his own; his knees did not cave in. One of his captors produced a strip of cloth. When another twisted the lad's arms behind his back, Rayun realized he was to be bound.

He held his wrists across each other, as he'd been shown by a conjurer in Kalimar's marketplace; the High

Councilor's son was privy to many sights and secrets denied to commoners. He winced as knots were tightened but willed his hands to stay in position. The fact that cloth was used instead of study rope left him with additional slack. With a simple hand movement, the cloth would fall away.

Rayun had no idea if this trick would be useful. He felt too weak to tackle six swamp people unarmed, and it was unlikely they'd leave him alone for very long now. The drums began their rhythmic pounding. He assumed he was once more slated to be guest of honor at the latest of their obscene celebrations.

Or perhaps, this time, the main course.

The swamp men led Rayun through the gathering crowd of celebrants. One swamp woman turned away as his gaze met hers; perhaps she was Kael. No matter. The crowd parted before his entourage, forming a narrow path to the serpent-head rock.

The dancing seemed to last for hours, although in fact the swamp people were working themselves into a frenzy far more quickly than on the night of his arrival. The youth felt himself lifted onto an altar-like slab of sculptured rock. He noted with relief that no attempt had been made to strip him.

Yet.

Rough stone gouged Rayun's back. His nose itched. He resisted the temptation to free his hands to scratch it. He needed a plan to get past this throng of whirling swamp people; a suicidal fight for freedom would only be his last resort.

Neva watched his every movement. Her eyes held

the same piercing look that had disconcerted the lad that first night, but there was something deeper in them now; whatever Neva was looking for, she intended to find, and soon.

Beside the ruler stood the medicine woman, her eyes cold and distant. Rayun guessed Adda was unaffected by the drums, awaiting only the proper moment for...what?

On the far side of the altar, Solon stood over him, holding in both hands a deep bronze bowl. The lad caught the swamp man's eye. Solon looked away, reluctant to meet his glare. At least one of these monsters had the rudiments of a conscience!

There was much about these people Rayun did not know, and much he felt he would never know, although he was certain there was a purpose to everything that had happened.

One thing seemed crystal clear to the lad. Tonight, he was to be sacrificed to some god or other. Jakor had often described similar rites during their travels together.

He and his mentor would never travel together again. Rayun regretted the childish outburst that led to their rift. His tongue probed absently at the gap left by his missing tooth.

If he only had a weapon!

Drums ceased; dancers froze. Neva stepped forward. Her razor-sharp claws ripped apart the left sleeve of Rayun's blouse. Solon stepped closer as well, keeping his eyes on the ground. Adda, too, approached him, making a gesture too swift for Rayun to see more than a flash of light. A cold sting struck the crook of his elbow.

He lifted his head enough to see the gash on his left arm. Blood bubbled thickly from it, slowly filling Solon's bowl.

"Be ready to stop the flow," Solon muttered, more for Neva's benefit than that of Adda, who would bandage the wound. "To take too much will kill him. Then where would we be?"

Horror chilled the young man's mind. If they didn't kill him outright, he would become part of their permanent larder, a perpetually refilled keg for their orgies. Perhaps they'd graft a spigot to his elbow. He giggled crazily at the thought.

Adda frowned at this unseemly reaction from a vessel of the royal blood. Rayun stuck his tongue out at her. She waved at him in annoyance, as one might dismiss an insect. Her hand still gripped the blade she'd used to cut him.

It was his own dirk.

That decided him. The opportunity he hoped for would never arise; Rayun had to make his own or die trying. He jerked free of his bonds. His left hand upset Solon's bowl, splashing blood; the right grasped Adda's thin wrist, twisting viciously.

The old woman screeched. Her brittle bones snapped easily. The dirk clattered on the stone altar next to Rayun. The youth shoved her away, towards Neva, who extended a yellow claw at his face. Ruler and medicine woman tumbled to the ground in a heap.

Solon stepped forward. By then, Rayun had recovered his dirk. He lashed out. The blade bit into thick, scaly skin, deep enough to elicit a yelp of pain. Solon retreated.

Rayun slid off the serpent head, switching the weapon to his left hand. With his right, he struggled clumsily to tighten his ruined sleeve around the slash in his arm. Adda slunk off to tend to her own injury; two female celebrants followed at her silent command.

The remaining swamp people stood frozen, circling the stone, shocked at the disruption. Sibilant whisperings rose in their midst. Then, slowly, the circle began to close in on the apprentice.

That suited Rayun. He knew his dirk was the only decent weapon in the village; fine steel needed constant care in this humid realm, something the swamp people were unwilling to deal with. These creatures would surely overwhelm him, but not before he'd done a considerable amount of damage. That was how Jakor would have wished to die.

At the outermost edge of the circle one swamp man, extending his claws in anticipation, felt a sudden prick at the small of his back. He waved a hand behind him to chase the insect away. The prick became a sharp bite. The swamp man reached behind him again, groping awkwardly for the pest.

His clawed hand encountered cold steel.

One brief scream escaped the swamp man's lipless mouth; further outcry was stifled as Jakor's burly arm encompassed his neck. His shout led to the swamp people's second great shock of the evening.

An outsider had discovered their village.

"Rayun!" the warrior shouted. "Are you all right?"

A broad grin split Rayun's pale features. "I am now!"

"Can you come to me? I'll slit this slimie's throat if they interfere, then start again with a fresh hostage."

Rayun glanced over the sea of ophidian faces, trying to read the mood. Expressions ranged from outrage to cool anger to disbelief such a thing could even be happening. The strongest reaction was Neva's; her yellow eyes radiated frustration and anger. Rayun decided he would need more insurance than Jakor offered.

He stared into Neva's eyes, nonplussed. The angry glow there quickly died. She leapt backwards, realizing what the lad had in mind.

She wasn't fast enough.

The youth grasped her forearm, swinging her before him like a shield. With his bandaged arm wrapped about the ruler's neck, and his dagger scraping the scales of her lower back, Rayun marched his captive through the ranks of her subjects.

"You're hurt," Jakor observed, when all four convened at the circle's perimeter. He released his own prisoner with a shove. The grateful swamp man scurried into the thickest part of the crowd.

Rayun lifted his injured arm, coated with sticky blood. The wound still oozed, but slowly; the improvised bandage did its job. "It's nothing. A good cleaning and a fresh dressing will take care of this scratch."

Neva squirmed against Rayun's grip, stopping only when Jakor pressed the tip of his sword against her midriff. "You'll never escape," she hissed. "No one knows these swamps better than my people."

Jakor ignored her. "My horse is waiting behind those trees," he told Rayun. "You go first. I'll watch your charming playmate. Another sword is strapped to the pack; it's yours."

Rayun nodded. "We'd best hurry. I don't think the natives are too enamored of their leader at the moment. They might decide they could do without her."

"They wouldn't dare," Neva snapped. Still, she kept her voice low so her subjects could not overhear.

Once Rayun was securely mounted, Jakor pushed Neva into the mire, then climbed up behind his apprentice. The warrior's sword flashed, slicing through the reins that tied the animal to the tree branch. Neva tried to call for help but wound up instead spitting out a mouthful of mud. Her second shout was more successful. As warrior and apprentice vanished down the rough, slippery trail, a horde of swamp people came to her aid.

"Hold tight to the mane," Jakor advised.

"An admirable suggestion," Rayun replied. "As long as the mane holds tight to this beast's neck."

Sounds of frantic activity echoed around them. For now, they were well ahead of the main body of swamp people. Even riding through the thick muck, they had a good chance of maintaining their lead – but only if they chose the right road to Numali. Rayun had been brought here in daylight and did not recognize the swamp's outer boundaries at night; Jakor's vision was less than keen; and the moon continued to stay hidden for interminable periods by a thick bank of clouds.

"We're cut off!" Rayun cried, pointing straight

ahead.

A swamp woman blocked their path not three me-ters ahead of them.

"Hush, you idiot!" the woman spat. "Follow me." She turned to make her way through the sludge.

Jakor raised a shaggy eyebrow at his apprentice. "You made a friend during your stay?"

"I didn't think so. There was one young female, Kael. She seemed to...like me."

"Enough to help you escape?"

"Or lead us into a trap," the lad responded grimly.

"Well, it costs nothing to find out. We're both armed."

He urged their mount to follow Kael down the mud-dy path.

At times the warrior's aging horse seemed unable to take another step. It sank hock deep in swirling muck under the double load. But Jakor always managed to cajole that necessary bit of extra effort from the animal, just as Rayun often nettled the warrior himself to main-tain his status as a legendary hero.

The first faint glow of pink dawn lit the eastern sky as they broke free of the marsh. The shouts of Kael's people had long since faded behind them.

"The road to Numali lies twenty meters further," Kael advised. She shifted a burden off her back that nei-ther had noticed, then handed it up to Rayun. "Here's what's left of your things. You should reach the town gates with the hour. My people won't try to follow you there."

Jakor nodded his thanks and dug a knee into his

horse's flank, urging it in the indicated direction. Rayun balked.

"We can't leave her behind," the lad protested.

Jakor raised both eyebrows.

"No, nothing like that!" Rayun added quickly. "It's just that...Kael, wait! Come with us!"

"With you?" Kael halted at the swampland's edge. Her pointed teeth flashed in a disconcerting smile. "You're a nice boy, Rayun. My uncle likes you, too, or the thought of what he'd done would not weigh so heavily on his mind. That's why I helped you. But, by Ophidius, you're an ugly creature! I hope you don't think I enjoyed what we did."

"I didn't mean...I wouldn't want...won't your people be angry with you?"

"Oh, Neva will be furious. But Solon will take my part. Swamp people don't carry grudges."

"What if they try to hurt you?"

Kael patted her abdomen. "They won't dare. I'm a sacred personage for the next nine months; after that, it won't matter that you've escaped." She vanished into the foliage.

Rayun gulped, his mind boggled by Kael's revelation.

"You really are full of surprises, lad." Jakor clapped a hand to his shoulder. "Wait until I tell the layabouts at The Sleeping Pig that my apprentice bedded a swamp woman! None of them will dare laugh at you then."

Rayun blanched at the thought. "I'll make a deal with you," he pleaded. "If you swear not to say a word of this, I'll...I'll...I'll let you pull out every tooth in my head!"

Jakor's laughter echoed over the swamp. Rayun refused to budge until he'd elicited his mentor's solemn oath – and without sacrificing another molar.

DOTTIE WILDMAN AND THE LOST WEST

CHARLOTTE LANGTREE

TEXAS, USA (MAY 1943)

The plane juddered, shaking Dottie Wildman awake.

Blinking the pain away, she looked around. She was strapped into the seat of a light aircraft, behind the pilot. *Piper J-3 Cub*, she thought. She'd flown enough of them to recognise one.

There was little room to manoeuvre. Struggling to sit up straighter, she took long breaths to calm her racing heart. Her arms tingled. She tried to move them, and realised her wrists were tied together in front of her chest.

What had happened?

The last thing she remembered was following a lead that Nazis were trying to rent a plane in some backwater town in Texas. She'd hightailed it from New York, where she was ostensibly stationed with the British Security Coordination and arrived in the Texas Hill Country with little more than a gun and her notorious wit.

It seemed neither had done her any good. Her gun was gone, and her wits were rattling around somewhere inside the banging drum her head had become.

Dottie winced as she tried to loosen the ropes at her wrists. A bout of turbulence turned her stomach, and she saw stars behind her closed eyelids. She swallowed.

"I know you're awake," the pilot said with an American accent.

Dottie arched her brow. "And I know you're not American."

He chuckled. "We have heard of you, Miss Wildman. My superiors will be pleased when I tell them I killed you. I may even get a medal."

Leaning forward to reach down the side of her boot, Dottie studied the view, though she couldn't see much straight ahead with the pilot in the front seat. They were still in Texas, at least. "If you've really heard of me, Mister …?"

"Breker," he said, a smile in his voice. "Ernst Breker. While we are in America, you may call me Ernie Breakman."

"Of course. Ernie, as I was saying, if you've really heard of me, then you'll know you should have killed me while I was unconscious. I've made it out of worse fixes than this."

The conversation paused as Breker focused on the landscape beneath them, and Dottie took the opportunity to think. The whole situation was ridiculous. She'd never understood why the Ahnenerbe were obsessed with ancient myths. The pseudoarchaeology they had been involved in since Himmler took control was something of a joke in most circles, but for some reason Command had taken an interest in it this time.

"What makes you think you'll be able to find Shady Creek, when so many others have found no evidence it ever existed?" she asked, more to mask the slight noise of her blade coming out of her boot than because she wanted an answer.

Breker scoffed. "We are the master race, Miss Wildman. We will succeed where others have not."

"Really, Herr Breker. Do you actually believe in a mystical town from the Wild West, lost in time and hiding some sort of magical stone? It's a fairy story for children; nothing more. I'm surprised the *master race* would fall for such nonsense."

"Fool!" Breker snarled, and the plane jerked. "There is evidence to prove its existence. When I find *la joya del tiempo*, there will be no more war. Germany will already have won!"

Dottie smiled as the rope began to break beneath her blade. "A time-stopping jewel won't help you."

"You have such little vision."

"Enlighten me," she drawled as she caught sight of another bright yellow plane flying nearby; it appeared Ernie was not alone.

"We have spent years researching the legend of Shady Creek. We have finally pinpointed it to this location, and we will find *la joya del tiempo*. When we do, Germany will swoop in and take control of your countries while you are all frozen in time."

Dottie laughed; she couldn't help it. "How did I go from running escape lines in France, to this?"

"You got caught," he snarled.

For a moment she flashed back to sharp knives, heavy fists, and tanks of cold water. "And I escaped. Looks like this situation does have some similarities, after all."

The knife sliced through the last of her bindings, and she leaned over to wrap her arm around his neck. Holding him in the headlock she'd been taught to use, firm against his struggles, she squeezed until he passed out. A quick check of his pulse told her he was still alive. It was too bad the higher ups wanted to question him, or she'd have finished the job.

Yanking him out of the seat, she took over flying the plane.

It handled like a dream. Her lips tugged upwards as she soared through the sky.

The other plane flew nearer, and she caught the pilot's eye. Flashing a smile, she swung the Cub into a sharp turn and flew over a hill. Below, a wide valley spread like an unfolded blanket.

If she could get Breker back to her superiors, she was sure he'd have some interesting stories to tell.

The engine spluttered.

Dottie blinked; the smirk wiped from her face.

It cut out completely. The ensuing silence drowned out the loud thud of her heart.

"F -"

She cut herself off and focused on landing. She'd

trained for this. It would be fine.

Forcing her breathing to calm, Dottie scanned the valley for a safe place to land. It was wide and flat, with plenty of open space. Aiming for a long stretch of grass, she glided the plane down and braced for impact.

Thirty feet from the ground, turbulence hit. The plane shuddered and creaked, and Dottie barely managed to regain control. The strong wind dissipated as quickly as it had arrived. She steadied herself and touched down.

They bounced once. Metal crunched; she guessed it was the wheel struts buckling from the collision. The ground was a little bumpy. Each mound of grass sent them jerking in all directions, until her brain had whiplash. Breker, unrestrained, thudded against everything in the cockpit. She doubted he'd be regaining consciousness anytime soon.

When they came to a stop, she paused to let her stomach settle and her heart slow.

A loud thud brought her to her senses. The second plane had landed, though a lot less gracefully than her. With a bent propeller and one broken wing, it wouldn't be taking off any time soon.

Dottie jumped out of the plane and set off at a run, then thought better of it. If the Nazis in the second plane took off with her Cub, she'd never be able to report back to Command before they got up to mischief. Doubling back, she ran to the nose of the plane and yanked the spark plugs loose. If they had any sense about them, they'd be able to fix it quickly enough, but she had little time to do anything else.

From the corner of her eye, she saw a beast of a man

unfold himself from the cockpit and point his gun in her direction. She ducked, and the bullet pinged off the nose of the plane. Dottie cursed. She had to move.

Keeping the Cub between her and the shooting men, she ran for the hills. A low mound gave her more cover as she scurried up a sharper incline behind. Gunfire echoed through the valley. Once, she felt the rush of air as a bullet grazed her ear.

Somehow, she made it to the crest of the hill and dove over the other side.

Sliding down the hill, growling as her panty hose laddered, she took stock of her surroundings. The land was dry and dusty, and dotted with shrubs. Spindly trees peppered the hills. A wide dirt path meandered across the ground and disappeared around the corner of another hill.

Feet scrambling in gravelly dirt, she fell the last few feet to land face down in the dust. She coughed and spluttered. A few feet away, a tumbleweed rolled across the path.

"Where the hell am I?" she muttered as she rose to her feet and brushed the dust from her skirt.

Voices shouted in German back in the valley. Dottie pulled her skirt above her knees and ran along the path, making it around the corner before shots rang out.

She stopped dead in her tracks.

Ahead, bustling with life as if it was perfectly normal, was a Wild West town straight out of Hollywood.

Dottie narrowed her eyes. She'd studied maps of the region during the flight from New York; she'd seen no mention of a re-enactment town. What the bloody hell was going on?

Men rode on horses, coated with dust from the road. They wore stained chaps, and battered Stetsons, and holsters at their hips. Bandanas hung from their necks. One, a scrawny fellow with a moustache, paused to spit tobacco onto the street.

Ladies shuffled in full skirts, fanning themselves to counter the heat. Their cheeks were rosy, and their eyes were hard.

A strong odour drifted on the breeze.

To Dottie's left, a small sign declared that she was now entering Shady Creek.

Dottie arched her brow.

Before she could decide her next move, a tall man approached. He, too, was dressed like a cowboy, with guns holstered at his waist. His spurs clinked as he walked with that stereotypical cowboy slope. As he got closer, Dottie could see a strong jaw shadowed with stubble, and a trim moustache resting on his upper lip. His eyes sparked as he looked her up and down.

"Howdy, Ma'am," the cowboy tipped his hat. "I'm Sheriff Jesse Boone. Pleased to make your acquaintance."

"Right," Dottie said, glancing behind her. "Why don't we take this inside your … office?"

With a nod, he stepped to one side and gestured toward a small wooden building with a 'Sheriff' sign swinging above the door. Dottie walked inside, the back of her neck prickling beneath the unashamed stares of every person on the street. Once the door closed behind them, she turned to Boone.

"You don't need to keep up the charade for me," she said. "I don't have time for it."

A crease appeared above his nose. "Ma'am?"

"The re-enactment. It's a waste of my time. I have three Nazis on my tail."

"My apologies, Ma'am, but I'm not sure I understand."

Dottie huffed. "Oh, stop calling me Ma'am. My name is Dottie. Dottie Wildman."

Boone tipped his hat again. "It's not every day we see folks like you here, Miss Dottie. What brings you to Shady Creek?"

She narrowed her eyes. "I refuse to believe you're really residents of some lost town people have spent decades searching for. Give it up. I need to use your telephone."

"Telephone?" Boone asked, shifting his weight.

Dottie growled.

Sweating in the heat, she pushed the hair back off her face and studied the room. Dust from the road coated the floor. A desk and two chairs occupied one side, all made of sturdy dark wood. The walls were bare but for several posters describing wanted men, and one woman.

Boone followed her gaze. "Train robbery. Don't know why I bother keeping those up, though; they'll be long gone by now."

"What do you mean?"

He cleared his throat. "What you said before, about Shady Creek being a lost town … What year is it where you're from?"

She narrowed her eyes. "1943."

"Well, I'll be …" He let out a low whistle. "Seventy years."

"What the bloody hell are you talking about?" Boone snorted

"What?" she snarled.

"Pardon me, Miss Dottie. I'm just not used to hearing profanities from a lady. Times must have changed an awful lot while we've been stuck in here."

Dottie took a deep breath. "Are you trying to tell me that Shady Creek really has been lost for seventy years?"

He nodded. "We've known something strange was happenin' for a mighty long time, now. Didn't at first, of course. But when time passed, and all of us stayed exactly the same age … Well, that just didn't add up. The folks here, they're the same ones as was here in 1873. That's when time stopped, we think. We never have been able to figure out what caused it."

A bullet flew through the open window and into the wall above Dottie's head. Boone ran for the door. Dottie followed, ignoring his warning glare. As soon as they were outside, the gunfire continued, focusing on them. They ducked behind barrels in front of Boone's office, and tried to pinpoint where the shooter was.

"Give me a gun," Dottie ordered.

Spotting a man taking aim from atop the hill, Boone fired back. "Do you know how to use one?"

"Of course."

Taking a Colt from his holster, she cocked it, took aim, and shot the hat from the shooter's head. "Damn it!"

"Friend of yours?" Boone asked, as bullets thudded

into the barrels.

"I told you," Dottie said. "Nazis. There are three of them."

"When this is over, you'll have to tell me what kind of varmint a Nazi is."

Down the street, a woman screamed. Several cowboys, also taking cover, shot at the German on the hill. Blocking out the noise, Dottie took aim again. This time, her bullet hit him in the arm. He yelped, dropped the gun, and scrambled back down the other side of the hill.

Boone rose to his feet. "Leroy! Gather a posse. Track him down."

"Sure thing, Sheriff." The lanky cowboy spat tobacco on the ground and settled his hat more firmly on his head.

Within a few minutes, Leroy had collected a rough crowd of gunslingers on horseback. They rode out of town, the horses' hooves kicking up dust from the road as the cowboys whooped and hollered.

"I think we'd better talk about these friends of yours, Miss Dottie," Boone said.

"Oh, we'll talk. You might want to send some men to guard the planes in the valley, though. That's their only way out of here, and I can't let them escape."

"Planes?"

Dottie closed her eyes. "Flying machines."

He whistled. "I'll be…. Alright, I'll send Luke and Doc on over to the valley."

"Tell them to be careful not to touch anything. We don't want any accidents."

He nodded and called to two men to give them instructions. When he turned his attention back to Dottie, his mouth was pressed into a tight line. "We have to talk about this. Now."

Dottie handed the Colt back to him. Her hand shook. "Is there a bar in Shady Creek? I need a drink."

"We can go to the saloon. It's not really a place for ladies, though."

"I can handle it."

Her mind raced as they passed through swinging doors into the dimly lit saloon. She didn't believe in ghost towns or timeless cowboys. Nothing in her experience suggested the paranormal was anything more than a load of nonsense. Yet here she was.

They went to the bar, and Dottie glared at a burly man leering at her legs.

"Look elsewhere," she said coldly.

The man sidled closer and put his arm around her shoulders. "Come on, darlin'. You can't fault a man for looking when you've put 'em on display like that."

Boone growled a warning. "Bill."

The vein by Dottie's eye began to twitch. Reaching down, she grabbed a sensitive part of his anatomy and squeezed.

Bill's eyes bulged and a high-pitched wheeze escaped his throat.

"I'm going to give you a free lesson, Bill," she said. "Even if I was stark bollock naked, that wouldn't give you the right to put your hands on me or leer at me like a piece of meat. Treat women with respect."

She let him go and turned away, then felt the rush of air as his meaty arm reached for her shoulder. Rolling her eyes, she sidestepped, jabbed an elbow back into his throat, and turned to thrust her palm into his nose.

Blood dripping down his face, Bill leaned on the back of a chair and snarled at her. Dottie raised her fists. She hadn't survived Nazi interrogation and escaped Ravensbruck only to be groped by a nineteenth century knucklehead.

Boone stepped between them and met Bill's glare.

"Bill, you're gonna walk yourself to my office and settle yourself into a jail cell. I'll deal with you when I get there."

Belligerence rolled off him in waves. "Why should I?"

"Because if you don't, it'll go worse for you when I track you down."

The two men stared at each other. After a minute of silence, Bill looked away. Wiping the blood from his nose, he turned tail and did as he'd been told.

Dottie and Boone ordered their drinks and settled at a table in the back of the room. Pleased that her hands were steady, Dottie threw back her shot of whisky and called for another one.

She pinched the bridge of her nose with two fingers. "What am I doing? I don't have money on me to pay for this."

"It's on me," he said, the hint of a smile in his voice. "Why don't you tell me about these Nazis?"

She closed her eyes. "I'll give you the overview; we don't have time for more, I'm afraid."

When Boone nodded, she continued.

"In my time, Germany is led by a man named Hitler.

He's decided that Germans are the *master race*, and they have invaded and occupied several countries. They've killed thousands. Most of the world has been drawn into the war."

Boone's mouth gaped open.

"The Nazis have a whole group within their ranks whose job it is to search for mythical artefacts to help prove their supremacy, and to aid them in the war. The Ahnenerbe, as it's called, seems to have sent three men to search for Shady Creek. I thought it was nonsense, until I met you."

"What could they possibly want from us?" he asked, downing his whisky as she had before.

"*La joya del tiempo*." She ran a finger along the rim of her glass as she thought. "Something else I thought was nonsense, but now I'm beginning to wonder."

Boone raised an eyebrow. "The jewel of time?"

"Legend says it's a small gemstone with the power to stop time, brought here by Spanish settlers way back when."

He laughed, then. The noise rumbled from deep in his throat and reverberated through the saloon.

"What's so funny?"

"Even if there is a jewel," he said, wiping tears of laughter from his eyes, "I doubt they'll stand a chance of finding it. I'm the sheriff of Shady Creek and I know nothing about it. Also, I'm pretty dang sure it won't help them like they think it will. Pardon my language, Miss Dottie. It's just, we've been stuck here for seventy years. It's not something you can jump in and out of, or control. Some *master race* they are, if they think a stone can win a war for them."

Dottie tried to keep a straight face; she really did. The whisky had warmed her, and Boone's company was surprisingly enjoyable. She grinned as he laughed and admired the way his smile brightened his whole face.

"We can't let them find it," she said. "The fact that it exists at all means they could find a way to manipulate it. This war has been going on for four years; we can't let them have any more advantages."

"Four years?"

She called for another whisky and downed it. "Four long years."

Boone shifted in his seat. "And they let women fight in this war?"

"Not on the front line. Women are mainly nurses or working behind the scenes. Some, like me, did a bit more. Maybe I'll tell you about it another time."

He nodded. "It's getting late. Why don't we bunk down for the night, and start searching for this stone come mornin'?"

"I could use a good night's sleep," she admitted.

"I'll arrange for you to have a room upstairs. I'll be just across the street in my office if you have any trouble. I'll have some clothes sent over for you, too. Everyone here knows we've been trapped in time, but at least if you blend in, they're less likely to bother you while we're asking questions."

"Thank you."

She yawned and focused on putting one foot in front of the other until she reached her room. Kicking off her shoes, she flopped onto the bed and closed her eyes, wondering whether the whisky had been a good idea on top of a concussion. It had been a heck of a day.

Sleep pulled at her, and she gave in.

The sun woke her as birds chorused the dawn. It took a moment for her eyes to focus. Sitting up on the bed, she became aware of a gentle knocking at the door.

"Who is it?"

"Boone. I brought clothes for you."

Tired and groggy, she opened the door and took the bundle of clothes from his arms. "Thanks."

She closed the door in his face and stripped off her uniform with some reluctance. The dress Boone had provided was dark blue, with a high neck and long sleeves. The hem skimmed halfway down her calves. A plain apron tied at her back added a waistline to the loose garment. Simple brown boots completed the outfit.

When she opened the door again, Boone's eyes widened.

"Thank you for the clothes, Boone."

"They belonged to my mother," he said. "She'd be happy to see someone getting use out of them."

Brushing past him into the corridor, Dottie shook her head. The dress swished around her legs as she walked, and the boots thudded on the wooden floor; the difference from her own clothes was distracting.

"You know this place," she said. "How will we find *la joya del tiempo*?"

Boone shrugged. "In my opinion, it's a wild goose chase, but if anyone knows anything it's likely to be old

Joe Higgins. We'll start with him."

"Oh?"

"Joe is an old widower who lives just outside of town," he said as they walked out of the saloon. "He keeps his mouth shut, so people are always talking to him. He likely knows everything about everybody in Shady Creek."

Outside, tethered to a wooden pole, two large horses drank from a trough as they waited. Boone released the reins of an Appaloosa and tilted his head at Dottie.

"I should have asked if you know how to ride."

Taking the reins, Dottie winked at him. She reached up to grab the saddle, then paused. "Side saddle?"

"Problem?"

Heat crept up her cheeks. "I've never ridden side saddle. I can give it a go, I suppose."

"I can change the saddle if you prefer, Miss Dottie," he said, clearing his throat.

"That might be best," she admitted, picturing herself sailing off the saddle mid-canter. She glanced down at her dress. "Although, I'm not sure how it will work with this skirt."

Boone's face flushed. "I guess I could find you some cowboy duds to wear. Bullseye Betty might have something that'd fit you. She used to do some trick riding, back in the day, and she's a heck of a sharpshooter."

"She sounds like my kind of gal."

Dottie waited in her room while Boone visited Bullseye Betty to borrow some clothes. When he returned, she changed quickly and nodded in approval. She strode back out to where he waited with the horses, enjoying the freedom of movement she found in the cowboy shirt, durable cotton trousers, and comfortable boots. Suspenders held the trousers up, while a faded red bandana hung round her neck. The Stetson atop her head had her resisting the urge to 'yee-haw' at the top of her lungs.

Flashing Boone a wide grin, she tipped her hat. "Howdy, cowboy."

His laughter drew curious stares from other residents.

"I could pass as Calamity Jane," she joked.

"Who?"

Dottie considered it. "Famous cowgirl. I guess you're a little too early to have heard of her here."

She took the Appaloosa's reins again and mounted onto the changed saddle. Sitting astride, she noted the differences from what she was used to back home. The reins were tied in a knot so she could only hold them with one hand, and the saddle was significantly larger. It didn't give her the close contact with the horse that she was used to.

"I can ride, Boone, but this is a little different to how we ride across the pond. Any pointers?"

He tilted his head. "Don't rely on the reins so much. Use your seat and your weight to guide him, a little neck-reining when necessary. Cactus is a good horse. Responsive. He'll listen to your body."

"Cactus?"

"He can be a little prickly if you rub him up the wrong way."

She laughed, and watched as he mounted his own horse, a pretty palomino. "What's he called?"

"Arrow. Been riding him about seventy-two years now, I reckon. We have a good bond."

He clicked his tongue and Arrow ambled forward. Cactus snorted and trailed after him. As they rode past the town sign, they nudged the horses into a fast trot and followed the dirt road as it wound through the sprawling hills. Boone tossed her a small pouch of jerky, and another filled with dried fruit. Her stomach growled, and her mouth watered. She ate greedily, though it wasn't food she'd normally enjoy.

Sweat coated Dottie's back by the time they reached Old Joe's tumbledown shack. The man himself rested on a chair out front, shotgun by his feet as he watched the world go by. His hair was white as the driven snow, and his skin was leathery from years of working beneath an unforgiving sun. When he saw Boone, he whooped and flashed a toothless smile.

"Well, if it isn't young Jesse Boone!" he bellowed. "What brings you out this way, Sheriff?"

Boone dismounted and clasped the old man's hand. "Good to see you, Joe. This is Miss Dottie Wildman."

To his credit, Joe didn't so much as bat an eyelid at her attire. "Mighty pleased to meet you, Miss Dottie."

"Likewise," she said, warming to him immediately.

"Joe," Boone began, "you know everything that happens around here. We need to pick your brain about something that's real important. I know you don't like passing on secrets, but I hope you trust me enough to know I'd never ask you to break a confidence if it wasn't life or death."

"Sounds serious."

"It is. It might mean a way out of our situation, Joe. A chance to catch up with time."

Joe's eyes bulged and filled with tears. "That would be a miracle, son. You know I'll help you any way I can."

They sat together on tree stumps outside Joe's shack and enjoyed the shade of several Texas live oaks. Dottie admired the low hanging branches and imagined that they were perfect for children to climb on, a pastime she'd very much enjoyed as a child herself. A sharp pang hit her midsection. She'd always imagined having children of her own, maybe watching them climb trees and have adventures as she had once had. It seemed nothing more than a pipe dream, these days. The world was at war, and she had to play her part.

"Joe, have you heard anything about a special jewel or stone?" Boone asked.

The old man shook his head, then froze. "Come to think of it …"

Dottie shared a glance with Boone.

"Oh, it was a long time ago," Joe said, his eyes glazed as his mind drifted to the past. "Someone found a gem up in the hills. They were panning for gold, though Lord knows why. Texas is rich in many things, but gold sure ain't one of them."

"Do you remember who it was?"

Old Joe tugged on his whiskers. "One of the old crowd, for sure. He'd not found any gold but came down from the hills talking about some shiny crystal he was sure would be worth something. Of course, soon after we all realised we couldn't travel no further than a few miles, and there was no way he'd be sellin' any jewel if he couldn't leave Shady Creek."

Dottie and Boone waited.

"Salty McKeever! I remember now. He wanted to sell it so he could buy a ring for Josie Morris."

"Where do we find him?" Dottie asked.

Boone sighed. "About six feet under. Salty was killed in a bar fight sixty years ago. We don't age, but we can still be killed."

"Well, what happened to his stuff? What would he have done with the jewel?"

Old Joe pursed his lips. "I reckon his only livin' kin was his brother, Grady. But he was lost in the mines shortly after Salty died."

Dottie pinched the bridge of her nose and bit her lip to hold back the curses.

"We'll search what's left of Grady's stuff," Boone said. "If it's not there, I guess we'll head up to the mines and see what we can find."

She nodded. "Thank you for your help, Joe."

"My pleasure, Miss Dottie."

A loud bang reverberated through the trees and Joe reeled back, clutching his chest. Bright red blood seeped through his shirt and between his fingers. The horses pulled at their reins and whinnied loudly.

"Dang it," Joe cussed.

Grabbing the shotgun by his chair, he took aim in the direction the shot had come from. A deep voice shouted in pain, and another called out in clear German.

"Nazis!" Dottie hissed.

Pulling the bandana from her neck, she helped Joe to the ground and pressed the cloth against his wound.

Blood soaked through immediately. Her breath hitched in her throat and her eyes stung. She looked at Boone and shook her head.

His Adam's apple bobbing, Boone knelt beside Joe and took his hand. "I'm sorry, Joe."

Old Joe smiled. "I grazed 'em good, didn't I Boone? You'll get 'em back for me."

"You know I will."

"Now, Boone. Don't waste any tears on me, boy. I'm going to see my Rose again."

Boone's voice rasped as he spoke. "You say howdy from me, Joe."

With the last of his strength, Joe patted Dottie's hand. His eyes closed, and his face relaxed. He was at peace.

"Damn it!" Dottie swore, her cheeks wet. She jumped to her feet, grabbed Joe's gun and turned to run after the Nazis.

Boone stopped her. "They're long gone, Dottie. We'll get them. I'll send a posse out."

"Let's go. They probably heard everything Joe said. We have to find *la joya del tiempo* before they do!"

"Help me move Joe inside. I'm not leaving him like this."

Together, they carried Joe into the shack and laid him on his cot. Boone's eyes filled as they left.

"I'll ask my deputy to bring a couple of men out and bury him next to Rose. He's waited long enough to be reunited with his wife. She was the love of his life."

Dottie mounted her horse and leaned across the saddle to squeeze Boone's hand. "I'm sorry."

"Let's find this dang stone and get rid of your Nazis," he said, his face drawn.

Spurring Arrow into a loping canter, he led the way back along the dirt road, kicking up dust in their wake. Dottie followed on Cactus and wished she still had the bandana to cover her face. The reminder made her glance down at her hands, still stained with Old Joe's blood, and her mind flashed back to her time in France and, later, Ravensbruck.

Her breath caught in her throat.

Nearing Shady Creek again, Boone called back to her, "When Grady disappeared, we had to take his belongings into storage in my office. He wasn't paying the rent for his lodgings no more, so Dora refused to keep anything in his room. We'll search through that before we risk the mines."

Main Street was quieter than before. They rode straight to Boone's office, and tethered their horses outside before rushing through the doors. Inside, Leroy waited for them, still chewing on tobacco.

"We got him," he said, nodding toward the cell in the back.

Dottie looked in the cell and saw Ernst Breker scowling back at her, a dirty bandage wound around his upper arm. "Well, if it isn't my old friend, Ernie. I told you, you should have killed me when you had the chance."

He glared at her, and she laughed.

"Where are your manners, Ernie?"

"You know him?" Boone asked, moving to stand by her side.

She snorted. "I met him just before we crashed into

your special time zone. He planned to kill me."

Turning his back on Breker in a pointed gesture, Boone spoke to Leroy about taking care of Old Joe. The younger man's face tightened, and his eyes shone. He clasped Boone's hand and left to follow orders.

Dottie focused on Breker. *"Wo sind deine freunde?"*

"Ich werde es dir nicht sagen," he snarled.

Boone raised an eyebrow, and Dottie shook her head. With a shrug, Boone stuck his head out of the door and called for someone. The man who entered was wiry and grizzled, with scars on his face. His eyes scanned the room.

"Thanks, Wyatt," Boone said, shaking the man's hand. "Watch this varmint for me, will you?"

Wyatt grunted his acknowledgement.

"Wait here," Boone said to Dottie. He moved to a chest at the far end of the room and returned with a small pack. Opening it, he spread the contents across his desk.

"I can't see a jewel," Dottie said.

"Looks like we're going to the mines."

She rose to her feet, and Boone grabbed her hand. Their eyes met.

"Tomorrow," he clarified. "We'll need a whole day if we want a chance of finding Grady's body. Right now, let's eat, and rest."

"Okay."

Leaving Wyatt to watch over Breker, they returned to the saloon and enjoyed a simple stew while a smiling gentleman played lively music on the piano. The lights were dim, and the food was warm, Dottie reluctantly re-laxed.

"How's the food?" he asked.

She pursed her lips. "I probably don't want to ask what was in it, but I'm sure I've had worse. It was … surprisingly tasty."

"I must say, Miss Dottie, you seem remarkably resilient. You're outside of your own time, fighting dangerous enemies, and you sure as heck seem like you'd die standing up."

She looked at him. "I assume I'm not supposed to take that literally."

"It means you're brave," he chuckled. "It's a compliment."

"In that case, thank you."

He tilted his head, the corners of his lips tugging. "Would you care to dance?"

Dottie glanced at the few couples twirling around the dance floor. Their movements seemed to be a type of waltz, but one somewhat removed from the version she knew. She pursed her lips as she tried to follow their steps.

"You don't need to know how to do it," Boone said. "Just follow my lead."

He held out his hand, and she took it. Her stomach fluttered. On the dance floor, Boone took hold of her right hand, and placed his other hand at her waist. She looked up into dark brown eyes and melted.

"Boone," she whispered.

The pianist started up again, and Boone led her in a lively dance. He pushed and pulled her body to follow his steps and spun her beneath his arm. She laughed, breathless with excitement. He winced when she stepped on his toes but didn't pause. As the tune came to an end, he lowered her into a deep dip, looked her straight in the eye, and winked.

Dottie's lips parted.

"Boone, I got to talk to you!" A voice boomed.

He held her gaze a moment longer, then pulled her back to her feet. "If you wait, I'll walk you to your door."

Heat in her cheeks, she replied, "I can find my way. Thank you for a lovely evening, Boone."

"Goodnight, Miss Dottie," he said, tipping his hat. "I'll see you in the morning."

As she settled into bed, snug beneath a soft woollen blanket, Dottie closed her eyes and smiled. She was half convinced she'd wake up in hospital having dreamed the whole thing, but she'd enjoy it while it lasted. Shady Creek was turning out to be quite an adventure.

She awoke with the dawn, and the merry birdsong beyond the window.

Washing and dressing quickly, she headed downstairs into the saloon to meet Boone. He was already there, dark coffee in hand. He smiled when he saw her.

"Morning."

She grabbed his coffee and took a large gulp before handing it back. "Good morning."

"Cactus and Arrow are outside. Are you ready to head to the mines?"

"Let's go."

Cactus whinnied as she approached and nuzzled her outstretched hand.

"Good to see you, too," she said, scratching behind his ears.

They mounted and moved at a brisk trot out of town, munching dried fruit and nuts as they rode. It seemed hotter and drier than the previous day. Boone pulled a spare bandana from his pack and passed it to Dottie, who wrapped it around the lower part of her face with a nod of thanks.

The sun was high in the sky when they reached the entrance to the mines. A pair of spindly trees stood at each side of the wooden support frame surrounding the dark tunnel. An old sign, cracked and faded with the years, warned trespassers to keep out. Wrought iron rail tracks disappeared into the gaping maw.

They dismounted and tethered the horses to a nearby live oak tree with a small stream running past. A large patch of grass in the shade of the tree ensured the animals would be comfortable until Dottie and Boone returned.

Striding to the entrance, Boone picked up a small kettle-like object that looked like it was made of brass. He shook it and nodded. "Still has oil. Let's hope it lights."

"What is it?"

"A lamp." He pulled a lighter from his pocket and used it to light the wick poking out of the kettle. After a few tries, a weak bare flame appeared. "It won't last forever. Shall we?"

Dottie followed him inside and paused to let her eyes adjust. Her mind flashed back to pitch black rooms and wretched sobs in the dark, punctuated by horrific screams that would fill her nightmares for the rest of her life.

A sheen of sweat broke out on her brow. Her heart pounded. Her fists clenched.

"Are you alright, Miss Dottie?" His voice called her back.

She swallowed her fears. "I will be. It's just … I'm not a fan of the dark. It brings back bad memories."

Boone's hand reached back for hers. "I can do this on my own. You don't need to come in."

"Yes, I do." She straightened her shoulders. "This is my mission."

They walked further into the darkness, crouching low to avoid hitting their heads on the wooden beams above. The lamp gave off the tiniest amount of light: just enough to see what was immediately ahead.

"What was mined here?" Dottie asked.

"Silver. But the mine shut down once we realised we couldn't access the outside world."

"Why? Wouldn't silver still be valuable to you?"

"Well, sure, but silver is mostly found mixed in with copper and lead, and we need mercury to be able to separate it. We ran out of mercury very quickly when time froze. No point in mining after that."

Dottie frowned. "So why would Grady come back up here?"

"He was hard up. I expect he was hoping to find something he could sell. It's rare, but you can stumble across a nugget of pure silver if you're lucky."

The oil wick lamp created a lot of smoke as they moved deeper into the mine. Dottie coughed, and pulled the bandana back over her nose, shielding her eyes with one hand. They walked for a long time, turning corners in both directions until she knew she'd never find her way out again.

"I hope you know how to get us back to the surface," she said.

Boone chuckled. "I've spent my fair share of time down these mines, don't you worry. I know the way back topside."

After what felt like an age, the mine shaft opened up into a natural cavern. The high ceiling was crowded with massive stalactites, the same deep orange colour of the rest of the underground mine. In the centre of the cavern, at the lowest point, a deep mineral-rich pool drowned the floor. Perhaps eighty feet above their heads, a small hole in the ground allowed a narrow shaft of light to fall down and illuminate the space.

"It's beautiful."

"Yeah, it's really something, ain't it?" Boone agreed. "These hills are filled with caverns. Sure is a sight to behold."

Following the rocky path around the outskirts of the pool, they manoeuvred their way to the other side of the cavern. Boone shone the lamp in every nook and cranny, searching for signs of the missing McKeever brother.

At the far side, they paused for a rest. Boone took some dried meat from his pack, and they shared it while enjoying the view. Taking his flask from his hip, Boone washed it down with a long gulp.

"Want some?" He offered the flask to Dottie.

She sniffed it and recoiled, her eyes stinging. "What is it?"

"Firewater," he said with a grin.

She swigged, coughed, then swigged some more. "It's certainly got a burn to it."

She leaned against the wall and sighed, resting her elbow in a narrow recess. When her skin touched something cold and smooth, she jumped. Turning to look, a skeletal face stared back. She yelped, and stepped back, almost falling into the pool. Boone caught her arm.

"Looks like we've found Grady," he said grimly.

Dottie stiffened her upper lip. "How do you know it's him?"

"The bandana. See? Nobody else has one with that patterning on it; he was famed for it. Got it from an old flame out in San Antonio, or so he told us. Yep, it's him alright. Here, hold the lamp."

Boone took a deep breath and reached into the recess. He moved the bones of Grady's arms from across his chest, revealing scraps of leather clothing which hadn't decomposed with the rest. In one skeletal hand, a pale gemstone glimmered.

"There it is!"

Boone took the stone and turned it over in his palm. "When Salty dug this out and took it above snakes, it must have activated the curse somehow."

Dottie blinked. "Above snakes? Curse?"

"Above ground." He explained. "And sure, it's a curse. What else would you call it? We've been trapped here for seventy years while everyone in the outside world moved on. I had a mama and two sisters in Bandera county. They'll be long dead, and no doubt always wondered what became of me."

She touched his arm. "Let's take it back to Shady Creek, Boone. It's time to figure out how to end this."

The soft scuff of a boot on stone was the only warning Dottie had before she felt the cold barrel of a gun pressed against the back of her head. Turning to look at her, Boone's eyes widened, and he raised his arms in front of his waist.

"Thank you for finding *la joya del tiempo*," a man said in heavily accented English. "We will take it from here."

"No!" Dottie cried out. "Boone, you can't give it to him. They've committed enough atrocities in this war."

Boone hesitated, and glanced at the stone in his hand.

"Don't do it, Boone. Please. I'll gladly give my life to stop Hitler."

Behind her, the Nazi tutted and pressed the barrel more firmly against her head. "I will blow her brains out if you don't hand over the jewel, and my colleague over there will deal with you. If you hand it over, we might let you live."

Boone's eyes met hers. "I'm sorry."

He held out his hand and offered the jewel to the German. As the Nazi reached out to take it, Dottie ducked and rammed her elbow into his throat. Spinning quickly, she grabbed the barrel of the gun and pointed it up at the ceiling of the cavern.

A shot fired. A piece of stalactite shattered, and the shards fell onto their heads.

Dottie kneed him in the groin and used the distraction to yank the gun from his hands. Before she could turn it on him, he tackled her and shoved her over the side. Screaming as she fell, she landed in the pool and sunk beneath the dark water. The muffled sound of Boone's enraged yell barely reached her ears. The gun slipped from her fingers.

She held her breath and righted herself, then swam to the surface. As she broke through, gasping for air, she saw Boone's hand reaching down for her. He'd moved to a lower ledge to help her out. She swam to him, her eyes scanning for the Germans and her shoulders clenched as she expected a bullet to hit them at any moment.

He pulled her out as if she weighed nothing and yanked her behind a protruding wall just before a bullet lodged into the rock face by her chest.

"They've got the stone," he whispered, "but they still want to kill us."

"Unsurprising," she said as her teeth chattered. "We've got to get the jewel back. We've got to stop them."

"We've gotta get out of here first. We're in a bad box."

Ducking low as they scampered across the ledge, Boone dragged her to a narrow tunnel leading further down into the darkness. In the opening, a small mine-cart waited. Boone lifted her into it and began pushing it along the track.

"Hold on, darlin'. This could be a bumpy ride."

As the cart picked up speed, hurtling along the track on a downward gradient, Boone jumped in beside her.

"Keep your head and arms tucked in!"

She did as she was told. "I can't see a thing, Boone.

We could crash!"

Air rushed past their heads, and the thunder of the cart on the track reverberated in their ears. Each jolt knocked them against each other, until they gave in and clung to each other.

"The track is well made." Boone shouted over the noise, his words shaking with the movement of the cart. "We should be alright, but you might wanna start praying."

Dottie's stomach churned, but a thrilling tingle ran down her spine. As they raced along the track, the excitement refused to be contained within her body. She raised her head slightly, grinned into the darkness, and clutched Boone's waist as she whooped. "Woohoo!"

"You're crazy!" He yelled, but there was laughter in his gruff rumble.

Without warning, the minecart hit something and jolted to a stop. Dottie and Boone were thrown from the cart and landed in a heap on rocky ground.

Groaning, and lifting a hand to the gash on her forehead, Dottie sat herself up with slow and cautious movements, cataloguing each ache and pain. Experience told her she'd escaped with nothing more than a few bruises and scrapes; she knew how to fall.

"Boone!" She called out.

"Over here!"

Her eyes accustomed to the gloom, and she saw the bulk of his shape curled up a few feet to her left. She ran over to him and ran a hand over his body to check for injuries.

"I think we could pick a more suitable moment," he

drawled.

Dottie pulled her hand back, grateful for the darkness that hid the bloom in her cheeks. "Are you hurt?"

He sat up, leaning on her arm, and grunted. "Might have broken a rib. Banged up a little, but I'll be alright."

"Can you walk?"

Not got much of a choice." He stood up, cursing and then apologising for it.

Dottie took stock of their surroundings. They were in a much smaller cave, with barely enough room for them both to stand in. It was narrow, but the ceiling was high above their heads. Perhaps twenty feet up one wall, a small opening let a little light through.

"Do you think we can fit through that gap?" Dottie pointed it out.

"I sure hope so."

She tested the wall, noting where it crumbled. As she found foot and hand holds, she manoeuvred her way higher, gasping as the hard stone scraped against her skin. She reached the opening, and grinned; it was larger than it seemed from below. Wriggling her way through the gap, she emerged into fading light and a cool breeze. Her wet clothes clung to her skin and she shivered.

Without pause, she turned around and leaned back through the gap to help Boone. He was almost at the hole, but the thin line of his mouth tensed with each movement. She offered her hand and guided him the rest of the way until he collapsed next to her on the dusty ground. Above them, the moon loomed like the silver nugget Grady had been hoping to find.

Rolling onto his side to look into her eyes, Boone

said, "I just gotta say one thing, Miss Dottie."

She rolled to match his position. "What's that?"

He moved one hand to cup her cheek and pressed his lips firmly to hers in a kiss that sent heat through her body. When he pulled back, she took a moment before she opened her eyes.

"That was quite a passionate statement, Sheriff Boone," she said, her voice thick and husky.

"I've never met anyone like you, Dottie. Nothing stops you."

She patted his cheek. "You're quite wonderful, yourself. Why don't we continue this conversation somewhere warmer, though? And maybe stop a couple of Nazis on the way?"

They climbed to their feet and looked around.

"Do you know where we are?" she asked.

"I think so, but we're a good walk away from the horses. We need to check on them. I sure hope those men didn't hurt them."

They walked over dry ground as night fell and the last of the sun's light faded in the horizon. By the time they reached the entrance to the mine, the stars were bright and clear overhead.

The horses were untethered, but they remained by the stream, happily munching on grass. When Dottie and Boone arrived, Cactus and Arrow greeted them with warm nuzzles and soft whinnies. Cactus nudged Dottie's arm, and nibbled on the ends of her hair until she scratched beneath his mane.

"It's good to see you, too, boy," she said, a sheen in her eyes.

"We should get back to town," Boone said. "Get you dry."

She shook her head. "No. We have to get the jewel back before they leave with it."

"Their friend is stewing in a jail cell under Wyatt's watchful eye. They won't be able to break him out without a fight."

Dottie mounted Cactus and guided him into a brisk trot, holding the reins loosely so he could pick his own path across the uneven terrain. "They won't try to get him out; they'll leave him there. Their mission is to get the jewel. They don't need Breker now they have it."

"Nice people. So how will we find them?"

"They'll go for the planes. It's the only way they can escape."

Boone snorted. "I get a feeling the stone won't let that happen. None of us have been able to leave for seventy years; why should they be any different?"

"Good point. We should still hurry though, just in case."

They rode through the night, pushing the horses into a ground-eating canter as soon as they reached flatter terrain. Dottie groaned each time they had to slow to allow the animals to rest, but she knew they couldn't run the whole way. They skirted around the town itself, cutting vital minutes off the journey.

It was still dark when they reached the wide valley where Dottie's plane had crashed only days before. Dismounting a short distance away, they drew guns and edged up the hill to peer down at the scene below.

"Dang it." Boone cursed under his breath. "My men

are down."

Dottie followed his gaze and saw two men prone on the grass beside the planes. A few feet away from them, the two Nazi officers faced each other and gestured with their arms. The moon was ripe, close to being full, and cast enough light to see the red flush on the Germans' faces.

Shaking off Boone's arm, Dottie slid down the hill and ducked behind the nearest plane. She kept her ears tuned to the heated argument between the two men, which seemed to be about the viability of flying the plane she'd landed. Boone's shoulder pressed against hers, and she smiled.

They stepped out from behind the plane, pointing their guns at the two men.

"Drop your weapons!" Dottie ordered.

The Germans looked at each other before carefully removing their guns from their holsters and tossing them aside.

"Now, hand over *la joya del tiempo*."

"Nein!"

With a hiss, the shorter of the two men launched himself at Boone and grabbed for his gun. The two wrestled, while the second man used the distraction to kick dust in Dottie's face. She fired blindly, but the shot went wild and pinged off one of the planes. He ran at her, knocking the gun from her hand. Her training took over.

Eyes stinging, she thrust the heel of her palm up under his chin while keeping her fingers shaped in a claw to scratch at his eyes. As he reeled back, she pulled her arm away then swung it back to slam the ridge of her hand into the side of his neck. He gasped, clutching his throat and falling to his knees. She whipped the edge of her hand against his temple, and smirked as he lost consciousness.

Turning, she saw Boone fighting with the other man. Boone knocked him down with a powerful haymaker punch, but the Nazi rolled across the grass and jumped back to his feet with a gun in his hand.

Dottie cursed. He must have rolled across his own gun that she'd made him toss aside!

He cocked the pistol. Boone's eyes met Dottie's. Time slowed.

Shouting her rage, she hurtled towards the German, coming at him from the side. As soon as she was close enough, she lifted one booted foot and slammed it into the side of his knee joint. The sickening snap of bone was barely heard above the bang of his gun and the blood-curdling scream released from his throat.

He fell to the ground and vomited on the grass, then lay face down and whimpered.

"Boone!" Dottie ran to her cowboy. "Are you hit?"

He grabbed his bicep with the other hand. "Just a graze. Dottie, I've never seen anyone fight like that."

She shrugged. "All SOE operatives are taught Defendu."

"Defendu?"

"Basically, kill or be killed," she said.

One of the Germans groaned. Dottie found the nearest gun and pointed it in his direction.

"Check their pockets for the stone, Boone."

He did as she asked, and grinned when he came

back with the jewel. "Got it."

"Look after it. I'll hold them here," she said. "You'd better get help."

As she looked at Boone, the man whose knee she'd dislocated made a move to reach his gun. Quick as a flash, Boone drew his own weapon and shot the pistol from his enemy's hand. The German cried out and clutched his injured limb.

"Nice shot," Dottie said.

"Be careful with them, Dottie."

"I will."

He nodded, kissed her cheek, and left to gather men in Shady Creek.

Dottie waited as the sun rose, her gun never wavering. Adrenaline faded, and lethargy threatened. She refocused her mind to stay alert.

When Boone returned with a dozen armed cowboys, and a very sour-faced Breker, she gladly stepped back.

Boone nodded at Breker. "I thought we could string 'em all up together."

Breker clenched his teeth.

"I'm afraid I'll need to take them for questioning," Dottie said. "My boss will have several questions to ask them."

"Damn you, Dottie Wildman." Breker spat at her feet, his veins bulging at his temple.

She stepped closer, leaned in, and smiled. "I told you, you should have killed me while I was unconscious. I earned my reputation, Breker. Never underestimate a woman."

Turning her back on him, she walked back to Boone.

"What now?" he asked.

She shrugged. "We need to do something about that stone. I suspect none of us will be able to leave with things as they are."

He took the jewel from his pocket and studied it. Without warning, he dropped it on the ground and took a small pickaxe from his saddlebag. With a few swings, the stone smashed into tiny pieces. Boone stomped on them with the heel of his boot and ground them into the soil.

A wave of energy rolled through the valley in the direction of the town. Dottie gasped.

"I'll be …" Boone let out a low whistle. "Seventy years, and that was all it took."

"Welcome to the 1940s, cowboy."

He gulped. "What'll happen now?"

Dottie took his hand and led him a little further away from the group of cowboys guarding the three Germans. "I'll need to find a telephone and let my boss know where we are. Once he's aware of the situation, he'll send help. I'm sure we can do something to help the people of Shady Creek find their way in the twentieth century."

"If you and your planes are anything to go by, I'll be a fish out of water."

"If you play your cards right, maybe I can be your tour guide."

Boone laughed. As she laughed with him, he took her face in his hands and kissed her as though she was his oasis in the desert. Behind them, the cowboys whooped and hollered, until Boone took his hat off and used it to shield their faces.

"Yee-haw!" Dottie said.

CAPTAIN HENNESSEY AND THE MYSTERIOUS PLANET ZETA X

DAVID GREEN

"Tamara, drop us out of light-speed. Jane, ready the view screens. Let's approach this new planet."

Captain Helen Hennessey smiled as her crew's fingers swept across their workstations before the words left her mouth. In truth, the women aboard the *ICP Starblazer* had got to work before the captain spoke, her officers well drilled. A woman had to be if she wanted a station on the Intergalactic Confederacy of Planets flagship vessel.

Under Captain Hennessey's command, the *Starblazer* had initiated first contact with nine new cultures, with all of them joining the ICP soon after. This planet, Zeta X, located at the far reaches of the Andromeda galaxy, would be their tenth. A landmark worth celebrating.

The *Starblazer's* sub-light engines kicked in. Hennessey rolled with the movement, leaning back into her chair as the vessel cruised through space. The view screen flickered into life, the endless depths of space reaching out in all directions.

"We'll have eyes on in five minutes, captain." Ensign Jane Galloway threw a smile over her shoulder, her eyes twinkling with apparent excitement.

Hennessey returned the smile, despite the woman calling her captain. They all did it. A sign of respect, they said, but she found the honorific a relic of forgotten times from before the Great Liberation. From when men led the ICP to the brink of disaster.

She quashed the frown working its way to her forehead. As if anyone could call the ragtag of planets that banded together to wage war on other systems the ICP. What it stood for today. More often than not, the so-called allies would descend into bickering with themselves, and missiles would follow. When they finally realised how unsustainable their cycle of intergalactic war proved, the ICP sent out scientific vessels to find new cultures on distant planets untouched by war.

They ended up fighting those, too.

"Too much testosterone."

"Sorry, Captain?"

Hennessey blinked and turned to her first officer. Yun-hee Kim met her eyes, a quizzical cast in her midnight-dark pools.

"My mind wandered," Hennessey answered, raising her eyebrows, and smiling. "Old age, eh? Ten new civilisations, Yun-hee. Ten! And to think, if the ICP hadn't changed, hadn't thrown off the shackles of tradition, we'd have never seen one."

"Tradition." Yun-hee stuck out her tongue. "Oppression, more like. It makes my stomach turn when I read the histories."

"As it should. Barbaric times, and ones we shouldn't forget. There are some lurking in the dark corners of space who'd welcome a return to those dark days."

"T-Minus three minutes, Captain," Jane announced.

Captain Hennessey's thoughts drifted again. The ICP represented the pinnacle of humanity, the reason all her nine civilisations had jumped at the chance to join after first contact. Their way of life represented true equality across gender, identity, race, and background. A soul from the backwaters of Pluto could climb the ranks to president of the ICP as much as one from the high-rises of New Tokyo on Earth. Everyone had a place, though science and reason dedicated many decisions. Four hundred years before, most of the crews for first contact missions consisted of men. After a century of misunderstandings, aggression, suspicion, and the occasional genocide, the ICP decreed female identifying crews would take charge of all proceeding first contact flights.

The galaxy hadn't suffered from an accidental genocide since.

Captain Hennessey turned to Lieutenant-Commander Moxxie Banks, the *Starblazer's* science-officer. She smiled as she did. Moxxie's porcelain doll-like appearance belied the fiercest mind and strongest arms in her crew. "Remind me of what we can expect, please. I've read the reports, but I'd like to hear them."

"Of course, Captain," Moxxie breathed, their voice like the tinkling of chimes. "Long-range scans suggest life-forms in a limited number, though we don't have an exact estimate. Evidence would suggest primitive souls live on Planet Zeta X, but there's the suggestion of trillian crystals in the space surrounding the planet."

"Which means starships have visited."

"Yes, Captain. We should gain greater insight from our own sensors when we orbit the planet."

Hennessey drummed her fingers against the armrest, fixing Moxxie with a blue-eyed stare. They matched it, unruffled as usual. "Speculate for me."

Their lips curved into a small memory of a smile. "Hard to say, Captain. I'd suggest it's ninety-nine percent certain a vessel orbited the planet in the last five-hundred years. Did it land? Did it leave? Only an away team will ascertain that."

"One day, Moxxie, you'll have to get off the fence you're always perched on."

They laughed, giving the captain a wink, too. "Wouldn't be much of a scientist if I did that, would I?"

"Captain, we're in range." Jane leaned across her workstation. Eager.

Hennessey clapped her hands together, rising from her seat in a smooth motion. "Bring it up on visuals. Let's take a look at Planet Zeta X."

The mammoth screen taking up the side wall of the bridge flickered, switching from the pitch-black of deep space to the image of a blue-green planet spinning at a glacial pace below them.

"It looks like Earth," Jane whispered, adjusting the

view screen so it focused closer on the planet.

"Trillian signal's strong, Captain," Moxxie murmured, staring intently at their workstation. "But not recent. Computer estimates four-hundred-and-fifty years since the last vessel sat in orbit. Atmosphere *is* Earth like. What's more, I'm detecting a congregation of life-forms on the coast of this continent here. Jane, I'm sending you co-ordinates."

"Received," the ensign answered, fingers flying across her workstation. "Coming into focus now."

The view screen zoomed in on the coast of the largest mass of land on Planet Zeta X, coming to a halt at around four hundred metres above sea level. Primitive structures sprawled across the coast, shanties made from metal, wood, and tarpaulin. A small city of souls, ready for first contact, waiting for Hennessey and her crew's help into a larger galaxy. She wiped the tear threatening to spill from her eye.

A shrill alarm sounded from navigator Lieutenant Tamara Williams' workstation, then fell silent. A sound they all knew.

"No." Yun-hee's words broke the silence. She shook her head, like she believed the movement could deny what they all heard. "That's impossible."

"Yes," Moxxie agreed, staring at her workstation. "It is. But we all heard it."

"No." Yun-hee turned her pleading eyes on Hennessey when the alarm chimed again. "It can't be."

Hennessey sucked air into her lungs. Her crew needed strength. Desired calm. Wanted a plan of action in the face of the impossible. "Tamara, the ICP recognition hail will keep sounding until you acknowledge it. I suggest you do, then take the bridge. Yun-hee, Moxxie, Jane, you're with me on the away team. It seems an ICP vessel left the trail of trillian crystals in orbit, and it's still on Planet Zeta X. Let's discover their story."

Hennessey strode to the elevator without another word, trusting her away team would follow, and glad they couldn't see her face. She wore shock like a mask, one she couldn't remove.

"Tell me what you've learned."

Hennessey stood on a transporter panel, waiting for her away team to follow. Moxxie had already taken up their position, scanning a data pad while Yun-hee helped Jane enter the landing coordinates into the transporter's nav-system. The ensign had given the away team ample distance from Planet Zeta X's major settlement, and Hennessey found the choice prudent.

Moxxie folded their data pad and met the captain's eyes.

"Many ICP ships went missing in deep space before the Great Liberation. I narrowed down the field to list AWOL vessels in just the Andromeda section." They bit their lip. A rare sign of nerves. Agitation, perhaps. Maybe both. Hennessey appreciated Moxxie's constant drive for answers, though their passion sometimes bubbled over into frustration. "I hit a wall of redacted files, Captain. I shouldn't, but I've lanced the firewalls. ICP won't know it's me, or us, doing it, but it's still illegal. I want you to know so you've full deniability. I can't stop the process now, and I'll be in soon."

Hennessey's chest fluttered. Not with anger, but with pride. She'd have done the same when confronted with a conspiracy. A wall of redacted files on missing pre-Liberation ICP vessels in the Andromeda system pointed to exactly that.

"It won't come to that, Moxxie." She gripped the science-officer's shoulder. "And I've got your back. They'll have to come through me to get to you."

Moxxie inclined their head, though Hennessey didn't miss their facial muscles relax.

"Ready, Captain," Yun-hee called, jogging over to the transporters, Jane in her wake. "Transport in 5...4...3...2...1…"

Hennessey breathed in…

... and held it as her molecules disintegrated. Her thoughts remained, drifting through space and time. The void, they called it. Her daughter's face flashed in her disconnected mind; first as an adult, the way she'd last seen her through the holoscreen a day before, then as a child, before her features aged to those of a grandmother. An age her daughter may never reach. She travelled in deep-space, on a top secret ICP mission, cut off from everyone, leaving Hennessey with old holo-logs and photographs.

Charlotte.

Her name rippled over the surface of her thoughts, flittering through the void. Time held no meaning when teleporting, neither did reality. They'd discovered the technology in the remains of some ancient, unnamed race on a planet beyond Pluto. A sphere hidden in the dark folds of space. The ICP had adapted it, but they never really understood it. Sometimes, people never returned. Lost in the void. On a transporter one moment, gone the next. Like dust in the great expanse.

Lights flickered in the darkness…

… and Hennessey breathed out.

She wiped tears from her eyes as rain lashed from above, plastering her raven hair to her forehead. The away team stood around her, blinking in the half-light of Planet Zeta X. With a shake of their head, Moxxie pulled out their data pad, though their eyes seemed far away, like they stared through it. Yun-hee squinted up at the sky, as if looking for the *Starblazer.* Jane studied her boots. No-one spoke of what confronted them in the void. Ever. Hennessey had resolved to explore its mysteries long before, and her work had led her nowhere, so she buried herself in exploration instead. *Maybe after this voyage, I'll study transporting again… but not today. First, Planet Zeta X.*

"Crew, are we together?"

She whispered the words, ones she always spoke after transporting. She discovered early on that gently does it after re-molecularisation.

"Reporting in, Captain," Yun-hee called, rolling her shoulders, and scanning her surroundings.

"Here, Captain," Jane replied, pulling a beeping imager from her belt, and holding it toward Zeta X's largest settlement. "Lifeforms approaching from the north. Detecting at least twenty-four entities."

"Captain!" The away team spun towards Moxxie, the alarm in their voice shooting ice through Hennessey's stomach. "I'm into the redacted files… Planet Zeta X… the ICP *knows* about it."

"They know?" Yun-hee asked, a v forming on her forehead. "And they've buried it? Why?"

"Continue, Moxxie," Hennessey commanded. Jane continued to scan the surroundings. Thick smoke rose from behind the trees on the horizon in the settlement's direction. Tall trees masked the approach, black plumes of smoke rising behind them. Her hand fell to her hip, where she kept her blaster. But she hadn't brought it. Protocol forbade it. Her eyes narrowed. *No matter. If there's trouble, we transport out.*

Still, a blaster would have made the queasy feeling in her stomach evaporate.

"The Pre-Liberation ICP assigned a vessel by the name of *Good Times* to investigate Planet Zeta X. They lost contact…" They broke off as whoops and yells erupted from the tree line. Deep, guttural, uncouth yells. "… and sent no one to locate them. Captain, the old ICP buried this themselves."

"Why?" Yun-hee asked, eyes searching Moxxie's face. "Did they carry some kind of weapon? Some kind of genetic disease to unleash on another race in one of their sick wars?"

Hennessey held up a hand, and her crew fell silent. Figures appeared in the distance, and with each step closer, the ice grew in her stomach. She keyed the communicator on her wrist.

"Tamara, come in, this is Hennessey."

"Captain." The reply crackled. Interference plagued it. "Your signal's weak, getting weaker by the second.

All okay?"

"We're on Zeta X, about to make first contact." Hennessey winced as static blared. It grew worse as the life forms approached. She didn't believe in coincidences. "Keep a lock on us for as long as you can. You may need to pull us out."

"Captain, perhaps it's wise to leav—"

Tamara's static bitten voice cut out.

"Damn it," Hennessey cursed, thumbing at her communicator. Only empty beeps responded.

"Captain…" The ice in Hennessey's stomach seeped into her veins, threatened to freeze her from the inside-out. Moxxie never sounded so plagued with doubt. "The *Good Times*… Captain Ted Masters commanded it."

Yun-hee thumbed her communicator, frantic fingers pressing away at it. They all knew that name.

Ted Masters. ICP Captain-extraordinaire, the pre-Liberation propaganda crowed. Hero. Leader. Legend. Women desired him, and many had their dreams fulfilled. Men wanted to emulate him, but most stood in his shadow.

All lies and misinformation.

Post-Liberation showed Masters for the man he was. A warmonger. Bully. Rapist, and xenophobe. A murderer of countless systems and civilisations. The old ICP no doubt thanked their luck nebulas he went missing.

And now it appeared his crew, filled with men just as toxic as he, had found Planet Zeta X, and stayed there, and the *Good Times'* descendents approached Hennessey's crew.

The cries and whoops grew with clarity as the group of dishevelled, long-haired, filth-encrusted men staggered towards them. Rain ran through their greasy, matted beards—the only cleaning they ever got, Hennessey reckoned—and they pointed at *Starblazer's* away team, leering as they did.

Hennessey blinked, glancing at her crew. The deluge had soaked their uniforms through, leaving little to the imagination.

"Look boys," a neanderthal at the front of the approaching group yelled, grabbing at his crotch, "women have fallen from the heavens above, and they've put on a wet t-shirt contest to say hello! You got any men with you? Surprised they let you pretties off your leashes."

"Oh, Christ," Moxxie muttered, thumbing at their communicator. Hennessey raised her eyebrows. Moxxie put little stock in religion.

Another caveman rattled a shining black box at them. Hennessey recognised it and sighed. A communications blocker, one pre-Liberation starships used in their constant wars. "No use trying to leave, ladies. No-one will hear you scream! We're armed, so why not be good girls, and do as you're told, eh?"

Yun-hee took a step forward, hands balled into fists, and Jane made to follow.

"Wait!" Hennessey commanded, dropping to her knees, hands above her heads. "Follow my lead and stay *calm.*"

The group of men cheered as they closed the distance, the rain-slick ground turning to mud at their feet.

"You have a plan, Captain?" Moxxie murmured,

falling in beside her.

"Always." Hennessey flicked her a smile. She eyed the filthy, walking masses of rags and hair. "We have the upper hand. Our brains."

"Can you women not talk, then?" The man holding the communications blocker asked, crouching down in front of the away team. Hennessey met his eyes in silence, and like she'd asked, her crew followed her lead.

The men had led them into the settlement, a shantytown of huts filled with men. Passing through, Hennessey estimated around five-hundred people lived there. Women kept to the shadows; naked, eyes downcast. Traipsing by the huts and peering in revealed them cleaning clothes or cooking over rudimentary fires. The men had whistled, and the meek women followed in their wake. Now a group of forty huddled together in the settlement's largest hut. It held relics from the *Good Times*; the captain's chair, mannequins wearing the old ICP uniforms and other useless paraphernalia. Hennessey's away team crouched before the women; shouted questions, and ripples of excitement drifted in from the men waiting outside.

"Chet. It's simple, isn't it?" Another interjected, just as filthy, holding a bitten-down finger up to the sky. "There's men up there like The Masters. They've sent us these women as a peace offering before meeting with us."

"Too right, Buzz," the one named Chet barked, hocking a glob of phlegm to the dirt-floor then climbing to his feet. Hennessey worked to keep the revulsion from her face. "Smart of them. They'd know we'd fight anyone without a peace offering. Win, too."

Buzz laughed and clapped Chet on the shoulder. Flakes of dirt and dust exploded from the blow, but the men didn't seem to notice.

"Pretty though, aren't they?" Buzz stated, ogling Hennessey's crew like they couldn't understand a word they said, or a look they threw. Probably didn't care either way. She felt Moxxie tense beside her and laid a single warning finger against their hand. "Which one do you like best?"

Chet ran a speculative eye across them. Despite her orders to remain calm and follow her lead, Hennessey's cheeks reddened. She knew from the histories that men treated women like meat, and in some systems, they still did, but the ICP had moved beyond that. Her heart went out to her crewmates; she hated the filth-encrusted man running his eyes over her still soaked uniform and knew her away team would feel the same. Hennessey chanced a glance at them and suppressed a grin.

They all stared back with hard eyes and no shame on their faces.

"Well…" Chet began, running a hand through his waist-length beard. "They all look a bit feisty, but it won't take long to knock it out of them. Fuck me, I can't decide, it's like The Masters above have sent one of every kind to try. And try I will. As leader, I get first dibs."

Buzz glowered, his bottom lip jutting through his dirt-encrusted beard as he sulked. Hennessey almost rolled her eyes. *Men.*

"You got a problem with that, Buzz?" Chet turned to the other man, stepping in close. Hennessey remembered the term; 'squaring up to someone.' She almost rolled her eyes again.

Buzz lowered his eyes. "No, Boss. No bother."

"Right. You women get your new friends cleaned and ready. Shout when they're ready." He nodded, rubbing at his crotch. "Can't wait to get started."

With a laugh, Chet left the hut, Buzz slouching in his wake, throwing dark looks over his shoulder.

"Barbarians," Yun-hee spat, climbing to her feet. A woman approached her, eyes downcast. "No, I don't need cleaning. We're not staying long. Can you understand me?"

The woman offered a slight bob of her head.

"How many women live here?" Moxxie asked, pulling out their data pad and sweeping it across the hut. The men hadn't bothered taking away their equipment.

The shy woman cast a sheepish look around the hut and whispered, "All."

"It makes me sick. Furious," Jane snarled, glaring at the entrance. "The men of the *Good Times* turned their women to slaves and kept every single one born since that way. We can't leave them, Captain."

"I don't plan to. I have an idea, and a part of it none of us will like, but I don't want any bloodshed, and it's the quickest way I see off this planet. Are you with me?"

"Of course, Captain," Yun-hee replied without hesitating. "What are your orders?"

Hennessey smiled as her crew formed up before her. She pointed at the entrance. "That communications blocker's the key. We disable it, we're in the clear. We need about two-hundred metres' distance, two-fifty to make certain. Moxxie, I'm relying on you for the first part."

"Yes, Captain," Moxxie replied, sweeping their gaze across the enslaved women.

"Good. Now hide yourself. Yun-hee and I will distract our friends, Chet, and Buzz. When their attention's elsewhere, disable them, take the blocker, and run. Alert us when you're far away, and we'll contact the *Starblazer* to transport out. You keep moving, and as soon as you can, join us."

"Yes, Captain."

"Jane, you move the women close together without touching. We'll try to bring them all with us, but they can't touch, and they may want to when the fighting starts. Comfort in fear and all that. But we know human contact during demolecularisation can prove disastrous."

"Aye, Captain."

Hennessey turned to Yun-hee, who raised her eyebrow.

"The distraction," her first officer stated.

"Yes, I wouldn't ask anyone else. It's… degrading."

"Interesting," Yun-hee smiled. "What is it?"

"Just follow my lead."

Hennessey nodded as Moxxie blended with the shadows and Jane whispered to the women, palms raised, face filled with empathy. Pulling Yun-hee in front of her, she filled her lungs with air.

"Ready!" she called; her voice airy.

Within a second, Chet pushed his way in, blocker in

hand, Buzz following.

"What?" he cried, anger breaking out in his face. "You've still got your clothes on!"

"Kiss me," Hennessey whispered.

"Kiss you?" Yun-hee asked, blinking.

Hennessey didn't wait. She pulled her first-officer close, pressing her lips against Yun-hee's. She tasted sweat on her firm lips as the woman tightened them in surprise before her body and mouth relaxed. Their tongues danced together. Hennessey ran her fingers through Yun-hee's hair and let them fall to her neck.

"Nice!" she heard Chet whoop. "A great gift indeed. Starters before the main!"

Hennessey cracked an eye open. The men stood closer, jaws slack, as they watched the women kiss. Behind them, Moxxie moved in, justice etched across their face.

With stunning speed, the science-officer dropped to the ground, sweeping out a leg. It cracked against the men's ankles, toppling them into a pile. Moxxie threw themselves onto them, grabbing handfuls of hair and smashing the Neanderthal's heads together and letting their limp bodies collapse to the ground.

"Run," Hennessey commanded, grabbing the blocker, and tossing it to Moxxie. They didn't look back.

She turned to Yun-hee, who stood with her eyes closed, lips parted.

"Good work, Commander," Hennessey coughed, examining her communicator.

"I didn't think that would work," Yun-hee breathed, red colouring her face.

"Well, men in our time have evolved," Hennessey replied, smiling at her first-officer, "for the most part. But those from pre-Liberation? If they weren't thinking about war, they had only one other thing on their mind."

"And what's that, Captain?"

Hennessey grimaced. "Sex."

"Ah."

"Quite. Jane, all ready back there?"

"Aye, Captain," the ensign replied, standing amid the enslaved women. Women Hennessey and her crew were about to liberate. She couldn't add Planet Zeta X to her tally of civilisations joining the ICP—the tenth would have to wait—but they'd give this downtrodden, innocent folk a chance in a new world. And that mattered most to Hennessey.

Guttural shouts of anger and surprise echoed into the hut.

"Yun-hee? Monitor the entrance. Those savages would have seen Moxxic running for it, let's hope they don't come in here." By her feet, Chet stirred, muttering as consciousness returned. She kicked him in the head, sending back to oblivion. "For all their barbarism, I don't want anyone else hurt."

The cries of alarm grew closer.

"How far do you think they got, Captain?" Yun-hee asked, dropping into a fighting stance.

"They'll make it. None can match them. Trust me."

Pounding footsteps slammed outside the hut.

"I trust you, Captain," Yun-hee muttered, "but one against five-hundred? Odds aren't in their favour."

Men pushed their way into the hut; filthy men, spitting their incomprehensible anger. Their eyes fell on Chet and Buzz sprawled before the women.

Their surprise brought them up short, made them silent. The hut held its breath.

"Captain! We've been trying to—"

"Tamara!" Hennessey cut off the Lieutenant-Commander as the communicator buzzed into life. She yanked Yun-hee towards the group of women and stepped back herself. "No time. Forty-two life forms around my immediate location to transport, and me. Right now!"

The men rushed forward…

… and Hennessey breathed in. The hut grew dark as her consciousness floated through the void. Relief, alien to the deep pockets of timelessness, fluttered across the surface of her mind, then scattered. This no*where* and no*when* had no purpose for it. A face formed. Charlotte's. Her daughters. Flickering between ages; from newborn to geriatric and back again.

'Mother. I need you. Come find me.'

Ripples of shock caused the blackness surrounding her unformed body to pulse. Panic, too, as her molecules separated further, threatened to drift into the unknown.

No. Hennessey's voice. No, her own. Echoing through the void. *I refuse to lose myself. My daughter needs me.*

Lights flickered from the depths of oblivion…

… and Hennessey breathed out.

Hennessey sat in the captain's chair as the *ICP Starblazer* orbited Planet Zeta X. To her right sat Yun-hee.

She'd spent the hours since returning from the away mission cleaning, housing, and supporting the women they'd liberated. Acclimatisation would take time, but they entered a better world.

Moxxie sat to her left, safe and sound. They'd teleported back in without a drop of sweat on her. Hennessey had waited. She'd leave no soul behind. The science-officer wore a frown since and hadn't joined the celebrations thrown for the crew's safe return.

"What did you see in the void, Moxxie?" Hennessey asked.

They gave a start, turning their frown on the captain. "I… we don't talk about that."

"I saw my daughter. Heard her calling for me, saying she needed help. Do you think it's real?"

Moxxie dropped their eyes, examining their fingernails as if deciding which one they admired best. Hennessey sighed. They wouldn't answer. No-one spoke about the void.

"Yes," Moxxie whispered. "I heard her, too."

Hennessey met her eyes, let the tears roll down her cheeks, and nodded. "Thank you."

Wiping her face, she walked to the viewscreen, and stood before her crew, Planet Zeta X looming behind her.

"You've served me well over the years. All of you. Nine civilisations brought into the ICP, and almost ten. But those women… they're my crowning achievement. We witnessed the past, and through it, we give those poor souls a better future." She paused, letting her gaze sweep across the bridge. Her crew sat in rapt attention. "On the way back here, in the void, my daughter spoke to me.

Moxxie, too. She needs my help. I won't ask you—"

"You don't need to, Captain," Yun-hee cut it. "We're with you to the ends of the galaxy and beyond."

"Aye-aye!" the bridge crew replied as one. Warmth flooded Hennessey. These were her family, just as much as Charlotte. Every one of them.

"Jane, set a course," she called, returning to her seat, and running her hands across the armrests, smiling at Yun-hee and Moxxie.

"Where to, captain?"

"Let's take Yun-hee's suggestion. The edge of the galaxy, and beyond if we have to."

"Aye-aye, Captain!"

The *ICP Starblazer's* light-speed engines whirled into life as Jane's fingers flew across her workstation and the bridge crew got to work, a flutter of excitement swimming through the atmosphere. It made Hennessey's blood sing.

"And Planet Zeta X, Captain?" Moxxie asked, leaning towards her.

"Yes," Yun-hee added, "what about them?"

Hennessey laughed. "Keep it hidden and leave the men to it. Let's see how well they cope without women."

The *ICP Starblazer* launched into light-speed and into the unknown.

Captain Hennessey and the crew of the ICP Starblazer will return.

THE AUTHORS

ASHLEIGH CATTERMOLE- CRUMP is an author from Christchurch, New Zealand. When she isn't writing, she is a mum, toy librarian, tattoo collector and chocolate lover. She enjoys writing flash and short fiction in a variety of genres, her work is upcoming in several 2021 anthologies.

DEBORAH DUBAS GROOM is a Canadian West Coast author. She's been published in anthologies in Canada, the U.S, the U.K. and soon, Australia. She's a member of the Langley Writers' Guild and the Federation of B.C.Writers. She has degrees in history and medical social work and considers anything after the industrial revolution to be current events. She's mom to an outstanding human being, Joshua, and grateful daughter of Helen and Stan. She's a sci fi/fantasy/vintage monster movie geek, and a secret superhero fighting the tyranny of everyday cooking.

SCARLETT LAKE is a riddle, wrapped in a mystery, hidden inside an enigma. From England she resides, tucked away in a log cabin found in the middle of the woods. There she writes in a little window nook with dogs at her feet, foxes frolicking on the porch and coffee in her hand.

SHELLY JARVIS began working on speculative fiction in the 2nd grade and never looked back. An avid science fiction and fantasy reader, she spends a portion of each day dwelling in other worlds. Shelly enjoys spending time with her wacky spouse, her wonderful nephews, and her rescue pups. She currently resides near Charleston, West Virginia, in the wild and wonderful mountains that have her heart.

Find out more about her books at:

www.shellyjarvis.com

and follow her on

Twitter @shellyjarvis

L. T. EMERY is a British author, with a love for Horror, Sci-fi and Fantasy genres. He is the proud father of one and husband to the love of his life. Outside of family life, he is an avid reader of novels, genre magazines, comics, manga and just about anything else he can get his hands on. With a particular love of long form fiction, he is currently working on a fantasy novel which he hopes to publish in the future.

He can be found online at:

https://ltemery.wixsite.com/home

twitter.com/ltemeryuk

You can find his works in Black Hare Press, Eerie River and Macabre Ladies anthologies.

DECLAN FLETCHER is an IT Project Manager from Warrington in the North West of England. He's been reading since primary school where he started with the Chronicles of Narnia. That started a lifelong love of fantasy and Sci Fi. He now writes in those genres too.

Fletcher is based in London in the UK and has worked in IT for just over 15 years

CHRIS HEWITT resides in the beautiful garden of England, Kent UK, and in the odd moments that he isn't dog walking he pursues his passion for all things horror, fantasy, and science-fiction.
Blog: mused.blog
Twitter: @i_mused_blog
Facebook: www.facebook.com/chris.hewitt.writer

GORDON LINZNER is founder and former editor of Space and Time Magazine, and author of three published novels and scores of short stories in F&SF, Twilight Zone, Sherlock Holmes Mystery Magazine, and numerous other magazines and anthologies. He is a member of the Horror Writers Association and a lifetime member of the Science Fiction & Fantasy Writers of America.

CHARLOTTE LANGTREE is a poet, aspiring novelist, and writer of short fiction. Raised in West Yorkshire, she has a deep love of hills, berry-picking, and her unique accent. She's been creating stories for almost as long as she has been alive, and has a profound respect for the magic of the written word. She has been published in several magazines and anthologies. In December 2020, she was named 'Author of the Month' by Paper Djinn Press. You can find her online at www.charlottelangtree.wordpress.com, and on Facebook at www.facebook.com/CharlotteLangtreeAuthor

DAVID GREEN is a writer based in Co Galway, Ireland. Growing up between there and Manchester, UK meant David rarely saw sunlight in his childhood, which has no doubt had an
effect on his dark writings. Published with Black Ink Fiction, Red Cape Publishing and Eerie River Publishing, David has been nominated for the Pushcart Prize 2020 and his dark fantasy series Empire of Ruin launched in June 2021 with "In Solitude's Shadow."

Website: www.davidgreenwriter.com
Newsletter: https://tinyurl.com/y6ah8brp
Twitter: @davidgreenwrite

Adventure Awaits

Volume 3

Earth Door
Cye Thomas
9789198671025

An Odd Collection of Tales
Cye Thomas
9789198684131

Graffiti Stories
Nick Gerrard
9789198671018

Punk Novelette
Nick Gerrard
9789198671087

Struggle and Strife
Nick Gerrard
9789198684049

Murder Planet
Adam Carpenter
9789198671032

Generation Ship
Adam Carpenter
9789198684063

Adventure Awaits

Cold as Hell
Neen Cohen
Hardcover: 9789198684094
Paperback: 9789198684056

Six Days to Hell
E.L. Giles
9789198684087

ANTHOLOGIES

Just 13
9789198684025

Lost Lore & Legends
Hardcover: 9789198684100
Paperback: 9789198671094

ADVENTURE AWAITS

Volume 1
978-9198684124

Volume 2
9789198684155

MORTEM CYCLE

Death House
9789198684117

Volume 3

Death Ship
9789198684148

Death Beyond
9789198684162

Find us at:
http://www.breakingrulespublishingeuro.com